THE
LADY OF THE
MOUNTAINS

THE LADY OF THE MOUNTAINS

SECOND BOOK IN
A SONG OF NIALLA
—— AS PART OF ——
A TALE BEYOND RETURN

MATIAN ELLIS
OSCUR BELLOC

ISBN: 979-8-9892029-7-3 (Ebook)
ISBN: 979-8-9892029-8-0 (Paperback)
ISBN: 979-8-9892029-9-7 (Hardcover)

Any references to historical events, real people, or places are used fictitiously.
Names, characters, and places are products of the author's imagination.

Cover, illustrations, and layout design by Brandon Richard Collebrusco,
working under the pseudonym, Matian Ellis

Second Edition, 2025.

Golden oaks grow high in the glare of an illuminate sun,

Where hope never fades and leaves never fall.

To my Grandma Berb.

Always.

CONTENTS

AUTHOR'S NOTE

As I write these words, I reflect on the fact that I have been conceptualizing 'A Tale Beyond Return' as a fantasy saga for nearly 18 years. I speak to you not from a place of certainty, but from a quiet, unwavering storm that sounds off inside me. What I share stems from an ongoing battle—not only between my mind and the blank pages of my stories-to-be, but also my soul as I wrestle with my own expectations to create something worthy of being read. Creation, whether through the written word or paint on canvas, is no simple task. It is a surrender and a fight all at once. Many days, I find myself sitting at my desk, staring at the immense responsibility I have set for myself, paralyzed by the weight of what I want to express but cannot articulate. I wish I could tell you the process is graceful, that the words flow as easily as the thoughts in my head. That would be a lie. Instead, the art of creation often feels like an exhale held out far too long, my lungs gasping for breath as my body fights to push through it. Creation is iteration and a willingness to learn from failure, so I did.

The struggle is not just external—facing critics or battling with self-doubt, although those issues do loom heavily. It is a deeper, more profound conflict that cannot be easily captured in words. My challenge lies in the clash between the artist I aspire to be and the person I am—between the man who demands perfection and the imperfect individual I actually am. This schism terrifies me. There are nights when I consider a section or chapter, questioning its worth and whether it captures even a fraction of the image born from my dreams. And so, I begin again, draft after draft, realizing the cycle never truly ends once a work is deemed complete. It becomes a constant negotiation between allowing the process to consume me and reclaiming control—between letting the stories take shape naturally and molding them into something recognizable, like a sculptor chiseling stone.

There is no map for what artists do, nor is there a clear road through the methods. When a path does exist, it is one that we, as authors, build and expand ourselves. The process can be messy, and often painful as we adapt our ideas to the medium. Even in moments of clarity—when a fragment of truth, a word, or the right line arrives to bridge a narrative gap—these instances can feel temporary and illogical. They serve to remind me why I pursue this craft: not for validation or praise, but for the quiet, sacred satisfaction of knowing that what I create, it is a part of me in a way that no single word today exists to convey the right chord. Endeavor is not a gift. It is not merely an act of expression. It is a discipline—one that demands everything and offers little in return, except for the knowledge we gain, for better or worse, beyond our true-born talents.

So, as my readers, may I offer you a piece of unsolicited advice? Should you ever find yourself ensnared in these struggles much as I have, remember this: You are not alone. The art of storytelling is not easy. At times, it is a relentless and silent war. But in the end, it is a battle worth fighting for with every ounce of imagination we can muster. Within these pages lies the culmination of those mistakes and hard-fought lessons. My pain and feelings will unfold, word by word, in a manner I hope does justice to the literary arts. We are far from the end of this journey, but neither are we at the beginning anymore.

Hope From The Unexpected,
Matian Ellis Oscur Belloc

MAPS

OF

THE

VALLEY

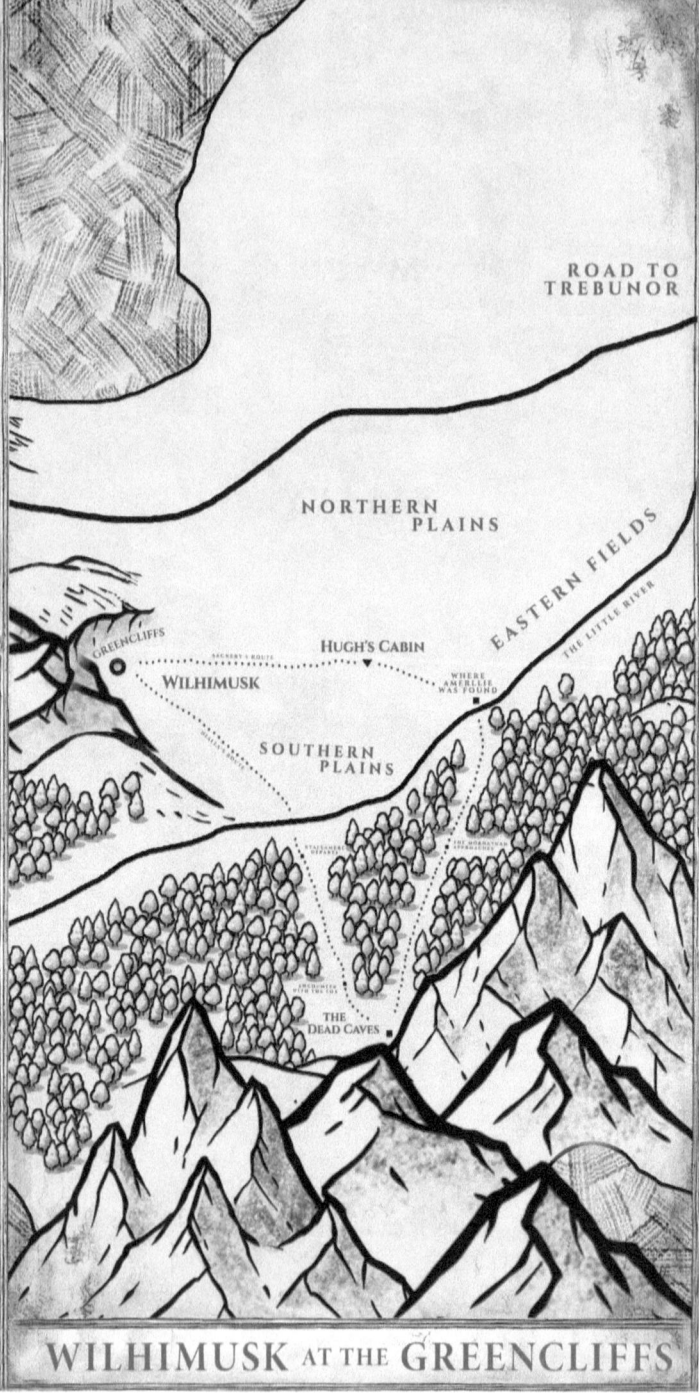

ROAD TO
TREBUNOR

NORTHERN
PLAINS

EASTERN FIELDS

THE LITTLE RIVER

GREENCLIFFS

ARCHERY'S ROUTE

HUGH'S CABIN

WILHIMUSK

WHERE
AMERLLIE
WAS FOUND

SOUTHERN
PLAINS

STALLOSKER'S
DEFEAT

THE WORNATHAN
APPROACHES

SWORDSMAN
WITH THE 101

THE
DEAD CAVES

WILHIMUSK AT THE GREENCLIFFS

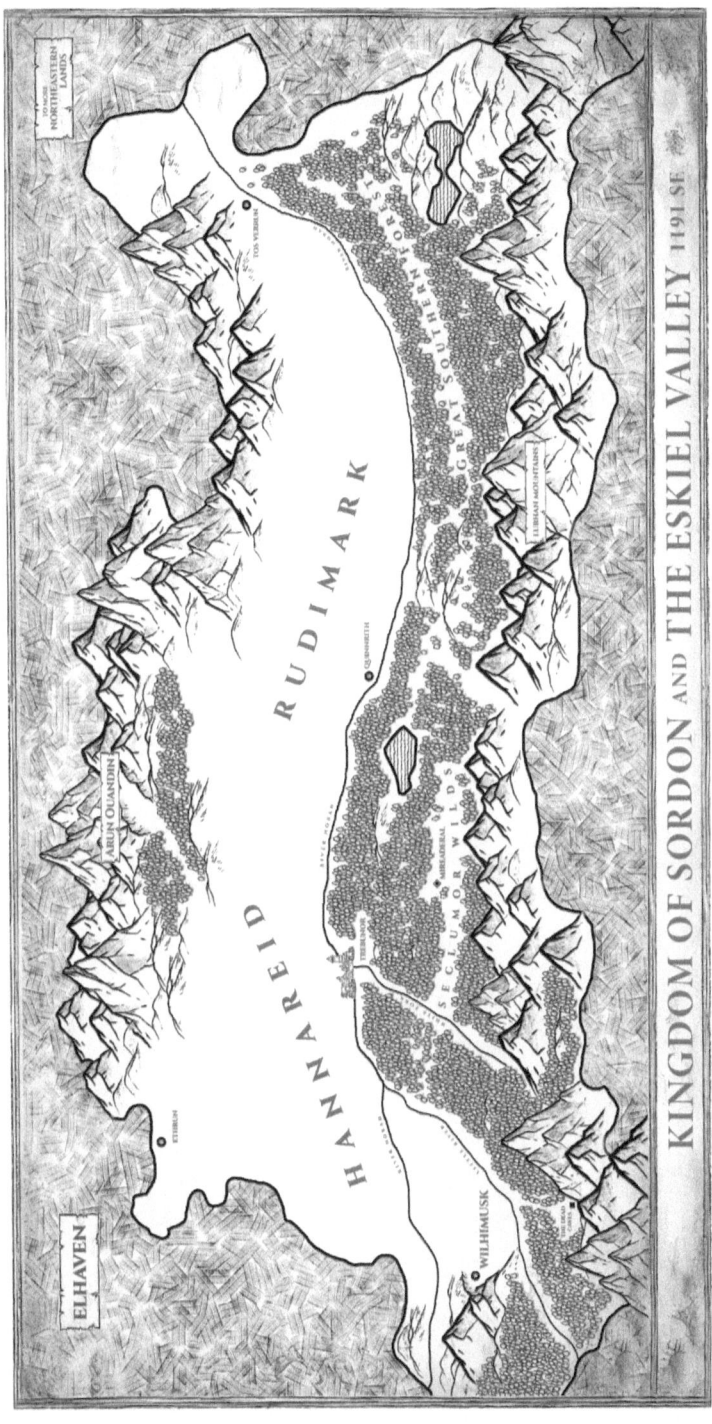

KINGDOM OF SORDON AND THE ESKIEL VALLEY 1191 SE

THE LADY OF THE MOUNTAINS

A TALE BEYOND RETURN

BY

MATIAN ELLIS

— Wilhimusk, Sordon —

Year of the Second Era, 1169

87 Years After the War of His Return.

In the waning days of his rebellion a thousand years before,
Icurian made a promise to the fox spirits with the best intentions,
For the Neshulha of Rarhavonn did not wish for conflict,
As theirs were a peaceful, if mischievous nature,
But others feared them—Heluvian and his warrior-servants,
The Vedrethal,
Their hunt for the foxes went to the far edges of Arún,
To the very place where the first trees grew into the world,
And ended all but their final songs.

— 1 —

AMERLLIE

Irimara paddles to the river's western shore, shaking the water off her fur and drying her back under the sun.

There's a distinctive smell that comes with the breeze. Irimara briefly catches it—like a cherry plume mixed with something sweet, maybe a little sour. It's strong enough for her to discern it against nature's flowery spring blooms.

"Sweaty cotton?" Irimara mutters, scrunching her nose.

She identifies the stench from her experiences with the Westermen expanding into the more eastern lands.

Curious but not overly eager, she follows the scent. Irimara maintains her distance, hiding in the grass and bushes. That is until she comes to a rock with a human's white dress flapping across its face, a few small stones keeping the wind from blowing it away.

Lowering her posture, Irimara skulks to it, wanting to stay

unseen from its owner, who can't be far if they're without their clothes. Humans are indeed strange that way. She's never understood them. She pokes the garments with her snout, attentive to that same sour smell she caught earlier.

Irimara pulls the dress off the rock before whipping it around her neck, her tail hitting its sleeves.

Her ears twitch, and she hears giggling nearby. Then, there's a melody on the air—a tiny, high-pitched tone, like a child's voice.

She peeks around the rock to see a girl dancing on the beach in her undergarments. She's no taller than a fawn and rather skinny, which Irimara expects is typical for a child her age. Her skin is pale but darker in areas from playing too long outside, and her hair is sandy blonde, grown past her shoulders and tied into large braids.

Irimara scrutinizes the terrain, looking at the wheat fields—the tillers and the planters—but none watch after the girl. She was left to play alone.

The fox's white fur reflects the light of the noon sun, making her glow like a beacon. The girl ultimately notices her, quickly eyeing the garb the fox had swiped off the rock. Irimara would've preferred to remain out of sight, but she can't help it now. She must accept the circumstance.

Not wanting to startle the child, Irimara takes a cautious step forward. Afraid to break eye contact, the girl winces.

Irimara takes another discreet step, followed by another and another. Yet, the child does not back down. *Will she call for help?* Irimara hopes not.

Eventually, the fox nears enough that she's only an arm's length away from the girl. By this time, she notes the child's hair is wet, standing half-naked on the grassy riverbank. She was in the water, going for a swim.

Irimara lifts her head, pawing the garments she's carrying. She pulls them off her back and tosses the girl her clothes.

The other hesitates as her large green eyes dart between the garb and the fox. Apprehensively, the child reaches down to steal her dress back, throwing it over her head and tying a belt around her waist.

"I did not mean to scare you," Irimara tells her. "This world is a dangerous place for the young and innocent."

"You speak?!" the girl asks. "A talking fox?"

"A fox? How precious," Irimara whimsically expresses. "I must look so to such eyes."

Irimara sniffs the child, licking her hand, which causes the little cub to giggle before scratching behind the fox's ears.

"Then what are you? I've never met a talking animal before," the girl glimmers. "Except maybe Gallandhal. Amerllie . . . That's my name! Amerllie."

"Amerllie?" Irimara repeats. "A name that originates in the Aarendelic tongue. But you don't look Ellúndar? Yet so close to the border, I wonder . . . Tell me, Amerllie, does the word 'Maithandír' sound familiar to you?"

"Maithandír?" Amerllie begs the question. "Yeavengeritt calls himself that, but he doesn't talk much about it. Lady

Miralifrim *does* tell us stories about the Míran, however. And about Ilhivendal. That's where she's from! Ilhivendal. She said her people were Maithandír but stopped calling themselves *that* for some reason."

"Familiar names to me, except . . . Who is Miralifrim?" Irimara prods further.

That's when Amerllie's gaze drops away, and her leg swings side-to-side.

"We're not supposed to talk about that to strangers," the child dithers.

"Strangers? Ah, I *am* Irimara of the Neshulha. There! Now you know my name, are we still strangers? You and I?"

"Yes? Because I don't know you," Amerllie confesses. "Nialla told me that animals—the good ones, don't often speak. Only the trees, rivers, and spirits do. That good ones like to sere-nade—loud and proud." She brings her hands together. "Can you sing like them?"

"Well, I do enjoy a song or two," Irimara returns, rubbing against the girl's arm to lull her worry. "You could say my kind was born from very special music. But Nialla? Another name?! Who *is* that? It is beautiful, how it rolls off the tongue."

"My best friend," Amerllie answers.

"Your *best* friend, is she? And what makes her your best friend?"

The child is about to open her mouth to speak, but instead, a cold breeze blows in, and her lips sputter.

"It's a secret," the girl finally states. "People outside the village aren't to know."

"The village? *Your* village? Home?"

"Wilhimusk—" Amerllie quickly cups her hands over her mouth, realizing her mistake.

Irimara narrows her eyes and inspects the horizons. "And that is where you live with your family? And this . . . Nialla?"

The girl's eyes widen as she shakes her head. "Why are you asking me this?" Amerllie demands. "Leave me alone! I don't want to talk to you anymore." She steps toward the wheat fields, toward the humans laboring under the sun.

Irimara swings around and blocks the child's path. "I thought *we* could be friends?!" she suggests, but the color washes from the other's face. Amerllie takes another step, this time westward from the river's course. Irimara notices and breathes deeply. *There it is! Wilhimusk, toward the Greencliffs. At least a distant view of it. The village is likely a day or two in that direction.* "Can I tell you a secret, Amerllie? You told me yours. It is only fair I tell you mine."

"You've got a secret?" the girl's ears perk up.

"It is a rather great shame for me," Irimara begins. "I am lost, little cub, don't you see? My travels have brought me to the far edges of the world, looking for a way out of the wilderness. I follow a set path, you could say. A journey from which my people never returned."

"People? Other foxes?" Amerllie asks. "Fox people?"

Irimara laughs. "Fox people? That is surely a way to describe us," she cheerfully accepts the comparison. "No. There were many others, but none exactly like me. Look around. What do you see? A bouquet of nature's sunlit blooms, each slightly different from the next."

Ethereal flowers erupt at the girl's feet in brilliant patterns. They appear like images reflecting off a mirror—too real and yet *not* real. Amerllie watches the stems grow while floating petals land on her head like a colorful rain. The blooms reach heights greater than most trees until their roots wrap around the child's ankles, frightening her until Irimara knocks her to the dirt and breaks the illusion.

Amerllie's face goes stark pale.

Irimara tilts her head and steps off the girl, letting her stand again. She reshapes the flowers until they form a circle around them.

Amerllie's eyes fill with tears. "Why did you do that?! That was mean!"

"I was overzealous. I didn't mean to—"

"You hurt me!"

Irimara folds her ears back, distraught. "My apologies? It can be a challenge to control at times. Though, aren't the colors pretty? Do you think your 'friend' would enjoy it, Amerllie?" She reorders the circle into a path that leads toward the Green-cliffs. "Why not bring her here, this Nialla? Let me show her," the fox challenges. "Then I can return home. Do you understand?"

Amerllie shakes her head. "She wouldn't like that I told you."

"And why not? She and I have matters to discuss," Irimara

tells the child. "Can you do that for me? Tell her to come, please?"

"I would never tell her about you," Amerllie shivers. "I'd tell Master Greywolfe! You won't—"

"Greywolfe?! Do you mean Sackery Greywolfe?" Irimara repeats with a crack in her voice. She allows the foggy illusions along the riverbank to dissipate. They're in the field again, with the sounds of calm water in their ears. "Now, that's an old name, Amerllie. Did you know that? A famous one. It's what his brothers called him. Alive—? How is *he* alive? And he *still* uses that moniker? They didn't tell me that, the old tyrants. Bad habits die hard, it seems."

"What?" Amerllie appeals.

The girl doesn't realize Irimara isn't talking to her.

"Vedrethal, my little friend. They never change, do they? And that makes sense," Irimara describes. "Warrior-servants? Protectors. Another 'friend' told me there'd be a test ahead. I wasn't sure if they meant *I* would be the test or the tested. Sackery of the Vedrethal—*Master* Greywolfe. Another survivor?" Irimara turns faintly from the child. "But why return here after what happened? Is it for this Miralifrim? Or maybe the 'best' friend? Nialla. She can't be the one, can she? A name so unlike theirs?"

"What do you want?" Amerllie sobs.

Irimara circles Amerllie. "I am looking for a girl with close ties to the ancient world!" the fox demands, staring onerously at the child's quivering knees. *She's afraid. Perhaps the Vedre-*

thal were right about fearing those like me? Irimara lets off a mild whimper as the wind fades.

"Me? I am a girl," Amerllie suggests, breathing fast and shallow.

"Yet not the one I am looking for, I am quite certain. Don't you see?" Irimara eyes the child one last time. "These aren't questions you can answer, little cub. You can run away now and set the pace if it suits you." She growls loudly to force the girl into motion.

Surprised and panicked, Amerllie dashes toward the wheat fields, crying for help. Irimara winces. She counted on the child running home, not betraying her to the other humans nearby. Unfortunate, but it doesn't matter. Irimara has another idea to isolate the one she seeks.

"Thank you for the lesson," Irimara whispers.

She allows the child to run a distance before taking the chase. It doesn't take long for the fox to catch up to her, pouncing on the girl's shoulders and knocking her into the grass, staining her lovely dress with dirty brown and unsavory green.

Amerllie kicks and screams, fighting off the attack. Irimara summons bright shades, like mist, mirroring the fox's elegant form and blocking any chance of escape. The images by themselves can't hurt the child, and Irimara doesn't particularly want to, either. But she won't risk letting the girl run and warn her people about the fox's presence—not if the old Vedrethal safeguards their little village. *It'll be far better for them to discover the child after I leave.*

Irimara keeps Amerllie on the ground, not letting her move. "The one I *want* has silver eyes, little cub. She'd not be much older than you. If it's not Miralifrim, then likely, it is your 'best' friend, Nialla. I will find her. And she will understand that witches and crones aren't the only threat."

Amerllie attempts to scream.

Irimara's shades drown out the noise. The others in the fields won't hear their wayward child.

Sackery isn't likely to leave his ward's side if he perceives an aimed danger. This attack must look savage enough to encourage a hunt away from the village. That means Irimara must do what she's never done before.

The fox witnesses her reflection in the girl's terrified eyes— teeth bared and angry.

In the end, Irimara locks her jaw around Amerllie's throat and squeezes, making it fast and painless. And the girl stops her struggle.

"I am truly sorry for this, Amerllie," Irimara whispers, blood in her mouth. "I am righting a wrong from years ago. You did nothing to me, but they can't know *what* I am before I finish my task. Not yet. Find peace in your passage to Iánturial's dark embrace."

All sound fades away as Irimara sits there with the girl's body. A tightness in the fox's throat makes it hard to breathe. Her tongue drops from her mouth while her heart pounds inside her chest. No reason can justify this offense. Irimara doubts *this* is what the Stranger intended when he told her to journey south and rectify her past.

Irimara rests her snout on Amerllie's stomach, hoping to feel it move again as she draws breath. She doesn't get that closure. What she's done . . . is done, and there's no reviving the dead. Killing the child is a test in its own right, as filthy as it makes her feel.

The fox grabs Amerllie's sleeve with her teeth and drags the corpse toward the riverbank. It's a long, encumbered venture that aches her paws and neck. Irimara mewls as she lays the girl across the soft sand. Now, she can only wait for the humans to worry and come looking for the remains.

— *Irimara of the Neshulha* —

— 2 —

A FATE NEVER OURS

He instructs his company in the practice yard, drilling them under the sun's intense heat. Sweat pours off him, making his skin glisten under his shirt.

Sackery falls into lockstep with his team and forms a circle, shoulder to shoulder. Individual skill in a fight might help his Jhalamar defeat an opponent, but to survive a battle, working together will take them further than any singular member of their ranks.

He shifts with them, countering the other team, led by Ivette. The woman mirrors his legwork, step for step, five against five, while another dozen or so study and watch—those not on duty in the fields, at any rate, or standing sentry with Captain Iben on the road leading into Wilhimusk. They play an elegant dance with wooden swords in hand, no armor or shields, so only raw muscle and nerve to protect them from strikes.

Sackery can see his reflection in Ivette's eyes.

Every bruise is a lesson, as much as every cut and misstep will harden these warriors for a true fight. For twenty years, he's taught these men and women in his traditions, pushing them to the edge, making them train until their bones scream and their knuckles crack.

Ivette is about to advance when five tolls from the bell tower come out of nowhere.

Sackery raises a hand and lowers his blade, stopping their mock battle. He waits and listens, and the bell sounds five more times.

The others are suddenly anxious. Sackery nods, and they hurry to the armory to equip themselves. It's an unnerving sound for them to hear in the normally quaint countryside. The tower of Wilhimusk only tolls for a few reasons:

Seven rings for when the morning calls, a welcome to the night's watch on the outskirts. As the farmers return from the fields at the end of the growing season, it rings four times, and everyone cheers, their wagons filled with a fresh harvest. Five rings are for safety—somebody spots a fire or other threats to the village. It was rare. Often, whenever somebody gets thrown off a horse or one of his Jhalamar injures themselves during a training session.

Sackery marches off to Elundjir's Hall at the village heart, the flat square outside its doors already busy with people asking questions.

"Master Greywolfe!" Iben rushes toward him from the

crowd.

"Captain?! Five tolls?" Sackery asks. "Why the urgency?" He doesn't wait for an answer. The old Vedrethal walks on until he reaches the west-east road out of the village, Iben following close behind him.

"A rider arrived minutes ago," Iben tells him. "Said there was some incident in the eastern fields."

"An incident? Who's on task out that way?"

"Pict and Hader, but the messenger didn't say what the trouble was," Iben answers, "only that he rode ahead to let us know they need help. I'll leave with the others to meet the caravan. With luck, we'll find them before it gets dark."

"Can you make ready my horse?"

"Master, I—?"

"Five tolls? Somebody's hurt. These are *our* people, Iben. I will ride with you."

"Chances are a plow tipped over into a ditch."

"Or a wild animal killed some cattle?"

"Always possible. Mountain lions like to tramp out of the Seclumor Wilds and bother the farmers."

"Maybe. But I won't have it said that the Jhalamar failed to answer when called," Sackery tells the Captain. "How far did our man ride?"

"About a day or two?" Iben answers with a question.

"From the group that planted by the river?" Sackery asks.

"Appears so," Iben acknowledges.

"Then, if the man rode ahead, we'll hopefully meet them

halfway back."

Iben nods and hurries to the stables. Sackery watches as the Captain pulls their people together, saddling the horses and mustering the Jhalamar to respond quickly. That is what Sackery trained them to do, a mirror of the Vedrethal, if a bit less skillful. But that's the difference between centuries of instruction and only a few decades, more than enough to match most foes in combat.

Sackery takes his mare's reins and leads the others down the road, the bell tolling five more times behind them.

They leave soon after the sun hits midpoint and don't see another living soul until twilight—farmers and their workers returning to Wilhimusk at the end of the day. Sackery questions them, but they don't know much more, so he lets them go with an escort. He continues with the rest, following the road east toward the Little River that nestles beneath the mountains, now dim in the cascading daylight.

Not long after dark, he notices lights from another group farther ahead but still distant. The air's so black that his riders spread their torches an equal distance along their column so everyone can see the front, center, and rear more easily. As they ride closer, voices call out to them:

"Over here! We need help! Please?! Over here!"

He eyes the lights and the dozens of folk gathered around them. Sackery can't see their faces, only their silhouettes. But there's also something else between them, a lone wagon. It looks intact enough and almost empty. So, it's not a broken axle that caused a wheel to fall off and crush somebody's foot. *And even if it did, I count thirty or forty sets of hands. They wouldn't need to send a runner to Wilhimusk for aid.*

Sackery feels a tightness in his throat.

Iben puts a hand on his shoulder, riding alongside him. "I do believe those are our people."

"Why do they covet the wagon like that?" Ivette asks.

"Do you hear them? They sound desperate," a third points out.

"Panicked!" hollers a fourth.

"What's happened?" the questions continue.

Sackery holds his breath and stops. "Something's wrong, do you feel it?"

"No. But I am not you," Iben frets. "Let's move!"

The group signal their horses and canter the rest of the way. As they reach the wagon, Sackery recognizes two shapes—Ankara and her husband, Nialla's childhood friends, and many of their neighboring farmhands. Some drop to their knees when the party approaches, their faces lament, crying into their sleeves.

Ankara runs to him, pulling him off his mare. "Sackery?! Please! It's Amerllie! My little—? My sweet girl! S-She—? Is she—?"

There's a heaviness to the woman's speech, full of terror. Sackery holds her close and looks at the others, the shadows from the torchlight dancing across their faces. Even in the dark, he can see the water in their eyes, their noses red, clearly distraught.

Sackery pulls away and steps toward the wagon. Inside, he discovers the body of the little girl, Amerllie, her name. He leans in for a closer look, torch in hand, noticing the marks on her throat and rips in her dress. Dirt streaks on the white cloth suggest something had dragged the child over the ground after she tried to run away. Amerllie? Another of Nialla's friends. A close one, at that, like a younger sister.

"Five tolls?" Sackery whispers. "Should have been six."

The girl's father meanders to his wife, leading her away and telling her to rest.

Sackery lets out an unsteady breath before passing off the torch and stepping a respectable distance from the body.

"Master Vedrethal?" the father asks, anger mixing with regret in his tone.

"I am so sorry," Sackery consoles him.

"Amerllie's dead," the man fights to say the words. "She's dead. I don't . . . I don't know what to do. Help me? Please! I don't know what to do. Tell me what to do! I-I don't . . . I don't know . . . Please, no . . . I don't know what to do! Tell me! Please."

Sackery hugs the man, letting him fall into his arms.

"You take her home," he tells him.

"And then?"

"We find what did this."

Amerllie's father collapses to the ground and lets out a terrible scream, punching the dirt. Sackery looks to Iben and Ivette, then at the settlers, who see them as protectors. These are the children of the people who followed Nialla from Trebunor. His charges. *I know all their names, their faces.* They appear to him now like strangers, shrouded by a sorrowful mask.

A cold breeze comes in from the west, causing him to shiver. Even the wind mourns the loss.

All that means is Nialla's awake. And *she* knows. The weather shifts with the girl's moods.

THE FOX IN THE GRASS

Nialla watches as Yeavengeritt carries the girl to the pyre, a white sheet covering the body as he lays her down. A hundred of their neighbors accompany them in these small morning hours, many bringing small paper lanterns to act as guiding lights for the girl's spirit to follow into Iánturial.

Her mother often says that ghosts are nothing more than the memories left behind by the lost. Looking at these people, Nialla only wonders.

She clenches the Ancestrum Stone that hangs from her neck on a thin silver chain. Sackery returned with the news only yesterday. Amerllie's death shocked the village. Daybreak arrives, and the mourners fill Wilhimusk with songs—quiet laments that Nialla doesn't have the strength to join.

Ankara and her husband, Amerllie's parents, hold each other close as Yeavengeritt lays a torch on the stacks, the flames catching as smoke takes the young girl's essence to a land beyond the black sea above them.

Nialla lets the fire strengthen before stepping forward, squeezing Ankara's arm. Her friend flinches at her touch.

"It is almost over," Nialla whispers, letting out an unsteady breath.

Amerllie was only a year older than Nialla's apparent age would suggest. She was friends with Ankara when the two were girls, but as the years passed, everyone she knew grew older, and she mostly stayed the same. *It is unfair*, Nialla often thinks.

"I don't want it to be over," Ankara sobs.

Nialla rests her head against the woman's chest. "Remember the love you shared."

Amerllie's father walks around and tenderly pulls Nialla from his wife. "Please," the man urges.

Nialla reads the fear in his eyes. He doesn't know what to do as his child burns on the funeral pyre, the smoke white and flowery. Yeavengeritt dressed Amerllie in perfumes and embroideries fitting for a noble lady, even though the people here in Wilhimusk aren't more than common folk with simple fashions.

"I am sorry," Nialla frowns.

Yeavengeritt steps next to the pair, long hair dancing in the wind, his face flush by the light's glow. "We can ask no more of the child now," the old man murmurs. "Won't you join me? I wish to offer your daughter a song my people had for dark days like these."

"Of course," the father speaks weakly.

"Do what you need to do," Ankara agrees.

Nialla wipes her nose with her sleeve. The air surrounding them is starkly quiet now, with only the fire alive, its embers floating higher into the sky. They have lived peacefully at the edge of the known world for twenty years. Beyond the valley, a hundred kingdoms vie for rule over the continent Arún. This land is only one tiny track, nowhere near the larger towns or cities of white stone towers.

Nialla's seen people come and go from Wilhimusk every year—some wanting a new life, others looking for somewhere to settle down. Refugees.

Life is precious in this place. Nialla enjoys the calmness most days. At the same time, it can also be deadly for the myopic fools who wander absent-mindedly. Amerllie wasn't a fool. She was born here and knew the outskirts well. She grew ten years in the time Nialla grew by one, and they've had many adventures exploring the fields and woods outside Wilhimusk in that short lifetime.

Nialla approaches the pyre where Amerllie lies. "I played the same games with your mother," she speaks to the breeze. Nialla lends it an ear with hopes the mountains would answer. But they don't. They rarely talk to her these days, and never for good reasons.

Yeavengeritt raises his hands and lets out a soft whistle that garners the crowd's attention. Five notes, clean and ambient. It builds to a tune which sounds out over the gatherers:

They say it's a place where the voyagers sail to,
A place where the mother sings and the father cries,
The youngest lament a parting of their ways,
A heart that beats when the gardens fade,
For the gates swing open, she walks on through,
To finally meet our bright lady true,
Ansolas, our bright lady true.

Beneath the stars where the ocean winds blow,
There's a shimmer, a glow that we all wish to know,
A beacon of light in the darkest of night,
Calling us home to the land that's right,
For the gates swing open, she walks on through,
To finally meet our bright lady true,
Ansolas, our bright lady true.

Ankara and her husband reconstitute their strength before wandering off with their neighbors.

Nialla looks into the fire one last time and sees her mother, Cyridel, on the other side, staring back at her through the kindled flames. She doesn't see Sackery anywhere. Cyridel's dress mimics the style worn by her people in Ilhivendal—the Míran of Naúmandial. Light and loose, so the fabric easily catches on the wind.

Her mother's eyes are disquiet, almost cold. She only blinks when the fire breathes, and the wood collapses.

Yeavengeritt sets a hand on Nialla's shoulder. "There's nothing else, little one." He kneels to her and rests his forehead against hers, embracing their anguish. "Return home. We will attend the mourners. Death is but a natural part of life."

"I don't want to leave her," Nialla clamors. "Our lives—?"

"Are full of questions without answers," Yeavengeritt admits. "Amerllie's struggles are over, however. Take comfort."

Nialla hesitates. Her mother takes her hand, and they ascend the Greencliffs together, the lament from the mourners rising with the smoke. It harbors a softer tone, although bright, like a candle that lights a dark room. Nialla repeats the words as she works her way up the path. "A heart that beats when the gardens fade." She wonders if it's true, folding her hands across her chest as they walk.

The plateau atop the cliffs is narrow and flat, overgrown with grass and flowers. Sunlight bounces off the pedals in the early morning. Nialla's planted hundreds over the years, and it is to her they'll listen. They are her ties to this earth. Memories. Tomorrow, she will seed another alongside the others for Amerllie.

"It would be beautiful if it didn't make me so sad," her mother weeps.

"Everyone's lost someone before," Nialla murmurs. "But this? It feels different."

"Bad things happen so often. Sometimes, I ask myself why they do."

"Because then people wouldn't recognize the good things,"

she tells her mother.

Cyridel looks at her with a pain that fills the space between them, her eyes reflecting a depth of sorrow that words cannot express. She nods and continues to the Houdicar, their House on the Cliffs.

They discover Sackery sitting on the doorstep as they walk around the corner. He flicks a knife, etching a simple face into a long, straight chunk of wood. *A hobby*, Nialla attests. He shares it with others from the village. The man argues it calms him during his excessively dull "retirement years," as he calls it. But she thinks he does it more to escape into his thoughts. Nobody will bother him if they believe the Vedrethal is attentive to other matters. Sometimes, they may even be right.

Nialla approaches the man and rubs her palms. "You weren't among the gatherers?" she asks.

"Funerals are unpleasant for me," Sackery frowns. "I've seen enough for a lifetime. Better to avoid them."

She raises an eyebrow, followed by a look strong enough to shatter glass. "Ankara was heartbroken. I didn't know what to say to make it better. I once promised her that Amerllie would be safe with me. And now?"

"The woman lost a child," Sackery admits, leaning forward on the steps. "Some things are beyond our promises."

"Nothing's ever been so quiet. And I despise it when everyone is . . . What's the word?" Nialla's voice quivers with a mix of frustration and sadness. "Subdued? They all wanted to voice their thoughts but couldn't find the courage."

"It's hard to know what's real when you can't read their eyes," Sackery agrees.

"But I can feel them all the same? Every glance, every whisper?" Nialla goes to sit next to him. Her mother watches from the distance before stepping aside to tend to the garden. "How do I make it better?"

Sackery wraps an arm around Nialla and brings her in close. "Life is too short," he voices. "Friendships grow strong and fast. We are not so different, but they *do* look up to us. Not because we've built our house above theirs. No. They followed us to make a home. You'll live a thousand years, but they'll live less than a hundred."

Nialla tucks her knees into her chest and buries her face into her sleeves. "Down there? Hardly anybody said a word to me. Yet I can still hear their cries," she admits. "When I drown them out, I hear the trees instead. And if not *them*, it's the birds, the bees, or even the dogs let off their leashes."

Sackery, displaying his characteristic patience, quietly sits as he lets her speak.

She closes her eyes and waits, still hearing the songs from the village below the Greencliffs.

"And what do you want to do about it?" Sackery finally asks.

Nialla looks up at him and bites her lip. "I don't know. Am I supposed to?"

"That's the hardest thing about this," Sackery chuckles.

"What is?"

"Admitting when you do *not* know," he imparts, his wisdom

shining through. "Nobody is ever certain. Do you under-stand?"

Nialla pauses for a moment. "I—I think so?" She forces herself to smile.

Sackery hums and squints at her. "Do you?"

"Yes? I understand you've gotten too old to walk down the cliffs," Nialla cackles, tagging him and quickly running away.

Sackery jumps up with surprise and chases her. "You little mouse!" the Vedrethal jeers, his voice bouncing off the rocks. He's fast, like a wolf after a deer, but she is more like a cat and dodges him gracefully. They run rings around their house, smiles and excited screams filling the air until Sackery corners Nialla in the garden. "Gotcha!" he exclaims, his triumph evident. She giggles as she tests his guard.

"At least I don't smell like an ox sent to the pasture!" Nialla mocks.

"You ride for two days," Sackery bursts, "and let's compare the stench!"

Nialla pushes him away as she breaks for it, but he snags her foot, sending them both stumbling into the dirt and fresh morning dew.

Sackery rolls onto his back, his merriment now somber as he catches his breath. "Do you see? Even on days like these, there's still some joy in the heart. Celebrate the lives of those you love, Nialla. Honor them by finding the happy moments. Don't cry for the dead who can no longer feel regret."

She looks at him and fights off a grimace, mustering a

warmth to her tone. "Maybe you're right? Amerllie would want me to laugh."

Sackery smiles and feels his throat. "It's a delicate balance for us. Most of the villagers? They came because of us," he admits more erstwhile. "And we couldn't live out here without them. Wilhimusk is our anchor. It safeguards us against strangers and outsiders. These people act as our shield."

"Trebunor provides for us," Nialla states.

"Only what we can't make for ourselves," Sackery acknowledges. "Arms and armor—what the Jhalamar use after I train them. Dresses for your mother, tools for me, and trousers for your skinny ass. Life here is beautiful and serene, but it can also be dangerous for those who don't respect it. Mistakes? Such as what Amerllie made. We're a fair ways away from Trebunor and Calidor. We live beyond the borders of most kingdoms—a wild, untamed frontier."

Nialla looks at him for a brief second. "Captain Iben said it was a wild animal that attacked her?"

"Any number of beasts could kill a girl that small," Sackery agrees. "A deer *can* if it's ornery. Or threatened."

"Did you see her wounds?"

Sackery winces. "I did."

"Will you tell me?" Nialla begs the question.

The man's head goes slant. His expression says more than he probably cares to admit. "The marks weren't from an animal trying for a meal," Sackery advises, sitting up in the grass. He looks over to Cyridel in the gardens, who glances at them, listening intently. "Predators attack because they're hungry or find easy prey. Amerllie's different. Deliberate. More restrained. A hungry animal wouldn't have left her body in any substantial state."

"And what does that mean?"

He surrenders a grim look. "I don't know?"

Nialla stares at him tenaciously. "You don't think it's a wild animal?"

Sackery pushes off the ground, his uncertainty palpable. "You share your mother's ambivalence. Do you know that?" He turns to the white smoke column rising from Wilhimusk below. Amerllie's embers will shine until the wind carries them toward the valley. "It's difficult to say *what* happened until I search for answers."

"You think something singled her out," Nialla realizes.

"She was your friend, Nells. I don't want to—"

"Why would anything *want* to hurt her?"

"Nialla, I—?"

"And what are we going to do about it?" she demands.

Sackery levels with her and sighs, his tone heavy and defeated. He takes her hands, a gesture of comfort and love.

"How long since our last great challenge? I should have guessed the peace wouldn't last," Sackery derives. He looks at her, the sunlight casting a shadow across his face. "But this is my task. Not yours, Nialla. Stay here and get some rest before the morning draws on too late. Amerllie's death has everyone riled. I'll get a party together and scour where they found her body. If we're lucky, whatever killed her left a trace."

Nialla swallows as she nods. And with that, Sackery goes inside the Houdicar to prepare for the hunt.

It's a cozy place they've built. People in Wilhimusk call it the House on the Cliffs. It's not fancy nor overly large but a simple cabin with sturdy walls, three beds, and a hearth. Sackery had cut the wood, made the frames, and set the foundational stones. Other buildings in the village are more substantial, like Elundjir's Hall. But this is *her* house, the place where she sleeps, where she belongs.

"My mother grew up in the stone palaces of Ilhivendal," Nialla whispers, "—among the fountains and lordly statues. Trees dotted the pathways alongside a hundred little rivers that flow down from the mountains." *Wilhimusk is as far from that as anywhere.* It's a farming community where the people work hard for an honest life. The Houdicar itself sits at the edge of the plateau, nearest to the Greencliffs, which are, in fact, an array of lush terraces facing the slopes of the Lurhan Mountains and Arún Ouandin to their east. "And the one place we thought we could be safe."

"But *are* you safe here?" a voice comes from nowhere.

Nialla snaps her head and lends her attention to the tall grass on the far side of the field. "Who—?"

"You cannot see me, but I *am* here. You *know* I am here. Feel the air around you, little cub—follow the wind, and you will find our true colors."

Nialla's heart beats faster as she notices two piercing yellow eyes near the plateau's solitary pond, their gaze fixed in her direction. She pushes herself off the ground and moves toward them, her steps purposeful and resolute, if not curious. "Are you trying to scare me?" she demands. *A voice?! But whose voice?*

She closes on the source, only for the yellow eyes to disappear into the grass. There's a heat to the presence. Nialla follows it, uncertain if she *should*, but decides to go after the feeling anyway. She fought the Crows at Mireaderal and survived. What can a feeling do to her that the witches couldn't?

As she reaches the pond, Nialla meets a profound stillness in the air. The water, as smooth as glass, imitates the light of the ascending sun. *Is this real?* She removes her boots and cautiously steps into the pool. Her reflection stares back at her with a brilliant glow about her silver eyes. Around her face, the water swirls and distorts her features, transforming her into a foxlike creature with a human body. It fills her with wonder and awe.

Nialla looks up to find a white fox watching her from the opposite shore. The creature doesn't move—frozen, like a painting on a canvas. Then, the fox tilts its head curiously, measuring Nialla's worth from a safe distance. Intelligence shines from the creature's eyes.

"What are you?" Nialla demands, her voice laced with a fearful hint.

"Not from the natural world," the fox speaks to her.

"Your song? It's like a drum filled with sand."

"And yours is like a kit that doesn't know when to run."

Nialla moves through the water toward the fox, almost getting within arm's reach before it lets out a mischievous laugh. The fox spins and darts away, quietly vanishing over the hill behind the grass.

Whatever the creature was, it left a mark. Nialla feels a tinge in her bones, an unmistakable imprint of *it* being here. She catches a whiff of a musky odor that lingers above the water. The stink is so minuscule that it quickly dissipates with the breeze.

"What *are* you?" she asks again.

"Nialla?" her mother calls. "Are you alright?"

Nialla fixates her gaze, her mind a whirlwind. Cyridel's voice breaks through, and she pulls her daughter out of the water.

"I'm not sure," she confesses, her words trembling with doubt. "I thought I saw something, but—?"

"Something?" Her mother asks, more confused than concerned. "What did you see?"

Nialla looks back, but nothing's there. "Maybe one of the sun's tricks?"

Her mother drapes a blanket over her shoulders, urging her to go inside and change into dry clothes. Nialla hesitates, a strange warmth spreading across her neck. Slowly, she turns, her heart pounding, only to find those sharp yellow eyes staring at her from the shade cast by the house under the sun.

Houdicar on the Greencliffs

— 4 —

IBEN AND THE JHALAMAR

Sackery didn't want to intrude until *after* the proceedings. Many who went to the funeral are now inside Elundjir's Hall, much of the village—a few hundred settlers and farmers, hunters and soldiers, weavers, and candle makers.

Jhalamar Iben stands vigil over the pyre's smoldering remains. Sackery, his steps measured, walks up to him with folded hands.

"We gave her a warrior's due," Iben mourns.

Sackery doesn't speak at first. He presses his palm into the burnt logs, feeling the heat of the embers. In all his long years, the Vedrethal had to witness many difficult moments that angered him. But this? His hands tremble, and his throat swells. "We should let the parents know they can collect the ashes," he whispers, drawing back, thumbing the fine soot that blackens his skin.

Since their arrival at Wilhimusk decades ago, Sackery had vowed to protect these people. But his promise has been shattered by this recent event. Amerllie, a summer child of barely nine full years, was snatched away, breaking their simple peace. He can feel it. She was Nialla's friend, a bright star in their lives after Ankara had grown into a woman and built a family and a home to call her own.

"Master Greywolfe?" Iben urges, bowing to the Vedrethal.

"When you finish your duties, enlist the retinue for a sortie," Sackery orders the Captain.

"Nialla sent you?" Iben begs the question.

Sackery frowns. "We won't let this happen again. A tragedy on our watch, so it's our task to make it right."

Iben holds his stare for a moment. "It could take a while," the other warns. "The woods are full of dangerous beasts."

"And monsters in the dark, don't forget," the aging warrior adds. "I'll burn them out of their holes if need be. Whatever it takes."

"Are you certain we are ready?" Iben queries, his voice laced with doubt.

Sackery turns his eyes to the man and puts a hand on his shoulder. Iben of Calidor is a veteran who once followed "Lord" Rasterforn to Trebunor. He fought in the Battle of Mireaderal and aided in the defeat of the Crows—survivors of Icurian's Rebellion that saw the Vedreron scattered and broken. Sackery accepted those who came with them to Wilhimusk and molded them in the traditions of the Vedrethal, his warrior kindred from another life. He named them Jhalamar to fit their role as Nialla's dutiful vanguard.

Sackery pulls away and touches the hilt of his sword, Aru il Endril. "We are going on a hunt, not marching off to battle," he tells the man. "But we'll learn the difference, I am certain. And that's enough for now. Whatever awaits us, the Jhalamar will face it like my brothers of old."

"That is rather high praise from you," Iben admits. "At your leave, I will muster the others."

Sackery looks at the girl's charred bones amidst the smoke. "Go ahead. Meanwhile, I will console Ankara and her husband."

"Be gentle with them, Master Greywolfe," Iben suggests. "The hardest thing for a parent—?"

"Is to grieve their children," Sackery finishes. "Believe it or not, I am not a stranger to heartbreak. A wise man once said that sons should bury their fathers, not fathers their sons."

"And pray it shan't ever happen to us," Iben nods. "Greywolfe?" He walks off and leaves Sackery alone by the embers.

Sackery steps heavily toward Elundjir's Hall, halting at the door. He lends his ear to the frame. The silence inside deafens him, broken only by the weak sobs of the mourners, a brief respite amidst the sea of tears that washes away the songs and food.

He rubs his throat, tension in his jaw, like he's choking on the air. As the Vedrethal musters his courage to knock, the door suddenly opens. Yeavengeritt greets him, a sight that catches Sackery off guard. "Master Vedrethal?" the man whispers.

"May I interrupt?" Sackery asks.

Yeavengeritt looks back and nods, opening the door wider to let him inside. Sackery walks through a hall full of families sitting at the tables, their eyes on him, the Vedrethal warrior, tall and broad-shouldered. A wary calmness settles the air as Ankara and her husband look at him as he approaches.

Sackery bows to the pair in a quaint sadness, his hands cold.

"My lord? We weren't—?" Ankara speaks. "Captain Iben promised to keep vigil."

"We didn't think you would come," the husband says, squeezing Ankara's knee. "You don't like funerals. We understand."

"I am so sorry for your loss," Sackery offers in a sullen tone. "Amerllie? She was a radiant soul. So polite. I released Iben from his watch outside." He kneels before them, gently taking Ankara's hands in his own. "The embers have faded. You may collect your daughter's ashes when you feel ready."

The woman takes a deep breath, unsure whether to invite the Vedrethal to mourn with them or ask him to leave so they may continue to grieve. But the question vanishes from the husband's eyes as he cherishingly turns to Ankara. "Your words mean the world to us," he says, wrapping a blanket around his wife's shoulders.

"I know this is a difficult time," Sackery softly urges. "If you'd allow me? I want to ask some questions."

"Questions? Of course," the husband falters. "Questions."

"Nialla told you to come?" Ankara realizes.

"She did, and I agreed. My riders are going hunting for what killed your daughter," Sackery tells them. "But I need to know what happened. Where to start? You were in the eastern fields by the river. What did you see? When did you see it? And who found the body?"

Ankara doesn't break eye contact. She stirs in her chair, watching Sackery, the candlelight flickering across her pale skin.

"Men were already out searching for what did it," the husband answers.

"They didn't find much," Ankara languishes. "She was just there, our little girl. Amerllie never looked so peaceful."

"Master Hugh, the wagon driver, was the one who found her. He lives a day's ride from the village at a small homestead off the main road. He and our field hands went to scour the shore, not a tracker among them. Vedrethal? Why do *this* to a child?! Was it some beast? A monster?"

"No monster I know would leave the body intact," Sackery describes, touching the pommel of his sword on his belt again. "This is different. We must hurry before we lose any leads. Iben musters the Jhalamar. And they'll have *me* with them." Sackery stands straight and rests his hands on his hips, anxious to head out and begin the search.

"Maybe you can see what we failed to?" the husband asks.

"That's my hope," Sackery admits.

"Nells always said we could rely on you," Ankara smiles. "Her? And Miralifrim? They don't know how lucky they are to have somebody so devoted."

"Miralifrim? How long have you known us?" Sackery whispers. "You don't have to call us by our false names."

"No. But we choose to," Ankara returns.

"We do it to show our respect for all you do for us," the husband agrees.

Sackery draws back, lowering his head. Should he feel ashamed then for allowing this tragedy to happen? He looks at the floorboards, listening to the whispers from the onlookers in the hall.

"Nialla misses you," Sackery offers. "You've grown up together."

Ankara shakes her head. "No. I grew up while my friend stayed the same. Then, I had a daughter who took my place in her adventures. After all this time, Nialla's still the girl I met in Trebunor. Maybe a little older? Nells won't ever get old. We all know it. Somewhere down the line, she will forget me. She'll forget Amerllie much sooner."

Sackery holds his breath, unsure how he feels about hearing the hard truth.

"You know that's unfair," he tells her. "Nialla won't forget."

Ankara slowly sinks into her seat. "In fifty years, Nialla will stand over my grave and realize she can't remember what my voice sounds like anymore." The woman pulls on her blanket to cover her face. "How old will she look? Thirteen? You'd think I'd get used to it, but—?"

"You never do," Sackery confides.

"I am afraid for her. Amerllie won't be the last. Everyone

Nialla knows will someday die. Mere notches in stone? A list of graves to dig or ashes to collect. It doesn't matter which. She'll continue while the rest of us become shadows of her past. You?! Me? All of us."

Sackery frowns as he offers her his palm. "Look at my hand," he instructs. "What do you see?"

Ankara looks at him oddly before doing as he bids. "I see an old fighter's skin," she describes. "Calluses? A slight shakiness?"

"From many years swinging a sword," Sackery admits. "They used to be steady. Now—?"

The husband leans forward and looks for himself. "Scars? Faded."

"A hundred battles—many won, a few lost," Sackery recounts as he pulls away, his tone laced with a fierce protectiveness. "Some more recent than others. I was always fortunate, but I worry how much longer that luck will hold. And I know, with every fiber of my being, I can't shield Nialla from the dangers out there forever."

"Like we couldn't protect *our* daughter from this nightmare," the father says, angry and aggressive. He doesn't mean it toward the Vedrethal. At least, Sackery doesn't think so. His cheeks are white like his wife's, losing their flush after a day of crying in each other's arms.

Sackery steps toward the door. "I will find what killed your Amerllie," he tells them. "You have my word."

Ankara surrenders a sorrowful nod, believing he'll do everything possible to keep his promise. "Thank you, Master Vedrethal."

Sackery leaves Elundjir's Hall and finds Iben and the Jhalamar crowding at Wilhimusk's palisade gate. About twenty men and their horses, grey cloaks flying in the wind. Ivette and two other swordmasters, Camdyn and Kinnen, complete a check of their provisions. None of them know how long this excursion will take or how far into the wilds it'll lead them.

"We're ready to go, Master Greywolfe," Iben tells him. "And we brought Ora from the stables. I thought you'd like to give the old girl one more ride before we retire her to the fields. She deserves a good rest after her years of service."

Ora's eyes light up with joy when she spots Sackery approaching. He takes her reins and jumps into the saddle, the beast burring at his touch, the comfort of a familiar rider on her back. "That she does, Captain Iben. Steady now." He speaks to the horse. "I have a favor to ask, old friend. I know you don't like going into the wilderness, but we have no choice today. Will you take me one last time?" His mare was only five when King Rasterforn gifted her to Cyridel at Trebunor, making the animal twenty-six this season. Under tender care, she can live for another ten years, but not if Sackery continues to bring her on these long and risky treks.

The mare lifts her head in agreement. *Or maybe she mocks me?* Sackery's never certain with the beast.

Iben clicks his tongue as he mounts his steed. "She's looking forward to it. Rest assured, we will get her back in time for a feast next week. I heard the stable master plans to give the old girl a bucket full of apples. She'd relish that, wouldn't she?"

Ora grunts approvingly.

"Seems like she does," Sackery interprets. "Ready, Captain?"

Iben turns to the Jhalamar and nods. He's assembled most of their numbers. A few will remain while the hunting party's away in the wilds. "Yes, my lord. Pict, Hader, Olynn, and Rod will stay to protect our ward and the villagers. Everyone else will follow your lead."

Sackery clenches his jaw. He looks back at Wilhimusk as Ankara and her husband leave Elundjir's Hall and approach the funeral pyre. They collect their daughter's ashes, urn in hand, and somberly close the lid. Later tonight or tomorrow, they'll go somewhere Amerllie had liked and spread her remains. They will do it alone without anybody else there to witness. It is a private matter only for close loved ones, a sacred farewell to those who died before their allotted time.

"Master Greywolfe?" Iben begs the question. "Are you okay?"

Sackery's eyes flash for a moment. He suddenly wants to draw his sword, like an itch in his throat. "Do you smell that?" the Vedrethal asks, turning his nose to a musky stench on the breeze.

Iben raises an eyebrow and lends his eyes to their surroundings. "No?"

Sackery looks to the top of the Greencliffs, where the Houdicar watches over the whole town. "Strange?" His breath quickens as the muscles in his arms tighten, a sense telling him that danger's close. "Something feels . . . out of place?"

"Something?"

And as quickly as it comes, the sense disappears. Sackery closes his eyes and tries to catch it again. "Maybe it's nothing, I don't know. Regardless? Bring me to the man who found the girl's body. His name is Hugh, the wagoner. He can point us in the right direction."

Iben nods. "I know his place." He lets off a sharp whistle. "Jhalamar? Let's ride out!"

— 5 —

WHAT DREAMS MAY COME

Nialla wakes to an odd smell, like musk after a rainstorm, stark and redolent. "But it's not raining? So, where—?" She looks out the window. Color breaks through as the sunlight hits the uneven glass, warming the air inside their little house. Nialla's slept a few hours at best.

Her mother lies beside her, asleep. She dozed off shortly after Nialla had laid her head on the pillow. They'd been awake since they brought Amerllie's body from the fields. She didn't even know how tired she was until now.

That still doesn't explain the musky stench *inside* the Houdicar. And the Ancestrum Stone hanging from her neck? It dithers and dims.

Nialla looks around. She notices the white fox sitting at the doorway to the house, watching the two of them slumber. There's a peaceful aura about the creature. Odder yet are the brilliant yellow eyes staring at her from across the room. The fox tilts its head curiously as they marvel at each other's presence.

Nialla nudges her mother's arm. "Mama? Are you awake?"

"She is dreaming a happy dream," the fox says, mouth unmoving.

"You? I saw you in the grass," Nialla speaks. "Those eyes?! What do you want?"

The fox straightens its posture and prances up to Nialla, jumping onto the bed and forcing the girl back into the corner frame. Those yellow eyes study her, closing the space between them to sniff the girl's hair and catch her scent before settling at Nialla's feet.

"I want you to understand," the fox says, narrowing its glare as if angry or impatient.

"But I don't understand?! What do you mean?"

The fox shakes her head and steadies herself, her eyes gleaming with a feverish fire. "How do you not know, little cub?" she wonders in a whispered tone. "My past? Your future. A story beyond the oldest tales, Princess Endúcar." She leaps onto a shelf above the bed, knocking aside several wooden figurines. One of them falls and clatters to the floor—a wolf statuette, breaking off one of its limbs.

Nialla swallows hard. She knows the title 'Princess Endúcar' all too well; it describes her father's lineage as a member of the royal house—the Endúcar, the Kings of Calidor and Maheira. *But how does this fox know to call me by that name?* It is far from being a popular secret with the talebearers and scandalmongers. *And how is she able to speak to me?* The creature's voice rings in Nialla's ears, though her lips don't move.

Is she one of the Shanashéron? Perhaps related to Gallandhal by some means? The white fur doubtless suggests the possibility. And yet? That doesn't seem right. The fox doesn't radiate a warm inner light. Instead, all the girl discerns is that musky stink thick in her lungs.

Nialla sits up in her bed. "Who *are* you?"

The fox grins pridefully. "Friend or enemy, what does it matter?" she answers. "I am Irimara of the Neshulha, a name you will learn soon enough." Gradually, the house around them starts fading into a misty blackness. Nialla's bed sinks into a shallow lake, and her mother disappears entirely into a cloud of butterflies. Shapes move in the shadows. Whispers echo. A hundred yellow eyes now watch Nialla from the darkness and the gloom.

Nialla clenches her fists tightly as her feet touch the lake's bottom. "What is this?" she demands, struggling to keep her head above the inky tide.

"A promise once made," Irimara states, appearing distantly through the torrent. Nialla rises on her toes and pushes toward the creature, step by step, ardently fighting for every breath, lost in a different world. But no matter how far she goes, she doesn't get any closer. Irimara merely sits on the shore, gawking at the girl with those bright eyes. "Icurian's words still hold some weight. They must! For all our sakes."

"Icurian?" Nialla begs the question. She reaches for the water's edge but feels nothing between her fingers. Her skin isn't wet, as if the lake isn't there! "What is this? I made no promise to anyone! Stop this?!" Her voice quivers. Nialla closes her eyes and tries to shove her fears into her gut, focusing on the gentle sounds reverberating off the water's surface. A coldness strikes her, but she throws it back until it becomes like the sun, hot and unbearable.

She opens her eyes to the lake engulfed in flames. Nialla loses her courage as her skin peels away. She wails a blood-curdling scream that ends up bubbling in her throat. For the first time, Nialla can't hear the songs. Her voice goes silent, and she collapses under the waves, air escaping her lungs.

"Time doesn't erase the memory!" Irimara growls. "Icurian failed us! And I demand consequence."

Nialla breaks the surface and gasps: "I am . . . not . . . a consequence!"

The fox draws back and vanishes, letting the fires quickly die with the cold and the mist.

Nialla is still in bed, clawing at her chest, blankets soaked with sweat.

Cyridel jerks awake and stares worryingly at her. "Another nightmare?" She feels Nialla's forehead with the back of her hand. "You haven't had one of those in a while."

Nialla's eyes flicker woozily, struggling to recognize the woman that gave birth to her. "No? I don't—? Was it a nightmare? It was so different."

Cyridel takes the girl by the hands. "Different? Different, how? Explain to me."

"Like I was a part of what I saw?" Nialla clarifies. "I don't know. It was so fast, it almost felt real—?"

"Not a passive observer?"

"I don't think so?"

Cyridel's face furrows intensely. "Your father used to have waking dreams whenever danger was nearby. One minute, he could be with us, and the next—? He was thrown back in history to watch events from before his time. He saw as the Flames of Morenarch burned the race of giants to ashes at Salahnair and Gwynedal. He witnessed the duel between Heluvian and Icurian after the latter's descent into madness."

Nialla's ears perk up, hearing *that* name again. "Icurian?" She had heard it before from the Crows of Mireaderal.

Her mother catches her tone and frowns. "A name we should speak of with more care."

"And how often would he have these terrors?" Nialla wonders.

"Your father?"

"Yes?"

Cyridel lets out a breath as she sits beside Nialla on the bed. She pads the dampness of the sheets and pushes them aside. "For all the time I knew him, it made his nights restless," her mother chuckles. "I should know. He destroyed my bedchambers after . . . well, after a moment. I only wish I understood then what I do now."

Her mother smiles as her gaze veers off to the side, fondly remembering another life.

"Did he ever tell you about a fox in his dreams? A white one that spoke Icurian's name?" Nialla asks.

"A white fox? No. Your father never spoke of a fox," Cyridel confides. "Foxes are tricksters, though some believe they are benevolent. But why would you hear Icurian's name from one in a dream? That doesn't make sense. His influence doesn't exist in these lands anymore. He's left them. Exiled."

"But that doesn't mean all his mistakes went with him," Nialla laments. "Clesturia and her sisters weren't the only ones hurt by Icurian in those days. His other crimes won't stay buried forever. They're rising to the surface like apples in a cauldron. Father was to handle them. He never had that chance. Now it's up to me."

Her mother lets out a stern puff of air akin to a parent discouraging their child's imagination from running free. "Others can handle those troubles," Cyridel mourns. "You aren't the only one. You *do* know that, right?"

Nialla's voice shudders with a deep sense of isolation. "But I *am* the only one cut off from the rest."

"Nobody's cut you off from anywhere," Cyridel refuses, pursing her lips together, uncertain.

Nialla stares at her mother, trying to find the best way to say what she needs to say. "For most of my life, Sackery led us on a long, aimless road. Yes? He brought us to the far ends of the world and back." She drops her shoulders, feeling like she's in a foreign place.

"To stay ahead of anyone with the patience to hunt us," her mother iterates. "Assuring if anything were to happen to the others, you'd remain alive. That was your father's wish, to save you from his enemies. And we've upheld it to this day."

Nialla frowns. "No? Something *else* found us. I know it has."

"Something?"

"A white fox with yellow eyes. Irimara? That's her name, she told me."

Cyridel surrenders a mildly concerned hum, stroking her chin. "I've only ever heard of such a creature in fairytales."

"And if one exists? At the battle twenty years ago, Clesturia said she had betrayed Icurian. She said they told Heluvian where to find the Neshulha, whom Icurian swore to protect. I didn't think much of it at the time. But now? I don't know what to think."

"It was a bad dream, nothing more," her mother whispers, wrapping her in a dry blanket.

Nialla pulls the covers over her head and covets the softer warmth before lying down again. "Maybe? But it felt so real."

— 6 —

MEMORIES, A DOOMED KING

Sackery's thoughts are like a small flame, a moment of peace, drawing him out of the darkness. The journey to where they discovered Amerllie is a few days' ride from Wilhimusk. Sackery, at the front of the company, allows his mind to wander, filling the silence with his musings.

A thousand years ago, Icurian and Sackery arrived on mainland Arún. He doesn't remember when they started calling him "of the Vedrethal," but it remains a mark of pride for him. It was the creation of a new tale. Sackery had lived most of his life an orphan, so he keenly felt the name's weight. Three years after arriving on these shores from Islinin, he hadn't yet embraced his role as the warrior-servant his adopted father demanded of him.

✳ ✳ ✳

Icurian carried him on his shoulders, deep into a hidden

valley far to the east, north of Iwon Vale.

"Our road narrows farther in," Icurian explained, lowering the boy Sackery to the ground. "We have a long way yet to go, son. I want you to walk the remainder. It'll make you strong for harder roads ahead."

"And what will we find once we get there?" Sackery had wondered.

Icurian smiled and began to shimmy through the tight passage. "A well-kept secret of mine. The others wouldn't understand. They'd see my friends and consider them a threat. I do not. I look at them and see life unfettered by time."

Sackery would pose a question. "Who are they?" he asked.

"A folk touched by a long, unending thread," Icurian told him. "Neshulha. Yes. That's their name. All creatures are born from the melodies. However, a few have closer ties to us than Heluvian would care to admit. Sackery? When they speak to you, do not look away. Meet them as equals, for like the Shanashéron, they are very proud."

Icurian and Sackery drifted through the mountains for weeks until reaching the final turn into the valley.

Sackery felt the warmth on his face as he looked over the lakes and autumn trees for the first time, rainbows arcing over the sky. Looking back, it was like a land out of a child's storybook, the pages illustrated by a religious hand, everything painted red, yellow, green, and blue.

"Welcome to the Rarhavonn," Icurian said. "A Land of a Thousand Colors."

* * *

He doesn't know why his thoughts linger on that moment. Maybe the smell he caught while leaving Wilhimusk reminds him of those days? The memory fades as Iben calls: "Hugh's hut is there! At the fork in the road."

Sackery halts the party and looks where the Captain points. "A farmstead?" It is a comfortable house with a triangular roof built into the hillside and a large rectangular door offset from its center. He notices tools left in the open, unattended—half-empty baskets with fresh pickings stored next to a garden under a large oak tree. The Vedrethal and his riders approach the grounds and stop at the cobbled footpath before the stables a few steps off the small entry gate. He counts five or six horses roaming the pasture on the other side of the fence. The wagon driver settled well into making his domicile an ample home.

"Hugh of Graffton," Iben speaks the name. "The man's a carpenter by trade. He joined us in Esgrelion during our trek south. Followed us from Trebunor after the battle with the Crows and mostly kept to himself these past few years."

"A carpenter and a wagon driver?" Sackery asks.

"Men of his skills are never without work for a community like ours, Master Greywolfe," Iben explains. "Hugh also builds wheels and acts as our seller. We normally see him escort harvests from the eastern fields to Wilhimusk. From there, he'll trade the surplus in Trebunor for goods we don't make ourselves."

"Clothes, tools—" Sackery lists, looking at the Jhalamar, "—arms and armor?"

"And a few added parcels often gifted by King Rasterforn," Iben states. "As thanks for our shared history."

"So, he is a coachman, a craftsman," Sackery demands, "and a tradesman?"

"Yes," Iben answers.

"He must be a man with many hands." Sackery dismounts Ora and dusts off his cloak. "Let's introduce ourselves." He walks up to the door, already open. Sackery knocks before entering the main room, candles on the shelves, casting the walls in a soft yellow light.

"Lord Vedrethal?" an older man speaks in the corner, looking up from a drawing board.

"Hugh the Craftsman?" Sackery asks gently, folding his hands.

"That is me. And this is a fine honor? I've never had our local garrison visit before," Hugh recognizes, setting his quill down on the table. "You don't often ride out this way for the mere sport of it." He sits up in his chair and squares his shoulders. "Would you like some tea? As a host, it's bad luck not to offer guests my hospitality."

"No tea for us," Sackery kindly refuses. "Thank you, regardless."

"Unfortunate. Then you're here because—?"

"Little Amerllie," he frowns.

Hugh leans forward as his eyes reflect the candlelight. "You and the Jhalamar?"

Iben and two others walk in through the front door. Sackery glances at them, eventually returning his attention forward to speak. "A child is dead," the Vedrethal tells him. "It was our duty to protect her, and we failed. Now, we must find what killed her and ensure nobody else gets hurt."

"A noble cause if a few days too late," Hugh states.

Iben walks to the man at the table with all the grace of a staarag hound in a larder. "Please."

Hugh sits back and crosses his arms, taking a deep breath. "That girl deserved more than what she got in this life. 'Twas no easy sight, I'll admit. And I would rather not relive finding her if it's all the same to you." The man hesitates as he stares at Iben, his voice a mournful tone. "But I know what others will ask of you. Folks of our little community want assurance. So, I will answer what I can."

Sackery kneels beside the table and tenderly rests his arm on the edge. "Where did you find the body?"

"By the riverbank," Hugh describes, "where the sand meets the grass."

"Recount the girl's condition when you found her as best you can, my friend. Even a small detail could prove useful to us."

Hugh bites his lip as he strokes his thinly grown beard. "Other than her throat lookin' like some animal tore at it? I remember dirt stains on her dress. Oddly enough, the linen was mostly dry. And that'd be fine if the girl's hair weren't freshly wet. I would think she went for a swim while her parents worked nearby. Oh, and there were bruises on her arms."

Sackery blinks as he takes in the picture. "Like some animal?" he repeats.

"Maybe a bush-yapper?" Hugh suggests. "Amerllie was small for her age. Most animals know to stay away from humans, but a daring sort could kill a child if it were determined. Though, with adults so close? It's a wonder why they didn't answer had she called for help."

"You're suggesting the others didn't hear the attack?" Iben questions.

"That is not what I said, Lord Captain," Hugh refuses, rising to get his coat. "What I meant is that I find it strange *if* the girl had called out, why didn't anybody run to rescue her? It's not some great distance between the fields and the river. Maybe the beast went for the throat first? True. But then, why the bruises on the arms?"

"She fought back," Sackery guesses.

"That is my take as well, Lord Vedrethal," Hugh agrees.

"Can you lead us to where you found the body?" Iben asks.

Hugh nods. "Of course. Let me ready my saddle, and I will join your company."

Iben and Sackery accept the man's pledge, leaving the house to rejoin the others outside, climbing onto their horses. Ora stirs nervously for a moment, jerking her head to the side. Sackery whispers to the animal to calm her down, but the mare spins in circles, quite unlike her. He feels a warm tinge in the air.

Sackery looks and spies a white falcon perched on the dwelling's roof—black spots on its wings and a violet hue to its eyes. The Shanashéron stares at him from above, an inner glow illuminating the thatching at the bird's feet. "Gallandhal?" he utters.

"Master Greywolfe?" Iben pleads, his voice trembling with a mix of fear and curiosity. "Isn't that—?"

"Yes. And it's been a while since the bird last appeared," Sackery acknowledges.

"Did she follow us?"

"I don't know. Gallandhal helped us find one of our hunters lost in the woods last time."

"I remember. We searched for three nights," Iben says.

"Only for the bird to arrive with the man trailing her on the fourth. And that was years ago? A Shanashéron would never reveal themselves without good reason."

Hugh comes with his steed and spots the creature on the roof of his hut. "Now, isn't *that* a sight? They say the white bird only appears in moments of greatest need. A lost soul who stepped off the path, looking for their way home. Guides to the wretched singers of the forgotten songs."

"She's a friend."

"I would hate for her to be an enemy," Hugh admits.

Gallandhal raises her beak proudly before taking flight toward Wilhimusk. *She must be here for Nialla to fly off with-*

out speaking a word. Sackery only has the old tales to help him understand the connection between the Shanashéron and the Vedreron. *How do they always appear when folk need them? Can they sense it? See the future?*

"It's a bad sign if the bird's here," some of the others fret.

"Did she come to help us?"

"Why did she fly away?"

"Do you think she'll come back?"

"Enough!" Iben shouts, raising his fist. "Are you soldiers or children playing with swords in the woods? Not another word from your troubled tongues." He turns to the wagon driver. "Master Hugh? Give us a lead."

"We follow the road east for half a day more, Lord Captain," the other answers. "I found little Amerllie near the ford to the Seclumor Wilds—a dangerous crossing during the flood season, let me tell you. For most of the year, the waters there are shallow. However, they tend to rise quickly during a deluge. Settlers had a calf drown two years ago when the current swept it off its feet and brought the poor creature a league down-stream."

"Is it possible the same happened to Amerllie?" Jhalamar Ivette breaks in to ask.

"Doubtful. We hadn't had a heavy rain in over a month, so the waters are pretty low."

"And the girl didn't drown," Sackery intercedes.

"I—? Understand," Ivette dithers.

Sackery looks at the woman with sad eyes. He offers her a

nod before steering Ora toward the wagon driver. "Take the front, my friend." All the Jhalamar in the company sit up in their saddles as he gives the order. "We'll follow you."

"As you wish, my lord."

Hugh guides the party toward the mountains. They ride into the night, their horses' stride echoing in the stillness, reaching the far eastern stretch by daybreak. Sackery orders the Jhalamar to dismount and form a perimeter once they arrive at the site. Otherwise, they could trample over the scene and make it hard for him to pick up the trail of whatever killed the girl.

It's a flat terrain, with low-cut grasses and very few trees on this side of the river. The early morning fog hangs low, adding an eeriness to the air. Settlers use this land to graze their herds, watched over by flock dogs and chaser hawks. Half-harvested wheat fields crescent the horizon in every direction during this time of year—not a good place for a predator on the prowl with too few hiding places. There'd be a fair chance a sentry would've spotted a threat.

Whatever beast attacked Amerllie did so in plain sight. *And nobody saw it happen?* Sackery weighs the question. He removes his gloves and rubs his palms together. Amerllie's death fixates his thoughts, that little flame growing stronger in the dark.

Hugh brings him to the sandy beach that hugs the water: "This is where I found the girl."

Sackery kneels and runs a finger around where the body had likely lain. "No blood?" He looks at Iben.

"We all saw her wounds," Iben describes. "Blood should have pooled."

"But it hadn't," Sackery returns. "Even for a child, a wound like hers? There should be *some* blood where she died. All I see are a few droplets around the edges. Maybe? I find that difficult to believe."

"What are you saying, lord?" Hugh asks, bewildered.

"I don't know?" Sackery admits. "I wouldn't think this is where she met her attacker."

Iben stays attentive as he walks a circle, telling the Jhalamar to watch the ground for more tracks.

Sackery balances on his knees and traces the imprint left behind by Amerllie's remains. He finds gouges in the dirt, something heavy dragged to the river from the grass. He follows the marks off the beach and into the field. Dried blood forms black streaks in the soil. Smaller prints alongside it, no larger than a fox's track. "Look here! Do you see this?"

Iben hurries over and eyes the marks. "Footprints? A canid? Maybe a jackal?"

"Too large. These have a narrower stride, with a thinner heel pad than a wolf or most hunting dogs. Maybe two and a half inches? Three? Large for a common fox, but it's the nearest match if memory serves me right," Sackery observes. "Which leaves us with more questions."

"Could a fox have killed a child Amerllie's age?" Iben begs the question. "Or *would* one even want to?"

"Maybe? If there's more than one working together and they

were desperate," Sackery frowns, unconvinced. "But I don't see more than a single set inside this mess. And we're not in winter. Had the girl died elsewhere, a fox isn't likely to drag the body, even short distances. Even if it was rabid? It'd still be unusual."

"Foxes mostly feed on small animals or insects," Hugh adds. "Their nature is to flee, not fight."

"Yes," Sackery murmurs.

He suddenly stops as the tracks take on a chaotic pattern. Amerllie and the foxlike creature seem engaged in a dance, their movements a breathtaking spectacle. Then, a new set of tracks appears in the mix, resembling those of an ursine but far too large to *be* a simple bear. They are still damp, too, almost fresh. From the river's direction—?

Sackery presses his hand next to it with the beast's paw more than three times his width.

"That's not a bear's track," Iben stipulates.

"No. Not any bear as we'd know it," Sackery agrees. "Three sets of tracks? And a dead girl? Maybe by a fox, or . . . something else?" His eyes dart eastward to the woods on the opposite shore. Those trees stand, shrouded in darkness—the Seclumor Wilds, named by the Maithandír who once inhabited these lands.

"Master Greywolfe? Sackery—?" Iben questions.

"Lord Vedrethal?" Hugh prods.

Sackery rises to his feet and strokes the dirt on his palm. "Amerllie was killed here. See the blood? And something dragged her body to the riverbank for *us* to find. A hungry animal that took a chance to kill a human wouldn't leave its prize with an empty stomach."

"Amerllie's remains were mostly intact," Iben ponders.

"Meaning what killed her didn't do it for survival," Sackery agrees. "It had a reason."

Iben and the Jhalamar turn to him, confused. "Intentionally? But a wild animal doesn't kill for sport—?"

"Not all the creatures in the Wilds *are* mere animals," Sackery corrects, his voice tinged with a sense of impending danger. "It is an untamed, ancient land, full of strange things, many of which go unnamed. Spirits? No matter how hard we search, you'd never find two that are the same."

"Like those we fought at our battle with the Crows?" Iben recollects.

Sackery grimaces. "Of a sort. Some there were peaceful, driven to desperation. Others? Naturally malicious. Icurian understood them better than anyone. It seems we're still following in his footsteps after all these many years."

"Not a place we want to be stranded," Iben notions.

Sackery doesn't respond. His father's voice echoes in his ears as he follows the larger tracks back to the Little River.

* * *

"Do not trust your eyes in this place," Icurian warned as they made their way through the Rarhavonn, his voice kept low. "The Neshulha protect themselves by weaving intricate illusions. They can appear as real as I am to you right now. Lifelike. Trust your instincts. Follow

*with what feels right. An image can only harm you if
you allow it to convince you it's real."*

*"Is that why you don't want the others knowing about
them?" an exhausted Sackery had asked.*

*"Heluvian fears what he doesn't understand," Icurian
said. "Sometimes things are better off if we just leave
them alone."*

* * *

Red clay gathers at the water's edge, with clear impressions
where the mighty bear-like beast strode. Sackery kneels to
touch the reeds pressed into the mud alongside the fox's trail.
His concern is that the larger tracks came back around while
the fox remained on this side of the river.

"What do you see?" Iben respectfully asks.

"More animal traffic? Older signs—boar, deer, wolves, and
wildcats," Sackery lists. "All of them, crossing at this ford. Most
are capable of harming a nine-summer child, like Amerllie. The
question is . . . Why make the trouble? So close to the fields,
would a wolf or a mountain lion risk it? Even feral animals
know to stay away from humans. Fear them like fire after a
thunderstorm." His fingers go numb as he muses. "And it left
the body mostly intact?"

His eyes keep landing on the shallower impressions on the
ground. As much as he'd prefer it to be a wolf or stray dog, only
the *fox* stays with the girl to a step. So, the prey they hunt must
be a fox—a fox that killed young Amerllie.

Sackery retraces the larger set of prints where they shadow

the fox's tread. *Was the bear following the critter? And if it was, why did it retreat into the wildwoods if the other hadn't turned back that way?* He clenches his fist and whispers: "Unless it intends to cut it off at its den?"

"Master Greywolfe? The sun's getting high," Iben states firmly.

"Our horses will need feeding soon," Hugh agrees.

Sackery looks, the colors in the sky turning a vivid white and blue. "Let's take a respite. We'll set out in an hour."

"I'll keep sentries on the lookout for any more wild animals," Iben suggests.

"Good. Do that. Master Hugh?" Sackery offers.

"Lord Vedrethal?"

"You may return home."

Hugh eyes Iben and the twenty or so Jhalamar circling the field. "We all serve by the Lady's Grace," the man tells him. "Amerllie was Nialla's friend. Ankara before her. You have a duty, and I won't dissuade you from it."

"That'd be most wise," Sackery admits.

"But may this common man offer some plain advice?"

"I am listening, Master Hugh."

"Be careful should you invade the wildwoods, Lord Vedrethal. Many things live there, as you know. Your hunt may not end happily should the trees decide you're a threat. Yes? King Rasterforn led seven hundred to Mireaderal to fight the witches in the forest twenty years ago. Less than half made it back."

"I was there," Iben growls. "And I survived."

"Please, Lord Jhalamar. Be cautious," Hugh says, raising his hands. "That's all I ask."

"He means well, Captain," Sackery calms the tension. "And thank you for your efforts, my good man."

"Always a pleasure to serve our Lady's Protector," Hugh smiles and steps away, horse by his side. "Good luck, my lord. May your task end triumphant." There's a heaviness to the man's shoulders as he departs down the wagon road.

Sackery nods and turns to the forest, thumbing the hilt of his sword, a tightness in his chest.

— 7 —

A BLUE SCRAP OF CLOTH

Cyridel removes her boots and dabs her toes onto the sandy patch of the Houdicar's garden atop the plateau. She closes her eyes as the sediment warms her feet. The wind pushes the trees aside until their branches fly in one direction, her dress flowing with the colors.

Nialla adores this place. Cyridel often finds her daughter here, making the sand dance at her fingertips. As dusk falls, the girl's inside, finally asleep.

Cyridel breathes deeply, opening her eyes as the grass waves at her. She listens as each blade cuts the air. It is the life from her dreams—away from others, in simple and cherished deference. Nature's purest sense. "Am I back home in Ilhivendal? No. But this feels close."

"Lady Miralifrim?" Yeavengeritt interrupts, his voice whimsical.

Cyridel looks at him dryly, counting the creases on the old man's face. "Any word from Sackery?"

"No. Not as of yet," the man shakes his head. "But you know what they say about messengers? They only come with bad news. His party remains afield. They'll be gone anywhere up to a week. It all depends on how long it takes for them to track the animal that killed young Amerllie."

Cyridel frowns. Sackery took most of the Jhalamar with him. He left only a handful behind to protect Wilhimusk if anything decides to attack them while the fighters are away. *Not that anything stands a chance against what meager force remains.* Such is the risk in this game they play with the lives of men.

"Thank you for letting me know, friend," Cyridel acknowledges.

Yeavengeritt bows to her and smiles. "I am ever at your service, Lady Miralifrim. I'll set the others to task for the night."

Cyridel nods, and the man leaves, fulfilling his obligation—a life debt owed to Nialla after she relit that little flame that brought him out of the dark.

Left alone in the garden once more, her thoughts wander. "Miralifrim," Cyridel utters. She had taken to the name years ago, the weight of it becoming a part of her identity. And why not? Nobody outside the Naúmandial Valley would recognize it. But it is *not* her name. She stole it from a woman close to her heart—the mother of her friend, Eéwen, from when they were kids in Ilhivendal.

Cyridel, in this grove, feels a yearning for her younger days.

Raindrops caress her face as a storm gathers, and she takes a breath, finding comfort in the subtle chill that comes with the breeze. Familiarity? This place of serene beauty stands so high atop the Greencliffs that only a few will climb the path. It isn't just her sanctuary, but somewhere she can look out to the greater world, an island in the middle of a grassy sea, the closest thing to home she has left.

So, it's a moment of surprise for Cyridel when she spots a solitary scrap of blue fabric hanging from the hedge. Puzzled, she steps closer and takes it, looking it over and running the threads between her fingers. She notices the intricate white patterns woven into the blue. And the natural finishes around the edges? All of it suggests a distinctive Ellúndar touch. It's no ordinary rag and certainly not something a settler on the frontier would choose to wear.

"Cyridel?" a voice whispers, although she almost doesn't hear it.

Her gaze shifts to the grass, following the sound, and Cyridel suddenly catches a tall figure standing in the shade of the tree. *Is it a man?* Broad-shouldered, his face hides under a worn blue hood. His stance is strangely familiar to her. She squints, trying to get a better look. He swiftly disappears into the rocks, leaving her with an abrupt pounding inside her chest.

Cyridel runs after the figure, her breath coming in quick gasps. The man is a blur of motion, but she's more agile and relentless. He darts through the rocky warrens and into a clear patch near the plateau's summit, a wide view over the mountains spreading out on the far sides of the valley to the south and east. And then, like a shade, she loses sight of him.

"Stop! Please?!" Cyridel calls out, her voice echoing in the vastness. "Please don't leave." She waits for a moment, but the only response is the dust in the wind.

She looks again at the blue cloth scrap, and her mind races in a hundred directions. There's no chance it could have come from Trebunor. Its embroideries are from the North, from Maheira—stars over a grand tower. Nialla's words repeat in her ear, "Something else found us," her daughter said. *Is she right? Has somebody found us? A friend? Or maybe a foe?*

Once more, the wind stirs, carrying with it a chilling whisper: "Elendsah," it utters, the voice fading into the very stone. Cyridel lingers for a moment, hoping for it to speak again. Nothing comes, and she feels . . . Grief? It is as if somebody tore a piece from her and left it to dry on a hot day.

A white bird perches on the rocks. "Gallandhal?" Cyridel murmurs, recognizing its purple eyes.

With a nod, the shape-changer regards her and suddenly takes flight again, disappearing into the clouds overhead.

Cyridel marvels at the bird's shape as the sun falls to the horizon. *Strange. How long has it been since the creature last appeared?* She counts the seasons, tallying each summer in her head. *Two years? No. Three?* That leaves her with a worrying question. *Why does the Shanashéron show itself after all this time?*

Without the bird to answer, she descends the warrens and

returns to the Houdicar. Cyridel discovers her daughter sitting in the garden's sandpit, softly humming to the roots. She should be inside. Instead, the rocks tremble as the girl's melody shifts the soil, and the flowery blooms glow like the sun reflecting in her eyes.

Cyridel sneaks behind Nialla while the other's focus is elsewhere.

Nialla reads her footfalls and turns. "Enjoying the warm spring breeze?"

Cyridel stops mid-step and crosses her arms. "Have you anything to do with it?"

"No. At least, I don't think—? A storm's coming over the mountains," Nialla admits. She smiles and slides to where Cyridel had buried her toes. "I am having trouble making the sand dance. And I don't know why. It doesn't want to listen to me. So, I must move the grains as one long, unbroken limb."

"You're tired," Cyridel frowns. "You promised to get some sleep."

"I did. But I couldn't. Maybe I am a little distracted?" Nialla shudders.

"Because you dreamed of a fox in the grass?"

"It felt so real. And yet? It wasn't. I know it wasn't."

Cyridel notices the look in the girl's eyes. She wants her mother to understand, even if she doesn't know how to express her thoughts with words.

Nialla draws a circle in the sand. She whistles a small tune, and the sand jumps like a phantom arm swimming like a snake to its burrow, reaching for her hand. Her patterns are simple next to what a weaver can do with a thread—still, Nialla stretches the muscle, and the images she creates become more elaborate. Cyridel does not doubt someday that her daughter may even give life to the sand and order it around like soldiers in an army.

"Have you gone to see Ankara?" Cyridel asks the girl.

Nialla blushes red and looks away. "She wouldn't want to see me."

"I don't believe that. Your friend? She needs you right now," Cyridel tells her. "You grew up together."

"She grew up while I mostly stayed the same," Nialla frowns.

"Her daughter's dead. Also, your friend! Nialla—?"

"I look too much like Amerllie. It'd only be a cruel reminder."

Cyridel sits beside the girl, resting a hand on her daughter's knee. "Is that what you think? No. You look too much like yourself to be Amerllie. Don't discount the feelings your friends will always have for you. Ankara could use the company of the one person who knows her better than anybody. Nialla? Can you look at me?"

Nialla tucks her knees into her chest and looks away. "Did she tell you that?"

"Does she need to? I can feel their anguish from up here. It's—?"

"Suffocating? Like breathing through a blanket."

"And the last time you felt that way—?"

"Twenty years ago, with the Crows," Nialla disquiets, her

voice laced with a hint of something else. *Bad memories?*

Cyridel drops her shoulders. "Do you think one of them survived?"

"No? I don't think so—? Do you think Sackery will find what killed Amerllie?"

"Should I even answer that? Of course, he will. Why? Are you starting to doubt after all these years?"

"No. But what if it's too much for our Vedrethal to handle?"

Cyridel leans in to kiss her daughter's forehead and smiles. "Sackery defended against those witches for almost two days before we caught up to him. He's a survivor—a devoted warrior, well-practiced in the battle arts. He now goes on a hunt like any other. And he's not alone. Remember? Iben and the Jhalamar ride with him. He trained them. Together? Nothing less than an army stands a chance."

"Or a very determined fox," Nialla murmurs.

"We've many enemies out there in the vast, open world. Some are worse than others. We'll deal with them as they come. Amerllie's case isn't anything but a desperate, wild animal on the loose." Cyridel doesn't know if it *was* an *animal* or a *monster* that killed her daughter's friend. Either way, Sackery will handle it. She has faith in the man.

"I don't know," Nialla mumbles, her voice less than a whisper.

"Look at tomorrow as a new day with a new sun," Yeavengeritt speaks, standing quietly under the tree by the Houdicar. Jhalamar Olynn and Rod are beside him in their full garb—Pict and Hader go to stand by the pond, equally armored. *Did they come back up the Greencliffs from Wilhimusk?* No doubt they overheard Nialla talk of her worries to Cyridel. "Pict and Hader will stand guard with you tonight. Olynn and Rod will watch over the village by the signal fire and belltower."

"All set to their tasks?" Cyridel asks. "Prepared for trouble?"

"With most of the unit with Master Greywolfe, I think it best," Yeavengeritt admits. "Yes?"

"The people below don't know what else to do," Pict offers.

"And there's not enough of us to cover the whole town," Hader agrees.

"We stand ready to defend Wilhimusk," Olynn boasts.

"Including our young lady atop the mountain," Rod finishes.

Nialla sits up in the sandpit and frowns. Even after all this time, most in Wilhimusk can't see Cyridel's daughter as more than the nine-summer child she appears to be, like Amerllie. Yet, Nialla will soon be ninety in a few years. Often, the girl acts older than she looks, with an energy that only an Ellúndar youth can bring to life. Other times, Nialla struggles with it. Cyridel notices it when she's around the older kids in the village. She tends to avoid them.

Cyridel stands and dusts off her gown. "Take to your posts, Jhalamar of Wilhimusk." She walks to Pict and Hader and squeezes their arms. "But I want you two to stay close to the house tonight. As a precaution for strangers and beasts stalking the grounds."

"Of course, my lady," Hader agrees, subtly narrowing his eyes, confused.

"Is there anything explicit you would like us to keep an eye out for?" Pict begs the question.

"A white fox with yellow eyes," Nialla describes.

Yeavengeritt nearly chuckles, but the man fights it off and lends the girl a kindly smile. "Ah? I don't believe there are many reports of white foxes in this country. Perhaps in the mountains? But the valley is a fertile, green land, little one. A creature with such a coat wouldn't last in the wilds."

"True," Hader offers. "Our native species has red fur with orange eyes and ears as big as spoons."

"Then she should be easy to spot," Nialla tells them, clenching her jaw. Cyridel reads the weakness in the girl's tone and how she rubs her throat. "It's something I saw most recently. Or was it a dream? I don't know anymore."

Jhalamar Pict, Hader, Olynn, and Rod look at each other, doubt in their eyes but unwilling to dispute it. The girl knows what she believes, even if everyone else thinks it's unlikely. "Remain vigilant for anything of the like, all the same," Cyridel instructs. "Please?"

Yeavengeritt regards Nialla with concern. "As you wish," he answers, offering her a respectful bow.

"We'll stay alert and wake you if we notice anything amiss," Hader promises, his voice steady and reassuring.

Cyridel pulls her daughter close, the touch of a mother's love, and brushes a few loose strands of the girl's unbraided hair behind her ears. "Good. You may leave." She tries to muster confidence in her voice, but she can't hide the worrying crack of her tone.

The others depart without further arguments. Pict and Hader will do their jobs, as will Olynn and Rod in the village below the Greencliffs. They are the Jhalamar—trained in the martial traditions of the Vedrethal by Sackery Greywolfe. They'll keep to their duty no matter the cost to themselves. *That* is their promise.

Holding her daughter among the flowers, Cyridel notices she still has the blue cloth scrap she found in her hand. *Was that man watching her? Where did he come from?* There's only one path up to the plateau. And to climb it? *That* somebody had to make their way through Wilhimusk and past the Houdicar. Cyridel would've seen the stranger had he come from that direction.

Yet, the man had a familiar presence. *And that voice?* It spoke to her before. She knows it. She's heard it countless times in her dreams, her memories. It can't be *his* voice. *He died.* And there are no such things as ghosts, Cyridel reminds herself, distrusting her feelings. *Then, how is he calling to me from the grave?*

Cyridel closes her hand and smells the torn fabric. "Galron?" she utters. Then, she tucks it into her bodice, next to where her birthstone rests against her chest. She touches it, the Fallenstar of June. And the stone warms, like welcoming an old friend home once again.

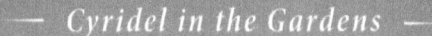

LIFE IS A QUIET THING

The water engulfs her leg until it stops at Nialla's knee. It's everywhere. Great falls delve into a deep black abyss from darker skies above. And in those depths, trees grow tall, their roots breaking through the torrents, massive branches stretching toward her.

Nialla wipes her eyes, hoping the dream will go away. It doesn't. And she holds her breath.

She spies the white fox sitting in the grass near the pond with a curious look. Pict and Hader flank her sides but don't notice the fair creature. Irimara glances at the Jhalamar before surrendering a nod to Nialla. "They won't see me if that's what you wonder. Not unless I want them to."

"Are these illusions real?" Nialla cries.

Irimara tilts her head the other way and lets off a low laugh. "A contradictory question, do you think? Is it real because you *see* it? Or should you *feel* it? Like a tide washing over you, drowning you in the darkest ocean with no way ashore."

"Because they seem real at a glance," Nialla feigns, clenching the Ancestrum Stone at her chest. "But as I focus, I notice these images lack spirit. Everything has a life to it, like a breeze coming through the valley. Do you know what it's like to hear a new song for the first time? Even the rocks hum, a mirror to our hearts. Your illusions aren't just a trick of the mind. They are manifestations born out of the imagination, flat next to the *real* thing."

Irimara sits up, her eyes bright against the shadows. "Few of your kind could ever tell the difference before."

"Maybe I am not like most others of my kind?" Nialla suggests.

"Perhaps. But what makes you so unlike your forebearers?" Irimara demands, her voice a challenge. "The mother? Or the father? As you sleep, aren't dreams made real to the passive eye?"

Nialla shifts uncomfortably away from the foxlike creature, her confusion palpable. "I don't understand."

"Of course you don't, little cub. Your eyes are open, but you remain blind," Irimara states. "You must do more than *listen* to survive the hardships to come. I will not be your only foe. Things far greater than me will find you. And when they do? They will rip the roots out from under you."

"I can see the dangers perfectly fine," Nialla iterates. She notices the birds singing faintly in the illusionary trees. Yet, they aren't flapping their wings or hopping from branch to branch. And as she turns her body, there's no echo about Nialla's movements. Muffled. "What must I do? Tell me."

"Be the first to rip them out," Irimara instructs. "Break the foundation. Reshape it anew into a fortress as if you are the Lord of Stone."

"Is that why you attack me now? To warn me?"

Irimara rises to all four legs and lowers her ears. She doesn't answer. Instead, the wind blows harder, and Nialla awakes in the field with the Jhalamar staring at her from the cabin's front steps. Pict and Hader rush toward her as she collapses to her knees.

"Nialla! How did you—?" Hader asks. "Are you okay?"

They pick her off the ground and brush the dirt off her dress. "I am fine," she says, wiping her tears.

"Good," Pict returns. "It'd be a shame if you were to die too soon."

Nialla's eyes snap toward them. "What—?" She takes a few steps back as Hader draws his sword and plunges it into her chest. Nialla gasps, falling backward into the pond. A black sheet enwraps her, and the water becomes an endless sea of tyrants that stare at her as she plummets toward the bottom. Nialla struggles to break Hader's hold as the man jumps in with her, a hand on her throat, the other still on the hilt of his blade, cutting toward her heart.

They sink farther into the abyss when Pict dives after them, grabbing her arms and pulling them tightly behind her back.

By chance of their absent-mindedness, they didn't bind her legs. Nialla kicks at the two, desperate to get away. She lands a hit square in Hader's face, but he shrugs it off as if it did nothing. Despite all her strength, the water diminishes each blow as the pair force her into the deepest parts of the dark sea. Their mouths crack open, and their eyes shine a golden hue. Tentacles burst from every orifice as their fingers become claws, ripping at her clothes and exposing her to the damp and cold.

Nialla lands hard on the sea's murky bottom. She rolls onto a knee, but a lamplight now shines on her from above, the weight of the glow pushing her into the muck. Outside the circle, she can hardly see the eyes watching her—dozens of dim pupils against the light, hungry and laughing at her nakedness. Their hands stretch toward her, demanding tribute. Even as she tries to escape, the sea floor opens like a great maw, but she forcefully beats it back with the flat of her heel and climbs to solid rock.

Nialla cuffs her ears and shakes her head. "Go away! Go away! Go away!" she shouts, air bubbling from her mouth.

"They won't go away," Irimara tells her. "They are your past. Your future! Your strife."

Nialla looks at the fox swimming toward her from the shallows. "Stop this? Make this go away! Please?"

"Please?! I thought you were a mighty one?" Irimara taunts, her grin a cruel slash across her snout, showing her teeth. The creature's grace dies as the dark waters surrounding them become illuminated by a red-orange star that burns Nialla's hair to a strand, her skin drying out like white ash. "Ignore your pride, Child of the Mountains. Take my place and ask, would you show *me* any mercy?"

The fox comes near enough for Nialla to touch her. Irimara merely skirts her fingertips and laughs.

"What did I ever do to you?!" Nialla shouts, her anger like the fire swelling her throat.

"Do you not know? How does it feel having everything burn away until there's nothing left but a scared little pup crying for her mother?" the fox demands. They're now in a forest, with trees feeding the star's flames. The yellow-eyed monsters around her enter the light, revealing themselves as people she knows. Pict and Hader among them. Ankara, too, alongside her husband and Amerllie—who's nothing more than an ashy figure vaguely resembling the friend that Nialla had known.

"Get out of my head! Why can't I push you out?!"

"Because *we* are a part of you," Ankara's shade says.

"We can't leave you," Pict decries.

"We can't escape you," Hader soon follows.

"You've taken us into your soul, and now we share your destiny," Sackery approaches. He's another shade, far younger.

"Our trust in you will kill us in the end," Amerllie's ashes whisper. "Much as it did for me." The shadow walks to Nialla and puts a hand on her trembling cheeks, sparking a dark limerick. "Little girl, little girl—watching all the boys. Little girl, little girl—visiting their dreams. Little girl, little girl—wooing them with her vows. Little girl, little girl—" Amerllie's form grows and grows. She now towers over Nialla, opening her mouth and blowing a kiss that reeks of deathly musk.

"—devouring their greed," Irimara takes over, her voice carrying a weight of ominous finality.

Nialla gasps for breath. The forest surrounding her expands as Nialla jumps to her feet and pushes through the flames, trying to run away. Each step becomes a league as she runs faster and faster to escape the nightmare. However, no matter how far she carries her legs, Nialla doesn't move, not an inch. The ground beneath her stays the same as the earthly maw opens again to swallow her foot, and she can't fight it any longer. Rock-like teeth erupt out of the dirt, and she becomes cocooned by its root-like tongue, ravenous and monstrous.

She drops into it as the fire engulfs the surface, saliva pouring over her, brimming her nose and into her nostrils. *Is this the end?* Nialla clenches her fist, outstretching an arm, looking for an anchor while begging for somebody to help.

To her surprise, a hand catches her wrist and drags her toward the light.

"Throw a cover over her!" Yeavengeritt shouts. "The last thing she needs is everybody seeing her bare." He brings a lantern close enough to blind her.

It's been the dead of night. Nialla woke in the middle of the pond near the Houdicar.

Jhalamar Pict, Olynn, and Rod form a perimeter around her, facing outward. Hader lays a blanket across her shoulders. Nialla doesn't know how she got here or how long she's been in the water. She lifts her hand and feels her fingers pruned, her skin stinging as she moves, aching and tender.

Her mother, Cyridel, rushes to Nialla once she's safe on dry land. "What's happened?" she asks, clearing wet hair from the younger's face. Nialla shivers in the cold. *But I don't get cold?* That alone, her mother quickly notices. "Frozen to the touch? Nialla? Nells! Tell me what happened?!"

Nialla's body shakes as her jaw stiffens. "I-I-I don't know. I-I can't feel m-my ha-ha-hands." She speaks through chattering teeth.

Her mother hurries to rub Nialla's hands back and forth together, creating friction in the motion. "It's okay! You're okay now. Let's get you inside by the fire where it's warm. Can you move?" Yeavengeritt and the Jhalamar close ranks around them, keeping their eyes outward.

Nialla nods. "I-I think so. Sure? Yes." As she attempts to stand, her knees give out from under her.

"That's all right," Cyridel weakly laughs. "We can carry you."

"I don't need to be—"

Without another word, her mother picks her off the ground as if she were a babe again.

Yeavengeritt and the others follow them, their hands on their weapons, undrawn. "Search the area!" the Maithandír orders. "Turn over every rock in the gardens! Ensure there's nothing out there peeping in on us." Nialla catches the light from the lantern, the *fear* reflecting in the old man's eyes as he glances at her.

"You heard him!" Hader shouts. "Form a line!"

Yeavengeritt leans toward Nialla's mother as they go inside the house. "What are we going to tell everyone?"

"Should they ask? Tell them my daughter had a nightmare," Cyridel answers. "All children have nightmares, don't they? Her, especially."

"Lady Miralifrim? She's not just any child," the old man states, suppressing the undercurrent of his tone.

"I don't think they need to know anything more," her mother decides, setting Nialla down on the bed and wrapping her in blanket after blanket. "And nobody can learn we found her like this. Understand? She means too much to too many people. How would the others react if they discovered she's not a stone in the river?"

The old man folds his hands at his stomach in deference. "Yes. I understand," Yeavengeritt fades, lowering his head. He then leaves the Houdicar to help coordinate the search, but he stops at the door briefly, a worried glance to Nialla on the bed.

He has soft eyes, full of compassion. Old and weary but upright and loyal.

Inside, Nialla's mother heats a few coals in an iron pan, sliding it under her blankets on the bed. She then begins steeping tea leaves in a ceramic pot, the aroma masking the stench of musk that's hung over the air these past few days. After letting it cool, Cyridel pours a small amount into a cup and hands it to the girl.

"I don't want it," Nialla refuses.

"No? But you *will* drink it," her mother instructs. "It'll warm your blood."

Nialla leans forward and lets the fragrance float down her throat and into her chest. She takes a sip, then another. It has a strong taste, nearly black, but the warmth spreads through her body and into her limbs.

"Good. That'll liven you right up. Now—*what* happened? You've had nightmares before, but you weren't asleep this time," Cyridel comforts. "Your father had rebounds very similar. So, *what* did you see? Something different? New? Or perhaps an old, tired terror rearing its ugly mug?"

Nialla shakes her head. "I don't know. It was—? I don't know *what* I saw." Every syllable leaves a bad taste in her mouth that even her mother's bitter tea can't overcome. "Shades? Faces of people I know turned against me. They tried to drown me."

"You never did like the water," Cyridel frowns.

"But then I was on fire? Like before? I thought I was, at least. Was it just a mirage? I don't think I truly *felt* anything."

Her mother gingerly nods. "A mirage? What do you mean? Like a vision?"

"Like a reflection through a misty haze? Daydreams made real. Vibrant? A little muffled at times? Everything came to me as if I could hear them from underwater. And all the while, the stench of musk, like dirt in the gardens after it rains. I don't know. It was like I *knew* the difference, but it was hard to tell. It all came at me so fast."

"And the white fox you told me about?"

"Irimara. She *was* there."

"In the dream?"

"She *was* the dream."

Cyridel frowns before pouring tea into another cup for herself. "Maybe you slept too much? We can figure it out after the sun beats the horizon. I'll stay awake with you for as long as necessary. Whatever dragged you into that fantasy won't have another opportunity. Not with me ready to stop it."

"But what if it does?" Nialla asks.

"It won't. That is my promise to you, baby girl," Cyridel reassures.

Her mother kisses the top of Nialla's head and eases her to the pillow. She's still naked under all the blankets, but at least she feels safe being confined by them. Memories of this encounter with Irimara harkens back to her confrontation with Clestruia in the battle with the Crows. There, the witches connected their minds in that fierce competition. Nialla won out by drawing on the memory of a man in a blue cloak singing her a lullaby.

Cyridel rests an arm around Nialla as the two lie together on the bed. The girl smiles as her mother starts humming that very tune, easing her worries. That humming shifts to words, bright against the Jhalamar making a ruckus outside in their heavy boots:

> *You dream of a world you've never seen,*
> *A life of love and dancing in the light,*
> *Beyond the ranges stand,*

A home you've never known.

Your heart is bound for more, my dear,
A power your blood adorns,
Beyond the river's rise,
A fate never meant as yours.

But you'll stand apart the world,
Where towers are falling down, beyond,
The valley heights,
Of a past you shall never know.

And you'll rise to the open fields afar,
A kingdom of stone and ash,
Beyond the mountain swells,
To a life you have never, ever known.

Nialla rests her chin on her mother's shoulder. "Did you change the words?"

Cyridel smiles. "Only a little. As with life, all things will change." She puffs her cheeks, taking a long pause between each breath. "And the song is old. After singing it to you all these years, I felt it needed something new to keep it alive. Do you like it?" The weight of those decades lingers in the air, a testament to the passage of time.

"Maybe? But it's not the same."

"Yes. Now, I leave a small piece of myself in the lyric."

"Like a tapestry whose story gets added to with each hand that sews it?"

"From my mother to me," Cyridel tells her. "And from my mother's folk, the Aenümorians."

"My Grandmother? Then, was it *her* lullaby? If she was the first to sing it?"

"No. I don't think—? Nadrial often serenaded me with it when I was little. And once you sing a song, does it still belong to you? You can revise and share words with others, but once they hear the music, it becomes a part of them. That's something you can never take back. It'd be like retaking a piece of their soul."

"Never take back?" Nialla repeats in a whisper. "I wish I could have known her."

"Have? And why can't you? I am certain she's still alive. Her father was Míran, like I am. I never knew him, either. He died in the Battle of the White Hills against the *hadorns* when our united forces, led by my father, Lurón, marched in defense of the Aens. Maybe someday, I'll earn some redemption, and you can finally meet your family."

"Do you think they'd accept me?" Nialla asks.

"Of course they would, little one."

"You believe that?"

"Without a doubt in my mind." Cyridel rests her hand against Nialla's chest, sharing the warmth of a soft touch. "Did I ever tell you? My parents met in that battle," she returns. "After the war, when the dust settled, Nadrial left with Lurón to live with

the Míran-Ellúndar. That is why we have the name Elendsah—you and I—even though we are a part of the House of
the Fallenstar, the Lords of Ilhivendal."

"Not my grandfather's name?"

"It is a tradition for Ellúndar children to take the name of
their likened parent," Cyridel nods. "Given that my grandmother's name was Aenümorian instead of Aarendelic, Nadrial
accepted the name of her father's house, Elendsah of Nrondon.
So, I took *her* name, too, while my brother, Erathil, took after
our father."

Nialla burrs unwittingly. "It sounds complicated."

"And that's not considering *your* father's account," Cyridel
laughs. "Endúcar? A name as much as a title. Everyone alive is
born of many families. *You* were born of more, distinct from
each other in every possible way—Maheiran, Aenümorian,
Ellúndar, Vedreron. *A power your blood adorns*, like in the
songs."

Listening to her mother talk helps Nialla's eyes go heavy. Her
thoughts about the white fox become distant following the
stories of armies and lineage. That is until she hears a whisper
from *inside* the walls: "Naught but a mutt?! You can't hide in
your mother's arms forever," it speaks.

Nialla looks up to see her mother's face, unaware, suddenly
turning bloody and rotten like a corpse. She wraps more blankets around her head to pretend it's not happening: "Why don't
you leave me alone?" Nialla breathes the words.

"And risk failure?" Irimara demands. "No, little cub. That'd be most unwise." She takes over the lullaby and forces it three octaves lower.

Nialla closes her eyes, wishing she couldn't hear the song anymore. "Please?"

"Find your strength, Nialla Elendsah. Remember? Hope comes from the unexpected."

Thunder cracks and the room flashes white.

— 9 —

THE OLD WAYS

Sackery waits at the edge of the Seclumor Wilds, a dense wall of trees and foliage ahead of them, cutting off their path where the grass meets the wood.

Iben comes beside him and kneels. "More of these strange tracks?"

"Look at the imprint," Sackery points. "See the ridges? Rough. Indeed, the same we found across the river." He paces back and forth, studying the dark of the Wilds. He hadn't ventured there for a few short years. And the last time he did, ready for a fight? Rasterforn and his people had to carry him out.

Iben glances up at the Vedrethal. The man takes a stick off the ground, using its tip to trace an outline. "Not a common beast, that's for certain," the man remarks, his voice hinting at his curiosity at the unusual spoors.

"And not a greater bear?" another of the company asks.

After they forded to the river's east bank, their troop regained the fox's trail. Every step of the way, these massive prints followed the smaller creature toward Wilhimusk before returning to the confines of the wildwoods.

Sackery remains stuck on the idea that a modest predator—like a fox—could kill a nine-year-old child. That concern stays with him like an old word at the back of his mind. All he needs to do is reach out and bring it into the light.

"A simple bear doesn't quite fit the mark," Iben murmurs, lowering his hand to the large print, which looks minuscule inside the depression. "And we all doubt an overly aggressive fox could be the sole malefactor. Like a mouse deciding to fight a boar? Unlikely, to say the least."

"You are right to ask questions," Sackery returns. "Please? Don't be shy."

"This beast could've easily gobbled Amerllie whole in a single bite," Iben takes his chance and suggests. "Or stepped on her without realizing it."

"Yet the girl's body was intact with only her throat gouged," Sackery reiterates, "and bruises on her arms."

"Which means?"

Sackery shakes his head. "That we aren't dealing with either a bear or a fox," he warns them.

Twenty men and women, Jhalamar all, look at him as he says it. Sackery can tell by their furrowed brows that he surprised them with the thought. For him, it's not so hard to imagine. He knows *what* lives in the forest. Some, like Iben, even saw them during the battle with the Crows at Mireaderal.

"You still argue these tracks belong to something other than a wild animal?" Iben asks.

"What do you think, friend? You saw what I did years ago. Things dwell in the wood and rock," Sackery describes. "Wilder beings. Emotional. And some? Folk like to tell stories about the odd nymphs that make a home at the edge of villages. Or the fiend-like creatures that lead the lost into caves, never to be seen again."

"They also speak of the Udvar—the unseen, evil shadows that manifest from human scorn," Iben adds.

"There's far more than shadows within those trees," Sackery pivots, rubbing his thumb against his sword's pommel.

"Then what are we dealing with, Master Greywolfe?" Iben demands. "Because if there's a monster larger than a bear out there—?"

"You already know *what* it is, Captain. At least, the bear of the two," Sackery tells him. "You met it twenty years ago. And I'd say it took a stroll outside its domain. Though, why did it leave? That is a question we should answer fast." He notices the Jhalamar with a twitch in their wrists. "Keep your weapons sheathed and watch your step. Just in case. I don't want us to come off as a threat."

"Afraid we'd trample over an innocent-looking flower?" Ivette offers in a half-jest. "Is that it?"

Iben darkly glares at the woman. "Jhalamar? Hold your tongue!"

Sackery frowns and cuts through the tension: "Don't confuse a half-considered remark for a challenge." He turns and places a firm hand on Ivette's shoulder. "We refer to it as the Mórhathan. And he's not a monster. Think of him as a Guardian with dominion over these forest lands. Nialla saw him as an ally during our battle against the Crows. Or that's how it seemed to me at the time."

"But not before mauling dozens of my countrymen," Iben seethes.

Sackery lowers his shoulders disapprovingly. "He's a fickle one. And that is where *we* must be cautious. Nialla convinced the Mórhathan to fight with us twenty years ago. That doesn't mean he will see *us* in a similar light. *He* only listened to *her*." His words linger heavily, invoking a wind of uncertainty over the unpredictable road ahead.

"So, what should we do?"

"Ready yourselves! Jhalamar?! Prepare for a march."

"March? Are we going on foot?"

"There are no safe trails for the horses in the Wilds," Sackery tells him. "They should go back to Wilhimusk. Whatever's in there," he points at the trees, "we'll face it like the Vedrethal of old—with swords in hand, boots in the mud, and our armor as our shield. You have a choice! Answer this? A test of courage. Swallow your fear! It will wreck the mind, turn you against your own."

"Greywolfe?" Iben prods, troubled by his tone.

"Don't trust your eyes in the dark," Sackery offers kindly.

"You know what killed Amerllie. This Guardian—?"

"No. Our friend wouldn't attack a child. The Mórhathan would likely only see her as an innocent. Defenseless? No wild animal caused Amerllie's death. It had a purpose. Whatever it was, it left a mark on the earth. And the Mórhathan came to investigate."

"You can't possibly know that," Iben shudders.

"You're right. And yet, it makes sense, doesn't it?" Sackery laughs.

"This beast hunts the same prey we do," another of the company reasons.

Sackery nods. "And no mere fox would pique *his* interest so much. So, the question is—?"

"When is a fox, *not* a fox?" Ivette riddles.

"When it has white fur and bright yellow eyes," Sackery answers, the word at the tip of his tongue. "Neshulha? Of course." He closes his fist, letting out his breath. "Another mistake. Another of your messes to clean up again, my old sire." He speaks to the wind, and, like an answer, it softly turns in his direction.

"What?" Iben asks.

"A sad tale from a long time ago."

"Like those gaflings from your stories?"

"Only a gafling won't make you think your best friend is suddenly your greatest enemy," Sackery explains. "Neshulha of the Rarhavonn, like the lyrics to an old song suddenly rewritten. Stay mindful of any familiar face from your previous life here, Captain. My adopted father once brought me to see them. They are beautiful and unnerving in one fell swoop." He scoops a handful of dirt that the Mórhathan had flattened. "Did one survive?"

"Sackery?" Iben prods again.

"Icurian's gambit. One that Heluvian saw through and wanted to avert," Sackery tells him.

Iben's questions fade, the tension rising as the Vedrethal provokes those names.

Sackery follows the Mórhathan's tracks to the very edge of the woods, heading in a southeasterly direction, the fox steady in its western course. He drops to his knees and lays an ear on the ground, picking out the faint thuds of the Forest Guardian's earthly footfalls.

"May I offer a notion?" Iben asks.

"You needn't ask permission," Sackery nods, returning to his feet and dusting off his cloak.

"We found one set of tracks left by the fox, correct? And the beast—eh, the Mórhathan only went as far as the outskirts," Iben lists, counting the steps on his fingers. "But why did the Guardian rebound toward the Seclumor Wilds?"

"You would have to ask him," Sackery admits, "but we can speculate."

"And how do you know the fox is one of these—?" Iben stumbles for the name.

"Neshulha?"

"Yes."

"A scholar's logic. Though more of a familiar sense? Some would call it 'a thread of thought,' I believe."

"And the beast decided not to follow the Neshulha toward the village?" Iben continues.

Sackery lets off a weighty grin. "I believe I understand your bewilderment."

"Oh, *do* you, lord?" Iben cheerfully asserts.

"You wonder why the Mórhathan would follow the tracks to their source," Sackery acknowledges, "and *not* their destination."

"It *does* seem odd," Iben admits. "But also, why—?"

"Why do we follow the bear and not the fox?"

"It would seem our quarry is in the opposite direction if the fox had indeed killed Amerllie."

"Perhaps the answer is more of a good feeling? Or a bad one." Sackery presses his palm into the breastplate under his garb. "But I agree. Our friend decided to retrace the fox's steps, moving south. Maybe back to its den? That's my guess. I thought the Neshulha died off centuries ago. For one to still be alive? And here, of all—" He hesitates.

"Master Vedrethal?" Iben asks, confused.

Sackery swallows: "—Places? Can it be that simple?"

Iben's eyes widen. "What do you mean?"

"We'll continue following the Mórhathan deeper into the wildwoods," Sackery decides. "See where the trail ends."

"Shouldn't we return to the village and head off the Neshulha? If it went toward Wilhimusk, that could only mean—?"

"No. That'll only scare it off and lead us to an open chase. And we may never find it if it does."

"But it's wiser to shadow the greater beast?"

"Probably not?" Sackery grimaces. "However, I don't see us having a choice." He eyes the darker clouds overlapping the falling sun, the unclearness of his plan causing the others to shift where they stand. "Another mistake," he repeats.

Iben and the Jhalamar surrender anxious glances among themselves. Sackery turns to them, unsure how to ease the worry on their faces. He's trained them all these years, but this will be their first true contest. Should it be true the prey they hunt is a Neshulha, they must prepare to go up against the terrors of their darkest dreams. *And if they see what I most fear?* Sackery's color pales at the thought.

"And how far will we be going?" one of the Jhalamar asks.

"On foot? Maybe a few added days?" Sackery warns. "A fortnight for the return."

"Without the horses?" Iben questions.

"Call it a lesson from the last time we went into these woods," Sackery iterates. "Then, we had numbers on our side. Seven hundred strong with shields, spears, and battle-hardened mounts. Less than half returned to Trebunor. Even fewer of the horses." He walks to Ora and pats the old mare on the snout. "No worries for you, though. Lead the others home and enjoy what life remains, old friend. We'll find our way through the dark and return when our task is complete."

Ora unhappily stirs as if she disapproves of his decision to split off from the herd.

"Doesn't look like she wants you to go," Jhalamar Camdyn points out.

"She's a stubborn lady," Sackery laughs. "But you'll let me, won't you? You carried me far enough."

"They'll find their way home," Iben agrees. "She'll look out for them."

Ora burrs as she nudges Sackery with her nose, letting out an uneasy snort. The Vedrethal smiles as he lays his forehead against the animal's cheek, trying to lend her some part of his courage. "She always does," he says. The old mare softens her restlessness and slowly meanders to rejoin the others of her kind.

"Your orders, lord?" Iben asks.

"Collect our gear from the saddles," Sackery instructs. "Once in the Wilds, we're on our own."

"Give us a few minutes," the man concedes.

As the company prepares to gather their equipment, Sackery raises his shoulders. There could be many reasons why the Mórhathan hunts the fox. He feels satisfied, however, believing the Guardian would simply refuse to allow a trespasser to offend its home territory. "We can only hope," Sackery whispers as the breeze picks up speed.

He lets out a hand and catches a few stray drops of rain.

— 10 —

GETTING OLDER

Nialla no longer wants to be near anybody. She isolates herself on the Solitary Hill outside Wilhimusk—bathed in sunlight breaking through the clouds, the only place she feels safe, even for a moment. Everything's still wet after last night's storm, from the wheat fields and flowers to the orchards along the northern bends.

Nobody can touch me while I am here.

Nialla catches a water droplet with her finger as it tips from a blade of grass. The bead trickles into her palm as she studies it, flowing like a dancer on a set course down her arm. Nialla wipes it away before gliding her hand through the greenery at her knees, sending driblets flying like a calm spring shower into the air.

Yeavengeritt rises to the hill's summit with his mouth open, taking deep breaths.

She looks at him and frowns. "You want to tell me every-body's watching as I sit alone? Getting nervous," Nialla predicts, cutting him off before he speaks. She tucks her knees into her chest and rests her chin on her arms. "They want to see what I'll do."

"Only because this looks unfavorable, my child," Yeavengeritt warns.

"Folks may judge me however they like," Nialla returns.

"Judgement? No. What I meant—?"

"It doesn't matter. Yeavengeritt? You mean well, but I want to center my thoughts."

Yeavengeritt steps toward her, only for Nialla to wave him off unkindly. The man surrenders a pause, nodding once she turns away from him and makes it clear. *I want to be alone.* The world is too loud, and she needs it to be quiet.

The old man's eyes drop as if wounded by her unwillingness to talk. He walks off the hill and makes for the Greencliffs, likely to fetch her mother and force the issue. Cyridel will tell Nialla to climb down from her *safe* hill by recounting a tale or singing her a song. She doesn't want to hear it. *How can I?* Even now, it isn't easy to focus.

Nialla can't unsee the image of her mother as a corpse. She hid under her covers until the rain died, the sun warming her sheets from the window. She ran out of the Houdicar to escape the feeling of drowning on dry land. Nialla understands it was an illusion, a trick on the eye played by Irimara. Her mother hardly believes her story. At best, the older humors the younger, making her doubt it's anything other than her usual waking terrors.

Sackery would believe me if he had stayed. Can it all be in my head?

Yeavengeritt and the Jhalamar found no trace of the fox anywhere nearby—no tracks or tuft of fur to lend credence to her claims.

"A silver for your thoughts?" Ankara whispers, coming up the hill and sitting next to her. A gentle breeze hits them, bringing with it smells from Wilhimusk—the baker's bread, the smoke from the cozy hearths that warm Elundjir's Hall. "You look like you could use a friend."

Nialla downturns her eyes to the base of the hill and spies her mother standing there. *How long has it been?* Yeavengeritt and their meager Jhalamar busily disband the crowd watching her from the village's palisade gate. "I am not the only one," Nialla welcomes.

Ankara rests her head against Nialla's shoulder like she used to do. They sit together for a while, neither one speaking a word. Nialla notices Ankara's hand on the grass and presses hers against it, realizing then how much her friend has outgrown her. Twenty years ago, the two girls looked the same age. And now? The difference is unmistakable. Ankara became a woman, found a husband, and had a daughter named Amerllie, who befriended the Girl on the Hill.

So much changed in the blink of an eye, with so much more yet ahead for me.

Nialla hardly recognizes Ankara despite living only a hike down the cliffs. Two people can't avoid one another for long in places like Wilhimusk. Too few live here, and the walls are too thin. It is as if this woman is a stranger wearing Ankara's face. Familiar, and yet . . . not so familiar.

Ankara tries to speak. Her words trail off before they can formulate.

Below the hill in the wheat fields, Nialla sights a bobcat endeavoring to hunt a rabbit. The hare circles the wild cat, fighting to keep pace with the fast little creature. Ankara notices her gaze and squints at the scene, but it isn't easy to see at this distance. For her friend, the rabbit and the bobcat are specks dancing around each other among the grasses. Eventually, the rabbit slows after minutes into the chase. That's when the bobcat leaps forward, catching the hare by the neck and killing it with one sharp bite. The hare would have done better to hide, not stay in the open, taunting the hungry beastie.

"That's life. Runners and hunters," Ankara finally speaks. "Good and evil."

"No. It's only nature," Nialla denies. "Food surrounds the rabbit with the roots and berries. The cat doesn't have many options for its feed. Just because one needs to kill to survive doesn't make it evil. You could say the prey mocking the predator during the chase prolonged the cruelty."

Ankara eyes Nialla. "Are you saying the rabbit is cruel?"

Nialla grins wide enough to show her front teeth. "Of course. Quite wicked things, those bunnies," she mocks. Ankara playfully knocks Nialla sideways into the dirt. "Just look at them! What do they have to hide under all that fluff?" She rips out a handful of grass and throws it at the woman. "You can't tell me they don't spend their days plotting against the field mice and sheepdogs. And what will we do when they take over the gardens?" Ankara laughs with her like she did when they were girls.

The joyful moment quickly fades as the pair lie on the hillside with the blue sky above them.

"Imagine if the rabbit and the bobcat could learn to live together without trying to kill each other," Ankara whispers, her voice filled with desperate hope, battling her tears. She sits up and wipes her face with a dirty sleeve. Nialla opens her mouth, her thoughts frozen on her tongue. "You want to say what happened to Amerllie was a tragedy, but I already heard it these last few days. And I'll likely hear it tomorrow, too."

"Do the words help?" Nialla quietly asks.

Ankara shakes her head. "No. It only makes this feeling I have worse."

Nialla frowns. She taps her teeth as she measures her next words carefully.

Ankara lifts her chin to hide the water in her eyes. It's hard to mask how much she's fighting the urge to let it out. Nialla feels the other's shortened breaths and drying mouth while her stomach churns. Tears swim down Nialla's cheeks as the emotion bleeds through the space between them.

"I saw her last night. Amerllie?" Nialla voices with regret.

Ankara looks at her in astonishment, furrowing her eyes while her jaw quivers and gapes. "It wasn't her," Nialla clarifies. "Just a memory playing out by this nightmare that's haunted me since she died."

"A nightmare?" Ankara dithers.

"Maybe a dream?" Nialla exhales. "It felt so real. And yet, so unreal."

"And you saw my daughter in this dream?"

"Yes? A dream of a fox, white as snow, with bright yellow eyes," Nialla describes. "She's called Irimara."

"A fox? That doesn't make sense—?" Ankara attempts to ask.

Nialla throws the woman a troubled glance. "Doesn't it? She's a trickster. Angry. And I think she killed Amerllie."

Ankara swallows hard. It's not a subtle reaction. Not abrupt, either. Her friend bites her lower lip as she holds back her surprise. "Why?"

"I don't know. Maybe to draw us out?" Nialla weighs heavily. "Make us vulnerable? I think she blames me. Something terrible must've happened to her, and now she's looking for retribution." Her hands tremble, so she presses her palms together to force them to play nice.

"Against you? But—?"

Nialla leans forward and gently squeezes the other's hand. A shiver runs down her neck and into her chest, each breath like shallow waves hitting a rocky shore, the air reaching her from a faraway place. "I asked myself 'why' too many times in recent days. And I still don't have an answer for all my questions."

"And you spoke to her? This creature in your dreams?"

"Only a little. Irimara came to me. Maybe I remind the fox of her past? Of all she had lost?" Ankara stares at her with those blue eyes, a shudder to her lips. "It wasn't Amerllie's fault. No rabid animal went after her. Irimara *knew* we'd react. That I would demand Sackery to hunt down whatever killed my friend. And I did exactly that."

"How would she know?" Ankara demands. "And how *do* you?"

"More questions without answers? We'd have to ask the fox," Nialla says as she looks softly at the woman. Ankara has ridges on her face that weren't there years ago. "My mother sent you to mourn with me, didn't she? I remember when I was the tall one. And these lines?" She touches the woman's cheek. "I don't know these lines."

Ankara smiles, taking Nialla's hand and bringing her close. "Neither do I."

"Maybe that's the harmony we seek?"

"I thought it'd be like a long walk among the flower beds. Fewer tragedies in that kind of life."

"Then would it be a life worth living without a trill in the strings?" Nialla asks. "Ours was always more than a tune. It's like an old story. Conflict breeds inspiration. Every struggle adds another verse to the chorus, a thread to the tapestry, or an instrument to the symphony."

"Is that all we are? Characters in a serenade?"

"Maybe?" Nialla swallows.

Ankara pulls away from their embrace. "I forget you're older than you look."

"Sometimes, I forget how young I am," Nialla breathes, the hairs on her arms standing on ends. Her chest suddenly twinges with pain, and the world around the hill shifts into bizarre, twisting shapes. She closes her eyes, almost like burying her head in the dirt. "Irimara?" she whispers, catching that musky stench.

Ankara takes her hand as Nialla opens her eyes. "Nells? Are you okay?"

They're now in a swampy land brimming with decay, but it's a corruption that feels wrong and unnatural. Nialla takes another breath, sensing the air's thin, lacking that unmistakable smell of rot that should come with such rancid earth. It's a lifelessness of a different breed. "No."

"Why do you look so pale?"

A cyclone, a force of nature, engulfs the hill, roaring a fiendish bawl as lightning takes swipes out of the ground, like fingers reaching from the sky to conquer what resides below. Giants as tall as trees rise from the horizon, their thunderous footfalls shaking the land. And the world hardens within a moment, encased in stone everywhere the wind touches.

"Are you seeing what I see?" Nialla asks, a weakness in her throat.

"I don't—? What is it?!"

Nialla lets go of the other's hand and rises to her feet. *How does she not see this? It surrounds us!* Then, it all vanishes. A bright flash of light at the base of the hill dispels the fog over her eyes. Nialla spies Irimara and her mother, Cyridel, opposite one another.

Her mother widens her stance while Irimara backs away, terrified, the fox's ears folded against her head.

Nialla's blood suddenly boils. "No?! I have had enough."

She twists a finger and concentrates on the ground under the damnable creature! *You will stop playing these mind games with me!* Nialla will show her what it means to be afraid. The hill vibrates and cracks, and the soil between the fox and her mother loosens, swallowing Irimara's paws until she's trapped and can no longer move.

Another figure jumps into the fray—a bright, colorless doe, and rushes toward the illusionist. Irimara digs herself out of the dirt and breaks toward the fields. The Shanashéron, in a flash, transforms into a white bird and chases after the fox, scorching the grass as she flies. *Gallandhal—? Where did she come from?*

For a moment, the two girls remain there, stunned. Nialla looks down the hill and notices the hard expression in her mother's eyes.

A CRY FOR HELP

Cyridel doesn't know what to do. Nialla went to sit alone on the hill outside Wilhimusk, worrying the settlers.

Yeavengeritt hurried to Cyridel with a plea to reason with the girl. "She's just sitting there! After last night? I thought it wise to inform you when she refused to listen." Jhalamar Pict, Hader, Olynn, and Rod follow them down the Greencliffs and through the village.

"Lady Miralifrim?" Ankara asks, standing with the others by the entrance archway.

"What is she doing?" Cyridel begs the question.

"Folks think she's looking out for when Sackery returns," Ankara suggests.

"And she isn't?" Cyridel directs the question to Yeavengeritt. The man shakes his head, not having an answer. "Then this is more than a bad dream. Ankara? Will you talk to her? Get her to confess? I will have the Jhalamar clear the onlookers."

Ankara stares at Cyridel long and awkwardly. "I don't know what I can say to her."

"You're her friend," Cyridel urges. "And you two haven't talked for years. Not really. With your loss, I think it's time. She feels abandoned. You two share more than history right now. You share that loss of Amerllie. I did what I could. Now, it's your turn."

Ankara shifts her weight to one foot—a small shudder as she takes a deep breath.

The warm grace of the Daughter of Ilhivendal doesn't lend comfort to the woman. Instead, 'Miralifrim' stands poised, as an Ellúndar *should* be. Cyridel won't deny that Nialla's nightmares are worsening every night, unable to separate her dreams from real life. As a mother, she doesn't know if it is this *white fox* the girl refers to or if it's simply the past invading her mind during her slumbering hours. *Or maybe it's something else entirely?*

Regardless, Cyridel has a duty to her daughter, no matter the trifles. She won't ignore the shadows under the girl's eyes.

"Maybe you're right? We need each other," Ankara decides. "How do I begin?"

Cyridel smiles. "Perhaps recite a memory? Or maybe sit with her? Anything to help the two of you."

Ankara shivers at the idea. The wounds are still fresh in her soul, gnawing at her every waking moment. "I don't know if I can do that," she murmurs, glancing at Nialla on the hill. Tears fall down her cheeks, dripping off her chin.

"You must," Cyridel urges. "That pain hurts you as much as my daughter. Something attacks us, moving around our defenses. Anything that can prey on *her* is a threat to all of us. Trust me. I have seen what her anger can do. But if she's afraid? *Truly* afraid? I don't want to see what happens. Our fight is now."

Irimara, Cyridel thinks the name. *That's what she calls the fox.*

Ankara clenches her jaw and raises her shoulders. She turns, mustering the courage to climb the hill, meeting Nialla at its crescent summit.

Cyridel regards the pair while the Jhalamar direct the villagers back inside their homes. It doesn't take much time, but enough for Ankara and Nialla to talk earnestly. As they speak, Cyridel catches a white figure on the edge of her vision. She turns, and there, a fox sits with a mellow stare—its yellow eyes a contrast to the green of the grass. "You're not a fox," Cyridel recognizes.

The creature tilts its head stiffly, taking a cautious step forward. "Neither are you," Irimara counters.

"I would never paint myself as a fox," Cyridel derides. "But I know your shape, Neshulha. My father told me stories about your kind."

A high-pitched resonance floats around this 'foxlike creature,' causing a ringing in her ears. Cyridel breathes and fights through it, but the noise is perverse. She struggles to keep her eyes open, wanting to pull back like standing next to a bonfire with an intense heat falling off it.

"Did he now? Most strange, indeed," the fox laughs. "And what about you? Your kind? Do the others here think of you as human? Perhaps? Not so much, I think. For me, what either of us calls ourselves doesn't matter. Your daughter, on the other hand?"

"My daughter?" Cyridel demands, narrowing her eyes. "So, it wasn't just her dreams?"

Irimara steps forward again, bold and unafraid. "Like a fox in the henhouse," the creature laughs again. She looks at Ankara and Nialla on the hill. "And *what* she is . . . that *is* worrisome. She is a fire left alone in the wilderness, feeding on the underbrush. Every song and whisper, she taunts the hunters looking for her."

"Like you? Nialla's my child," Cyridel boldly asserts, "and you won't go anywhere near her again."

"Circumstances drive us together," the fox refutes. "She's nobody's mere child."

Cyridel's nostrils flare. "And what does that mean? She *is* mine—I birthed her, kept her warm. Nursed her."

"You made sure your cub survived. Nothing more. A mother's thankless job."

"We did more than survive," Cyridel seethes. "And what about you? We knew those like you would come for her."

"For a reason," the fox says, raising her snout. "I merely found you first." She circles Cyridel like a predator, measuring its prey before an attack.

Cyridel approaches the fox, but the creature quickly draws back and fades into a mist. The world transforms into an orchard with cherry blossoms floating on a gentle breeze. Beyond the trees are mountains and stone towers, with boats on the little lakes and bridges across the rivers. And at the summit, a house high above the city's sprawling reaches.

"What is this?" Cyridel mutters. "Ilhivendal? The one place I know I am not."

Another's voice echoes through the trees. "Do you hear it? Below the starlight, above vast ancient groves—" it sings, deep and beautiful. Cyridel turns, knowing *that* voice. *But that's impossible? He's dead.* "—Where a people sing of stories, and the coming tales of old."

Cyridel swings into the next verse: "Where the fair dwell in gladness as the mountains stand our walls."

"And the fearless forever rise," the other finishes, "against our wicked foes."

Standing before her is a man in a blue cloak and silver eyes. "Galron?" Cyridel asks as he walks to her, joyful and content.

Galron takes her hands and smiles that brilliant grin, soft with his touch. "You know that's not my real name, friend." His eyes reflect the same uncertainty she found when he awoke that first day they met—the Man in the Forest, the Stranger that came to her, chased down by the Morkül like a wild deer.

"Friend? More than friends," Cyridel decides. "Endúcar! Your true name?"

He frowns. "I wonder if it's even *that* anymore."

Cyridel reads the wrinkles on his face. "You're old now? Older than you were. How? You aren't here! Not really? You're an image."

"An image made real to the eye," he confirms. "But that does not mean I am not here. Irimara? She can use memories as weapons against her foes. Protect herself when all else fails. Images real enough to threaten but not to kill. Not on purpose. Any pain is the mind filling in the blanks."

"And that's what you're doing to Nialla? To *me*, this very moment?"

"I don't—? No. That's not me. She and I are not the same."

"Liar?! Why do you play these games? You already said memories are your weapon."

"Only bad memories," the false Galron confides. "And the fox? Her power cannot twist your thoughts into something you know can't happen. She'd call it . . . imperfection. I would say that some emotions are too strong to fake. Our fears can ravage the mind. They can destroy our hearts and make us lose faith in the ones we love."

"Which means? You—?" Cyridel demands. Then, her eyes widen, realizing the answer. "I have no bad memories of you."

Galron smiles. He falls away as if he's weaker now than he was moments ago. "She won't let this fantasy go on much longer. So, right now . . . I *am* your Galron. Call me a ghost if you must, for I *am* a ghost. A memory? And a father who *will* protect his child!"

The image of the man she loves draws his sword and charges toward a light behind him. The illusion collapses, and Cyridel is next to the hill outside Wilhimusk again. Even as a memory, Galron doesn't fail to prove his worth. Cyridel smiles at the thought. That smile becomes a scowl when she notices Irimara watching her, bewildered. The creature's yellow eyes do not blink, like she's anchored in a trance.

"What was the point of that?" Cyridel asks the fox. "Do you know who *he* was? The father of my daughter."

"How did you—? He was right, wasn't he?" Irimara returns, her foxlike face diminishing into eerily human features. "Of course, he was. It doesn't matter. Nothing changes. Your daughter inherits the crimes of her forefathers. She holds the mantle created by Icurian—*his* deeds. You set the girl on a pedestal. You must now live with the consequence."

"And what consequence is that?" Cyridel demands.

She marches toward Irimara. The other jumps away before she could reach the damnable creature, however. She's fast—even for a fox, naturally quick on their feet. Irimara circumvents her with blinding speed. Every time Cyridel catches a glimpse, the fox disappears into the haze.

"You cannot see me if I don't allow you," Irimara mocks her.

"I don't need to see you!" Cyridel fights. "Your grief is like a stench."

"Do you think you can smell my anger?"

"My question is, can you mask it from me? You're like a wet dog drowning in the river."

As she pushes through, the ground shakes, and Irimara gets caught, sinking into the dirt and unable to move. A bright streak darkens Cyridel's vision, burning the grass between her and the creature. Gallandhal emerges from hiding and jumps into the fray as a doe, barreling toward the Neshulha like a wild spirit in a frenzy.

The fox yelps and breaks free of her snare, racing as fast as she can from the hillside.

Nialla shouts from the crescent. "That was her!" Ankara follows as the pair rush to Cyridel.

Gallandhal slides behind a rock and remerges as a familiar bird, chasing after their foe. Nialla squares her shoulders when she reaches the bottom of the hill, only to relax, letting the ground underfoot solidify again.

"That was unpleasant," Cyridel murmurs.

"What was that? Why did—?" Ankara asks. "Are you okay, my lady?"

"Perfectly fine," Cyridel answers.

"Did you see her?" Nialla begs the question. "She was here?! Irimara, clear as day."

"I only saw your mother talking to herself," Ankara admits.

Cyridel's eyes land on the woman with surprise. "Only to myself? But it felt so—?"

"Real? Hard to tell the difference," Nialla describes. "I felt the air change! When I looked down the hill, I thought—?"

"The images must trick the senses as much the eye," Cyridel frowns. "A worrisome thought."

Nialla takes a breath and crosses her arms. "Did she make you see anything? Faces of people you know?"

Cyridel feels a chill on her neck. She notices her daughter swallowing hard, clearly nervous about asking the question. "Only what I knew was impossible," she admits, eyeing the two white specks disappearing into the fields. "And Gallandhal? I spotted her loitering about the grounds only yesterday. She was keeping an eye on us."

"Gallandhal?" Ankara repeats. "That doe that ran into the fields?"

"No, the bird," Nialla corrects.

"Didn't we see her last . . . oh, maybe three years ago?" Cyridel asks. "Why now?"

"Maybe four? She just appeared," Nialla replies breathlessly. "I hardly realized before the fox ran away."

Cyridel notices a tremor crawl up the girl's arms and into her throat. She glances at Gallandhal as the creature returns from the chase, having lost the fox in the rows. The bird finds a perch on a nearby fence to catch her feathery breath. "Then we better find out why now she's come. Ankara? Go home to your husband. This talk is ours." Shanashéron, like Gallandhal, are many things—spirits of many shapes, guides to the lost, and loyal friends to those who've earned it.

Ankara flinches. "But I don't want—?" The woman looks to Nialla.

Cyridel merely shakes her head. "Please," she says, encouraging her to leave.

Ankara bites her lip, uncertain. The woman eventually nods and shuffles back to the village. Cyridel must do what she can to protect the life that grows here at Wilhimusk. Yet, as she watches the woman walk away with a heavy step, Cyridel wonders if her efforts parallel a dam cracking under a great river's weight.

"Why send her away?" Nialla asks.

"Because she still has a life to lead," Cyridel tells her, "no matter her pain."

"Irimara—?"

"You were right. No wild beast killed Amerllie," she professes. "This fox? She has a vendetta. That much is obvious."

"But why? What did I do?" Nialla tearfully asks.

Cyridel turns to Gallandhal. The white bird flutters her wings and straightens her posture on her perch. "You did nothing, little one," the Shanashéron voices. Nialla folds her arms over her chest, still feeling at fault somehow. "Irimara wants some-body to blame. She attacks you because you are vulnerable."

"You speak as if you *know* this fiend," Cyridel notices, raising an eyebrow.

"Our two races were rivals in the distant past," Gallandhal answers. "Before my kind helped wipe them out."

"Wiped them out?" Nialla begs the question. "You mean, killed them?"

Gallandhal opens her beak and hesitates for a long while. "We were at war. Too many dead to count," the bird speaks in a low tone. "Heluvian and Icurian sought any advantage they could over one another. The Vedrethal, the Shanashéron, the Rolirnadilin . . . Everyone took sides. All but the Neshulha."

"Icurian protected them," Nialla whispers. "Clesturia? She told me how the Crows betrayed the Doomed King—?"

"Yes. By showing Heluvian where to find the Rarhavonn," Gallandhal regrets. "Their home."

"And he killed them?" Cyridel asks.

"Not at first. First, the foxes ran," Gallandhal answers, "as far as they could. South? As far south as south can go. And for a while, the Neshulha hid, safe in the wildwoods at the edge of the known world. Sackery's brethren were relentless in their hunt for them, however."

"But you said they didn't choose a side?" Nialla begs the question.

"You no doubt felt Irimara's wrath, my dear friend," the bird explains, smoothing out the feathers on her chest. "Tricks and illusions were all the strength they had. Imagine creating armies that aren't there or making you think your companions want to silence your songs forever?"

"She makes you doubt the world around you?"

"Yes. By distracting all your other senses."

"Power enough to turn the tide of any battle," Cyridel realizes.

"Heluvian feared such power in Icurian's hands," Gallandhal mourns.

Nialla pauses for a long while. Cyridel notices the shift in her cheeks, the girl working through her feelings. First is anger, and *that* lingers for a while before subsiding into a sudden dull pain in her chest. Nialla raises her hand to her throat and presses against the tenderness of her skin, a mute sadness. She looks up at her mother with a sudden fear, then levels with the Shanashéron.

"Gallandhal? Did you have a hand in the scouring?" Nialla's voice quakes, rippling the grass on the hillside.

The bird draws a long breath and shivers from her beak to white tail feathers. "I have no defense of the hard decisions made in those years. But I will say that Heluvian lost my faith in the goodness of his cause after the butchery. My kind were never friends to the Neshulha, but many of us too gladly fell into the fervor."

"You didn't stop it?" Cyridel wonders.

"And what could I have done?" Gallandhal defends. "I was alone."

"What about Sackery? Where was *he* in all this?" Nialla musters the courage to ask. "Is he a murderer?"

"Murderer? Could *he* be anything else? He fought in many battles, often in search of his father," the bird explains. "Icurian raised him, trained him for most of his life. Heluvian understood Sackery was the only one Icurian would never kill, the only man that could go after the Doomed King and *not* die. Your friend did many horrible things, fight after fight. Sackery most often put his duty above his compassion." Gallandhal stops for a moment and stares intently at Nialla.

"Irimara would be afraid of him," Nialla realizes.

"Afraid enough to kill a child to lure your protectors away," Gallandhal agrees.

Nialla lets out an arm and motions to the white bird. "That's not the man I know," she argues.

Gallandhal jumps onto her wrist and surrenders a sorrowful bow. "War breeds the worst in us, little one."

— 12 —

THE FOREST GUARDIAN

"Do you see it? Another impression in the bark?" Iben points.

Sackery looks, counting the sixteenth mark on the trees along their path. "Like the others? The Mórhathan roams south. Not far now." His tone falls to a whisper, uncertain if getting close to the creature is safe. Last night's rain washed out the tracks on the ground, but they weren't the only signs to follow.

"You seem nervous, Master Greywolfe," Iben adds, watchful.

Sackery considers the man and the Jhalamar. He looks at their faces. Grim. Some are older, like Iben. Others? Still young as he once was in the years that Icurian had trained him in the ways of a swordsman, a warrior, and a servant to his father's ambitions. Hard years after he left the ship that carried him from Islinin to Arún, the boy who would become the first of the Vedrethal.

"I am not nervous," Sackery denies. "I am . . . cautious."

"As you say," Iben frowns.

Sackery purses his lips, unsure if the man believes him. *It doesn't matter.* "Let's go a little farther before we rest," he tells the party, knowing their exhaustion. Sackery looks skyward but can hardly tell where the sun falls behind the mountains through the dense forest canopy. "We'll make camp in the next clearing."

"I don't like being so close to the monster's footpath," Iben warns.

"Then you better not lay where the Mórhathan's likely to walk," Sackery laughs. "Three days since Wilhimusk. There's no going back until we find what killed Amerllie. Creature or beast, I won't tell Nialla otherwise. Like us, our 'friend' hunts it, making for the fox's den."

"And what if the beast doesn't want us following it?" Iben asks.

"Again, with 'beast' and 'monster' from your mouth," Sackery grimaces. "Don't you know? It's bad manners to insult our host, Captain. These wildwoods are his home, and we are his guests. He is the primordial king of this place, born out of the rock and wood." He walks on, leading the others through the underbrush.

"Then *what* should we call it? Mórhathan? What does *that* even mean?"

"It's Iírdun, the Vedreron tongue, for the Great Bear," Sackery translates. "Guardian of the Forest, as the old tales stipulate. It ruled these lands longer than the race of men could speak.

Ruled before the Vedr fell from Anánturial. Before the dragons even took Islinin. So, we'll call him the Mórhathan, for it is *his* chosen name."

Later, when they stop for the night, and the shadows among the trees darken, Sackery forbids the party from lighting any fires. Free to wander the Seclumor Wilds, he doesn't want to gain the attention of the strange beings that inhabit the caves among the thickets.

Mellow tunes for kindly spirits are what the Mórhathan allows—something to soothe the animals and keep the predators away.

Iben and the Jhalamar hum as they find their places in the clearing to sleep.

A rustling in the bushes, a tiny hedgehog crawls out, attracted to the noise. It sniffs Iben's boot, poking the man with its nose. Sackery sits back, amused. The man feels the critter and stops his lullaby, opening his eyes and reaching for the hilt of his sword.

"Careful now," Sackery warns him. "Let it be. Remember?"

"I don't want it crawling on me while I sleep."

"And why not? It won't hurt you."

"Because I—" Iben stops, his eyes widen.

They hear a low growl. Sackery notices two amber dots among the trees, along with cracking timber. The party all wake to the sound, their hands going for their weapons, much like Iben. "No!" Sackery shouts to keep his people from antagonizing their host.

He stares mournfully at the Mórhathan as it lumbers into the field. Clearing his throat, Sackery doesn't break eye contact. The bear sneers pointedly as it snaps its great jaws to scare the Jhalamar surrounding him. "Vedrethal?!" Iben frets.

Sackery raises both hands, showing his palms. "Easy now, friend. We are not here to hurt anyone." The bear rises to its full height on its massive hind legs. "Least of all your wards! Do you remember me? Yes, I think you do. My scent, at least. We've come for answers about a girl from our settlement. Something killed her."

The large creature groans and cracks, intrigued as it lowers its posture and steps past a hardened Iben to confront Sackery.

He remains passive so as not to aggravate the wild forest lord. The other closes the distance, smelling the Vedrethal's breath, inevitably pinning *him* against a boulder with its snout. Sackery lets it happen, holding back his instinct to resist. It isn't a fight he could win, even if he tried.

"Master Greywolfe?" Iben begs the question.

The man regrets it when the Mórhathan abruptly pivots and roars at the Jhalamar Captain.

Sackery puts a finger to his lips and lets out the softest hush he can muster. "It's all right. We're not in danger."

"Are you sure?" Ivette asks with a tremor in her voice.

The Mórhathan turns back and studies him for a spell with those amber eyes before pulling away with an unhappy grunt. Sackery sighs, wary of the creature as it withdraws to the shadows. "Pretty certain." He watches as the Forest Guardian weaves through the wood and brush as if it were a part of them.

Nobody speaks for a long stretch. Iben is the first to question, "Are we good, then? Are we safe?"

"Certain odds work to our favor," Sackery admits. "Seems we set camp next to his haunt for the night. Quite fortunate."

"Fortunate, how?" Iben demands.

"Because the Mórhathan is aware of us now, and he recognized who I am," Sackery tells him. "He understands our intent and will let us follow his path."

"Let us?" Iben repeats. "How do you know? If this is some guess—?"

Sackery dusts off his cloak and returns to his spot in camp. "Because we're still alive." He glances at the trees where the forest lord plods. Sackery can only imagine what soul could go against such a force and survive. "And I would like to keep it that way."

The party settles into their bedrolls. It's not like they can do more before daybreak. Sackery stays up a little longer to keep watch on the woods. The Mórhathan circles the clearing from behind the trees, unseen. But he can feel the creature's footfalls through the dirt, rattling the buckles and metal on their gear.

It'll be a short night. He'll steal an hour for himself before rousing the others to begin another day's march.

— 13 —

OLD ENEMIES, NEW FACES

Cyridel watches her daughter from a distance. The girl tends to the Houdicar's garden, with flowers numbering in the hundreds, one for everybody who fell in the battle with the Crows at Trebunor and Mireaderal. She's planted more since then. Dozens? Each is a memory of a face the girl doesn't want to forget.

Yeavengeritt joins her, cuffing dirt in his palms, nesting a young sprout. Together, they replant the seedling next to its siblings.

Nialla sings to it in the way only she can do. The air shimmers as the colors across the field brighten. They handle the young plant with such care as if it were a newborn just brought into the world and carried into the daylight, a testament to promises made.

Gallandhal glides down from above and lands on a rock

next to Cyridel.

The white bird considers her for a while, then quickly glances at Nialla among the vibrant blooms. "Shanashéron," as the old stories call her race, guides for the lost. Twenty years ago, the bird led Nialla, Rasterforn, and the Men of Calidor into the wilds to fight the witches that tormented the land. She has come and gone ever since, disappearing a few years at a time before showing up again. Where does she go? Why does she return? These are questions that Cyridel has always wanted to ask her. However, she feels a profane sense of intrusion whenever the opportunity arises.

"What are they doing?" Gallandhal asks.

"Holding on," Cyridel replies, studying the bird's soft curves.

"Why?"

"Do I need to answer?"

Gallandhal lowers her head, and a slight blue hue breaks through the white of her glass-like frame. "I suppose not," the bird admits, letting the air flow, whistling across the rocks like a flute carved into the earth.

Do I now take the chance? Cyridel wonders.

"When you change forms," the woman asks, "is there a limit to what you can do?"

Gallandhal turns to her with a heaviness in her violet, almost purple eyes. "What do you mean?"

"I mean . . . What *do* I mean? I've seen you assume many appearances, even human ones. Can you be anything? Anyone?"

"The shapes we take are our own," Gallandhal answers. "Never would the *shanashé* take another's as a mask or steal their face. There is no greater crime among my kind, for it would be like ripping their soul from their body."

"And none of you ever tried?" Cyridel begs the question.

Gallandhal's eyes flutter for a moment. She opens her beak and is about to speak, only to shut it before swallowing. "This talk is not for decent company. So, we shall not speak of it any further, Daughter of Ilhivendal." *Meaning it happened, and her people felt shame for it.* Cyridel weighs her thoughts carefully. "We only take *our* forms, with *our* faces. Many prefer birds. Others? Deer, mice, wolves, cats, fish, and more. Most simply have preferences for certain shapes over others. It all rests on the individual to decide."

"And do you miss it? Your home?" Cyridel speaks openly. "Have you ever gone back?"

"To Silhashan? No. I have not returned. Those mountains are very far away, and the winds are quite treacherous," Gallandhal answers. "Years back, I would never make it with my injuries from the witches in the woods. Could I now? Perhaps. Though I remain wounded."

"You looked like a cloudy glass vase, cracked and faded in all the wrong places."

"Imagine going blind while still able to see. It was like flying at night until I heard your daughter's voice."

"Due to her little songs?"

"She stands apart from the world."

"Have you ever thought about asking *us* to take you?"

"Many times, friend. Many times. Some days, it is all I think about."

"Then, why don't you?"

"Through shadows deep, we find the light," Gallandhal recites a strong melody, "brave the night, embrace the fight."

Cyridel steps back with a dull pain in her chest. "Those words? How—? My mother said those words."

"As the chorus of a song she wrote," Gallandhal tells her. "Rise up again, fly high and free."

"Catch the wind," Cyridel whispers.

"Feel the beat," the bird finishes. "We all have our roles."

"You couldn't have learned that song anywhere but Ilhivendal."

"Unless somebody had carried it all this way to my ears," Gallandhal remarks.

Cyridel looks to Nialla by the house, padding the soil with Yeavengeritt, where the young flower will root itself, replacing one that grew too old and withered on the stem. It distracts her from recent events, and that is good. The girl needs a moment to let her troubles go and be a child again. She may be older than most in the village, but she'll outlive all of them.

Her curse, Cyridel imagines, and then frowns.

Gallandhal puffs her chest feathers as she hops across the rocks, watching her watch Nialla.

Cyridel forces a smile before returning her attention to the bird. "A dangerous thought. Sometimes, I wonder if I did right by robbing her of the life she could have known. 'A life of love and dancing in the light,' as the lullaby goes. It's hard to see her grow from the baby once at my breast."

"She wouldn't be safe where she belongs," Gallandhal comforts.

"Is she *safe* here?" Cyridel begs the question. "At least in Calidor or Ilhivendal, she'd have others. Here? She's so alone. Ankara? Our dear Amerllie? She's grown up with them for these twenty years, but she must live with the idea that everyone she knows will someday die while she's still a child. Everyone in the village? Me? Sackery? How long can she suffer this way before it breaks her? Our songs do not ease the years gone by."

"Should I ask you the same question you asked me?" Gallandhal laughs. "Why not return? Despite the dangers, it could do her some good."

"Because her father didn't want her to grow up in his world," Cyridel tells her. "A world of politics and debates."

Gallandhal raises her head. "And what about your world?"

"Among the Míran? Ilhivendal seemed so cold and empty when I left," Cyridel admits. "My father died when Icurian attacked us. My mother shut herself away after that, and my brother was always more of a stranger to me. Maybe if I had stayed with Nialla? She could've brought new life to the city my grandfather built. My home."

"Then you have my answer for why I choose to stay," Gallandhal offers, nodding toward the girl. "She brings life here."

Cyridel looks up and notices many birds gathering to Nialla by the flowers—some large, like hawks, while others are small, like summer robins. A yellow goldfinch lands on Gallandhal's rock and jumps around, tweeting a lovely little song as if seeking appraisal by the Shanashéron.

"Another illusion?" Cyridel asks.

Gallandhal shakes her head. "No, it is real. Do you hear it?"

Cyridel lends her ear to the wind and listens as it carries her daughter's voice:

> *I whisper to her, never to hear me,*
> *And so, I shout across the distant valley,*
> *She turns to me, a sparkle in her eyes,*
> *So, I ask, do you know, my fair queen?*
>
> *She climbs the mountain, walks the high streams,*
> *She likes to reach for the clouds above her,*
> *She wants to dance away all her loneliness,*
> *And I ask, do you know, my fair queen?*
>
> *One day I called to her, and she answered,*
> *She smiled and laughed like she was glad to see me,*
> *And she descended her silver palace,*
> *So, I ask, do you know, my fair queen?*
>
> *There was this moment when I found her,*
> *Lost in the forest, the road before her,*

She was crying with darkness all 'round her,
And I ask, do you know, my fair queen?

Then she saw me, bright and joyful,
Among the flowers and the fields aplenty,
She kisses me, a cherry in the white bloom land,
So, I ask, do you know, my fair queen?

We dance and sing now, all together,
Through our troubles and our triumphs,
For what else is there but love and beauty,
And she asks, did you know, my fair king?

"What is that song? I don't know it," Gallandhal utters. "Powerful words."

"It is a pretty tune the settlers brought with them from Calidor," Cyridel tells her.

Nialla rises from the young sprout and walks to them, the cheerful finch jumping to the girl's finger and settling on her arm. "I always enjoyed the Northern melodies the most." She halts before them, her skin flushed with color. "It's in my blood."

"You could hear us from over there?" Gallandhal begs the question.

"I always did have a good sense of things," Nialla admits. "My mother's gifts." She looks at Cyridel when she says it, the silver of her eyes glowing in the sunlight. Cyridel pulls the girl close and kisses the top of her head, startling the small finch off her shoulder.

Gallandhal remains motionless, a heat radiant off her like a piece of glass left in the sun, her colors almost like a rainbow.

Nialla breaks away and moves to the edge of the cliffs. Her gaze sweeps over the village and the valley below. Cyridel follows her closely while Yeavengeritt keeps a respectful distance. Gallandhal takes to a new perch on the tree overlooking the Houdicar.

"Irimara?" Nialla asks. "Am I able to help her?" She tucks her hands into her sleeves.

"Nialla?" Cyridel hesitates to question.

"She told me about a promise, but I don't remember—?"

"Because it wasn't your promise to keep," Gallandhal intercedes.

"And she wants *me* to? I don't—? How did she know to find me? Here, of all places?!"

"You aren't the only one with questions," the bird mournfully admits. "How did the fox survive all this time? Where did she come from? Why now? My kind and hers are sisters, born from the same kiln. That brings a grudge that likely fuels her bitterness in these events."

"But who made the promise? Was it Icurian?" Nialla states. "Before or after he became the Doomed King?"

Gallandhal flattens her wings against her sides. "Icurian loved them. He also failed them."

"Your father once said," Cyridel breaks in, telling her daughter, "that Heluvian called Icurian the Doomed King to mock him. He used it to say that all his efforts were ill-fated—a doomed man, doomed to fail. That's what he said. A cruel prophecy that repeated every time someone uttered his name."

A soft burr in the wind creates a chill between the three of them. Cyridel feels it and crosses her arms to fight it off. Nialla's face darkens, letting her anger show. She closes her fist as her nostrils flare, the dirt shifting at her feet.

"Gallandhal? Why *did* you come back?" the girl demands, looking at the Shanashéron. "What made you return to Wilhimusk? You were gone for years! You couldn't have guessed I was in danger." There's a coldness to her words, a bite that holds barely contained resentment.

Gallandhal's light dims for a moment. "I am your guide," she offers. "Just as Vanhashal attends your father, I am tied to your being now. I feel it when you're afraid, child. Irimara, confronting you as she did, sent ripples across the world. Others likely felt it. They will surely follow."

"Irimara said much the same," Cyridel realizes.

"And what are these ripples?" Nialla asks.

"Like echoes? Drops of water to a cavern's lake. The kind Icurian used to make with every step he took," Gallandhal describes. "Trust me when I say *that* is the kind of attention you should avoid. Your father ran toward such threats and changed history. You—?"

"Don't speak about my father," Nialla orders. "I grew up on the stories."

"All of them?" Gallandhal shifts, looking at Cyridel.

Cyridel wonders what she means, feeling a hint of guilt under the bird's tone.

"So, you came to warn us?" Nialla asks. "A little late, maybe?"

"No, it isn't. I will help you through this battle," the white bird iterates. "That is my promise."

"And finish what my forefathers began? No. I am not a murderer."

Gallandhal lowers her head and hesitates to speak. Cyridel notices and frowns as Nialla sways back and forth, uncertain. Irimara *is* dangerous. She's also a victim, wanting to correct the outrage done to her. Nialla seems to understand even as Gallandhal struggles with the idea. A mother can tell with their child, although her daughter's tone should make it obvious to the Shanashéron.

Cyridel drops to a knee and takes the younger's hands. She wipes a tear from Nialla's cheek and smiles. Her breath is quick and shallow. "It's all right," she whispers to the girl. "You're all right."

"I won't do it," Nialla weeps.

"She already calls you her enemy," Gallandhal stipulates.

Cyridel looks into her daughter's eyes, so much worry and doubt showing through like a deep shade reflection. "Irimara hurts. Now she's lashing out at the only one she can right now. Nialla? You can feel her pain, the same as I do. You can talk to her, listen to her. Make her feel heard and put all this nastiness behind us."

Nialla quietly pulls away from her mother, staring regretfully at Gallandhal, her thumb pressing into her palm.

"How do I find her? Where do we start?" Nialla asks, weakness in her throat. Her eyes drop groundward. "What can I do? How do I fight the shadows she pits against me?"

Gallandhal hops down to a lower branch. "Shadows by themselves cannot harm you. Should you let the fox sing you a tale, she'll trick you into hurting yourself. Don't let her, whatever you do . . . Do not let her convince you otherwise. You are your father's daughter, little one. Your voice is loud. Use it, and she might listen." The white bird looks at her and raises her beak. She spins her head toward the horizon where Irimara had run off after their confrontation at the Solitary Hill. "The fox will likely retreat to her den, so we'll follow the trail she leaves behind."

"You can lead her there?" Cyridel demands.

"Without a doubt," Gallandhal admits. "I can already guess where she'll go."

"And I can face her?" Nialla begs the question.

"Yes. But what that means is entirely up to you," Gallandhal returns.

Yeavengeritt, standing quietly all this time, suddenly coughs. "I will enlist the remaining Jhalamar to join you."

Gallandhal shakes her head. "Going without others by your side is the wiser choice," she suggests.

"You want her to go alone?" Yeavengeritt demands, a crack in his tone.

"Alone. For everybody's sake," Gallandhal acknowledges.

"I don't know if I should," Nialla whirls apprehensively. "I'd feel better if my mother could anchor me."

"As would her mother," Cyridel agrees.

Gallandhal burrs and releases a low whistle. "Not better. No. It'd be a mistake. Go without taking anything the fox can use against you, little one. One second, your mother is an ally by your side. And the next? She's the knife in your back."

Cyridel raises her shoulders angrily.

Nialla catches her arm and holds it. "Alone? Anyone familiar would be another illusion."

Gallandhal nods. "Do not give Irimara tools to use against you," the white bird cautions. "And should the panic set in and you lose yourself for even a moment, a friendly face will seem twice as inviting. Your wits are your strength. Trust nothing. Nobody."

"Even you? Is it that easy?"

"Never."

"And how far is it?" Cyridel asks.

"Far enough," Gallandhal answers. "Irimara will race to put distance between us. We only scared her, and she may want us to follow. When she rallies, she *will* haunt your daughter again. That is the one certainty I can offer you, my friends. A chance to cut her off at the source."

"At her den," Nialla glowers.

Gallandhal nods sullenly. "It is unfortunate, indeed. A choice may lie ahead."

"A difficult one," Nialla realizes.

Cyridel steps forward to better view her daughter's face. "Are you sure you want to do this?"

Nialla's mouth trembles and her fingers stiffen. "No?" She shakes her head.

Looking at her daughter's boots, Cyridel notices they are wet, with grass marks on her skirt. The intricate patterns sewn into the fabric have become worn and faded over the years. Nialla rubs her hands together. The girl rarely feels cold. And the last time she did—Clesturia, Alanssia, and Raenia were playing on her fears. *Another stain to wash out? A fox instead of crows this time.* Cyridel frowns.

"Don't drown on dry land," Cyridel advises. "Follow Galland-hal. Do what she tells you."

Irimara dared to confront Cyridel on her own. The fox had made her see Nialla's father as if he were alive. However, the image worked against its creator. Galron's visage broke free of the tricker's reign. And that defiance surprised the fox enough to help drive her away. Irimara twists memories to her needs, but she must play by a set of rules. Cyridel doesn't know or understand what those rules are . . . Not yet. That's for Nialla to discover. That's how she can fight, by *not* fighting.

Yeavengeritt approaches the girl and squeezes her shoulder. "You'll walk with the heart of Wilhimusk with you. Ask whatever you need, and it's yours."

"Provisions?" Nialla wishes. "And a horse to carry me?"

The old man nods. "You'll have them," he promises.

"Should I bring a knife?" the girl questions.

Cyridel looks at her worryingly.

"You *are* the knife in the dark," Gallandhal finishes.

"No," Cyridel recites. "She is my daughter. A light in the darkness where the flowers grow." And with a less than confident nod, she walks away to ready the materials for her daughter's task. Cyridel descends the Greencliffs and calls the villagers to Elundjir's Hall.

The Wilhimuski seem eager to help when Cyridel tells them about her daughter's intent to leave. After some debate, the villagers accept, with others offering to join Nialla on the road. Cyridel isn't sure if it's loyalty or faith they put in the girl. Nevertheless, the woman praises them for their courage. Most understand Nialla must travel this road alone.

It reminds her of how much Galron disliked the attention others gave him. Cyridel often laughed when her kinfolk first saw the man who came to them, lost in the forest, the world behind him. "A hard one to miss," they would describe passing him in the streets.

"You didn't ask for this," she tells Nialla at the edge of town. "And I don't know what you'll face. Trust your instincts. Trust what you *feel*, not what you see out there. You will need your father's gifts and mine to win against this foe."

"And if I lose?" Nialla begs the question.

"Do you think you'll lose?"

"I don't know."

"Then be careful how you define your triumph."

"I won't hurt the fox," Nialla proclaims.

"She killed Amerllie," Cyridel reminds her, testing her resolve. "Your friend? That's a deep wound to ignore, even for the most noble among us."

"Because she's lost. And if what Gallandhal said is true—? I don't know what to do."

"Irimara might use that against you," Cyridel warns.

"She didn't deserve what happened. After everything that Gallandhal told us?" Nialla expresses, stern and defiant. "I will finish this—not just for our sakes, but for hers, too."

Cyridel kisses the girl's cheek and wraps her hands with cloth for the road. "You can't always change the past, Nells. No matter how much you understand another's pain, it doesn't always mean you can mend their wounds."

"But there *must* be a way to make it right," she resolves. "Somehow? I don't know how, but I—"

"Just come back alive," Cyridel tells her, handing the girl a pack of food as Jhalamar Hader leads a horse to them.

"Here you go, my lady," Hader speaks. "This is Ryallamere, a new addition to the herd. He has a strong back and a brave soul. And he is fast."

Nialla smiles. She goes up to the animal and presses her head against its snout. "You are a mighty one, aren't you? His name's familiar?!" The horse suddenly grunts as if he understands. "Ryallamere? I once met another by it." She turns to the Jhalamar. "Is he not from our stock?"

Hader nods courageously. "He's a royal breed, this Ryallamere. He's to replace Ora as Sackery's mount. Another gift from King Rasterforn the last time Hugh traveled to the Trebunor market. The Sordheiran Guard stopped us at the Bridge Gate, escorted us to the Royal Palace, and told us to accept it on our Master's behalf. Captain Iben ordered him stabled with the fielders so we could surprise Lord Greywolfe."

"He's wonderful," Nialla says, grateful.

Cyridel looks to the horizon and the sun cusping the trees. "It'll be dark soon."

The girl clenches her jaw and bites her lip. She looks at Gallandhal: "Then we should make haste," Nialla tells the white bird. "Sackery already has days on us, and we must beat him to the finish." She turns to the young stallion. "Ryallamere? Will you take me where I need to go?"

The animal stomps his foot, almost like accepting it as a challenge.

"Do not fall behind," Gallandhal instructs. The bird takes off southeast, toward the mountains and the Southern Wilds. Nialla mounts Ryallamere, determined to keep pace with the Shanashéron. "And hold on tight to that warrior of a beast!"

Cyridel holds her breath as Nialla taps the horse's side. "Run as fast as you can, for as long as you can take me! Do not stop until the sun warms our necks and the wilds block our road." She whistles. Ryallamere breaks into a sudden gallop and races down the trail out of Wilhimusk.

She waits for the dust to settle as her daughter vanishes beyond the wheat fields behind the hills. "All my joy goes with you," Cyridel whispers, like a prayer to the sky. It makes her wonder if Nialla is perhaps too much like her father. From their short years together, she misses the smell of his skin and how his eyes could lead her into dreams, the promises they made to each other there, sworn in body and mind.

Cyridel takes the blue scrap of cloth she found, kept in her bodice, and thumbs over its cross-stitch patterns. It's just a worn rag torn from somebody's cloak that passed by the bushes above the Greencliffs. *But—? How did it get there?* She still doesn't know. Cyridel wraps it around her wrist and ties off the ends.

For some reason, she wants to keep it with her.

It only feels *right* with Nialla off to confront Irimara.

— 14 —

ILLUSIONS TO POWER

"Dal Rarhavonn," Irimara whispers. "That's what Icurian called our home."

She wills the images to life—familiar shapes in the trace light between the trees, the faces of long-dead friends from her younger days. Irimara makes the shades move as she remembers them. Nothing overdone. They'll ward the clearing, discouraging the animals from getting near so she can breathe.

Yet a brave red fox catches her scent and slips through her circle, following it out of curiosity. The handsome guy does a little dance when he finds her. Excitedly, he shows off his bushy tail and waits for Irimara to return the greetings. "No," she tells him. "Leave me alone."

But the other remains, confused and insulted.

He attempts to approach her.

Irimara contrives the shapes of human foresters from the

surrounding trees. They encircle them, one by one, with axes and longbows, their eyes mad set on the lone male fox. He scrunches his nose, sensing that something's very off about these men. The illusions Irimara creates don't have a scent to them. Even while he can see the shadows and puffs his tail, his instincts don't tell him to run.

"I am not some minx to fawn over," Irimara barks. "Leave! Begone."

She makes the huntsmen yell as they charge toward the pathetic creature. He quickly grasps an understanding and darts away.

Now she is alone again with only smoke for company. It's like talking to a reflection, cold and distant.

Irimara reshapes the smoke into a single human-esque figure. The change is quick and seamless. She renders the girl's visage with the same raven hair, white string braiding her locks atop a soft face and pale eyes.

The image opens her lids and looks at the Neshulha.

"What are you hoping to see?" it asks.

"A reason to keep doing this," Irimara returns. "Stop blinking, won't you?"

The girl-like figure ignores her and blinks anyway. Irimara arches her neck and circles the sketch, studying it closely. She makes small corrections. Irimara lengthens the hair, tying it into larger braids with heavy bangs, growing her nose to the right size, and smoothing the slant to her smile.

The last one defies the human obsession with symmetricity

over nature, Irimara muses.

All the while, the image maintains her silver stare.

"Look straight," Irimara instructs.

Nialla's figure shifts her body toward the fox defiantly.

"Stubbornness?" the fox describes. "Mimicking your kind also mimics a personality I don't wholly control."

"Maybe that is by design? I *am* a Singer of the Songs," the false Nialla suggests. "It *is* my blood."

"Or there is only a single chord to draw from," Irimara counters. "It is difficult to create something out of nothing. Like an artist to a canvas, there must be inspiration, but sometimes, even the brush doesn't know what it'll paint. There. Now you look identical. Like true sisters."

Irimara looks over her work. *It is nearly perfect*, she decides, but it is only a false impression.

"Is that why my father's shadow turned on you?" the girl asks.

"That was a step too far in the wrong direction," Irimara admits. "The mother is not a fool. She is of the Ellúndar and Vinvidurfólk—Míran and Aenümorian, the Fallenstar of June. She could sense my deception. It was dumb of me to take the chance."

"But you did, didn't you? Took the risk and were chased off by the Shanashéron," the false Nialla states.

"Where did the 'bird' even come from? Their kind slaughtered mine. *He* told me I would face the past," Irimara shudders. "Is this what the Stranger meant? Or did the Exile know from the start?"

"Perhaps this ordeal is yours as much as mine?" the girl weighs.

"Or maybe you are an illusion pretending to have wisdom you do not," Irimara growls.

"And should I? You said it yourself, old friend. It can be difficult to control us."

"Old friend?" Irimara begs the question. "You are my enemy, false cub. Why do you—?" She pauses only momentarily, letting the other's voice fill the air. *It isn't right*, she frets. *It's nigh impossible.* "How can you argue with me? You *are* me?!"

"Questions that lead only to more questions," the false Nialla states. "Look at me, what do you see?"

Irimara focuses on the figure as it shifts against her will, a youthful face turning into an older, more experienced one with a scar on her cheek. The fox shakes her head and forces the image to dissipate out of utter shock.

"A mind stretched across time to speak to me now," Irimara realizes, only the emptiness left to hear.

She had rarely been able to compel her illusions to do what their living counterparts wouldn't do. *It is much easier to mimic the dead or those blind by duty.* Her kind *do* have workarounds, if only temporarily effective. Force an image to see what they *want* to see as one solution. Stripping away the parts that offer them a choice is another, even though it strains Irimara's creativity to redefine the details of their personalities.

Next, the fox draws an image of the mother—Cyridel, the Lady Miralifrim, as the villagers had called her. Shaping her with light and shadow creates insight into how she overcame the attack. She burns brighter than her daughter. The woman understood *what* Irimara had fabricated wasn't real. The same is evident with the girl, only to a lesser extent, so the fox took advantage of those brief lapses in judgment.

Nialla allowed what she saw to overwhelm her. *Is it her youth?* A cub's mind is open to suggestion, the imagination filling the empty spaces left by the fear of the unknown.

The mother and daughter are remarkably similar, almost like staring at the same person—only minor differences in the broad strokes. Nialla shares the round face of her father, with his silver eyes and wide shoulders. Irimara had created Endúcar's shadow from the mother's dim memories, eighty years older than when she last saw the man. The fox made sure to include everything the woman could recognize. All but a few details weren't in harmony with the *real* person. A mock duplicate, Irimara would describe it.

And with that in her mind, Irimara calls all three to stand side-by-side—the mother, the father, and the daughter. A family separated by tragedy, lost on opposite ends of the world, dreaming 'what if' they could be together again.

Irimara raises her snout and stands in awe of them. "So, you are the total of Icurian's ambitions?"

The father's visage breaks free of her control and steps forward. "You shouldn't play these games with me, Irimara," he warns. "You go a step too far. And killing the child? That is more than a simple blunder."

"Somebody must pay the cost," Irimara argues.

"You took the life of an innocent," the mother resists. "A gentle creature! Pure-hearted."

"Do you think I should doubt my actions? My cubs died in the slaughter!"

The father draws his sword and points it at the fox. "You have a purpose here, friend. Remember what we said?"

"Do not mistake me," Irimara barks. "I serve my role willingly."

"Then why run from the fight?" the false daughter asks.

"I do not run," the fox denies, "rather, it is to lead *her* in the right direction."

"And *what* direction is that?" the false mother demands.

Irimara shuffles backward, afraid of the answer. "The only one that matters."

"She carries us to a Crossroads," the father declares, "to the roots of the Grandfather Tree."

"A place my kind hid at the end of their days," Irimara confirms. "A place where time and space overlap. Gets confused."

The father draws back and sheathes his sword. He nods, satisfied with the fox's answer. After holding his stare for a moment longer, he returns his attention to his false daughter. "An entry point into our world that could prove a danger to us if we don't shut the door."

"And what's on the other side of this door?" the false mother asks.

"Waters that lead to darker places," Irimara states.

The fox halts the scene, having all three hold their breath. Walking up to the older Nialla, Irimara has so many questions. Yet these figures surely don't know the answers. They can't perceive anything that she doesn't already know. At least, they shouldn't. *They sing their songs as I sing mine.*

Irimara turns and summons nine little fox cubs among trees, shades of her children. She watches them play in the grass. Ourimarus is there, her mate, rolling in the dirt and soiling his brilliant white coat with ugly brown. Irimara prances up and meets him, nose to nose, and chirps a happy song.

As her tail flicks, the figure of her mate imitates it. Irimara tilts her head, and the other repeats in a mirrored form. That is all these illusions are—a mimicry of life. As the last Neshulha, she can easily duplicate shapes. Nothing is as perfect as the original, like a painter trying to match another's work of art. Still, this portrait of Ourimarus feels real, with scruffy fur, a large snout, and a soft golden stare that lifts her heart.

A rustling of leaves echoes high in the wildwoods, breaking her focus. She releases the falsehoods and jumps into the bushes. Overhead, a white bird's gaze pierces the forest canopy like rays through a watery ceiling.

"Shanashéron?" Irimara whispers.

At the village, the creature had thrust itself at the fox. Irimara, caught off-guard by the sudden advance, couldn't do anything but escape. She's witnessed enough of her kind burn to death in *their* light. Shanashéron may distinguish themselves as guides to the lost in the dark, but they are prideful and vain. And that pride will lash out at anything the bright shapeshifters consider abhorrent.

Irimara stirs uneasily among the bushes as the white bird lands on a tree branch, scanning the dense forest floor. The old scars under the fox's coat chafe, remembering the pain. She holds her breath, afraid to make a noise.

I remember my friends on fire, hunted by the Shanashéron and Heluvian's noble Vedrethal.

The last thing she wants is to go head-to-head with the bird. Its delicate appearance is another illusion, just not that of the fox. *A light show.* Yes! It provides a warmth Irimara cannot replicate, but that doesn't make it any more *real* than her false impressions and mirror shapes.

"Nobody would follow you if they saw the ugliness under that plumage," Irimara whispers.

She moves into cover under a tree's root as the bird jumps to another branch.

Irimara buries her snout into the underbrush as she watches the Shanashéron finish her watch. The creature takes flight and returns in the direction she came, letting out a song that causes the trees to bend out of her path.

The bird must be attempting to scout the way, staying high, searching for the fox's trail. Irimara sees a chance to sow mischief if she's careful. While she cannot let the bird find her footpath, Irimara *must* lead the daughter east toward the caverns—the Dead Caves, where the real challenge awaits.

Irimara will hide her prints in the dirt and replace them with a more obvious trail. She'll move freely through the wildwood without drawing the bird's attention. The problem for Irimara is then masking her coat. In these Seclumor Wilds, white is a dangerous color to wear. Monsters and beasts inhabit the trees, looking for small creatures like her to make a fast meal. Rarhavonn had predators that contended with the Neshulha as rivals—the staarag, dracaons, ramkins, and the dread Aüth-bringar-in-the-Night.

Our advantage was casting shadows to draw them away from our dens.

Such energy isn't without its limits. Irimara knows all too well. She can emulate the willpower of the beings she musters. *That* is essential—without which, those of her kind would exhaust themselves, risking their lives, playing out every motion and gesture an image can produce.

And to fool an onlooker, the illusion must be as real as possible, especially if the projection is wholly unreal.

However, the Neshulha are not like the Shanashéron. For Irimara to alter her appearance as this Gallandhal does, she must conjure shapes around herself and match them with her movements for all who behold her. It is akin to a hunter wearing a deer's hide, and it causes her no small bother. Irimara shudders at the thought.

A coldness creeps into her bones as she darts away, ready for the final stretch.

— 15 —

THE MIRRORED FOREST

Nialla races across the vast southern plains, only stopping when Ryallamere needs a break.

Gallandhal flies ahead when they reach the outskirts of the Seclumor Wilds, the mountains stretching for leagues to her left and right. In front of her is a worn, moss-covered road. "This feels familiar," Nialla whispers, dismounting from the saddle. She uncovers an old waymarker in the underbrush.

The last time she came this far into the wildwoods was to confront the Crows at Mireaderal. Nialla recalls their names— Clesturia, Alanssia, and Raenia. Twenty years ago, the witches killed dozens of Rasterforn's people at Trebunor. Hundreds more died in the battle that soon followed.

Irimara isn't *them*. She killed *one* and only *one* person— Amerllie, *her* friend. And that is where Nialla draws a line.

Gallandhal returns and perches on the waymarker. She folds

her wings to her sides. "The road ahead is clear," the white bird says.

"Is it? Are you certain?" Nialla begs the question.

"I am never sure of anything in these woods," Gallandhal admits. "But I saw no sign of our quarry."

"That doesn't mean she's not out there," Nialla warns.

"Perhaps waiting for us to lose our way? Unlikely with me."

"Or watching us as she leads us beyond the point of no return. How far do you think?"

"At least another day's march? Maybe two if we're slow? You should leave your horse. He won't be safe once you step onto the road. Powerful beings live out this way," Gallandhal tells her. "Even the spirits in the rocks would leave if they could."

For a moment, a soft hum floats toward her from the trees. "Voices?" Nialla takes a breath and closes her eyes, listening carefully, but the hum fades as soon as it comes.

"Why are you suddenly pale?" Gallandhal notices.

"You didn't hear that?" Nialla asks.

"All I hear is the wind causing the trees to whistle. A subtle music, but not a worrying one."

Nialla frowns and pats the stallion under the mane: "Ryallamere?" she whispers the name. The animal burrs and tilts his head to her, brushing her with his snout. "Thank you for the ride. You are a brave one, aren't you? And so fast!" She hadn't realized then, but a few miles back, the beast ran into a bush when they broke through the edge of the Wilds, leaving scratches on his side. "I am sorry. You *should* return to the village."

Ryallamere lets off a prideful grunt, acknowledging the wounds. *A lot like our favorite Vedrethal,* she thinks. Still, the animal hesitates, but now isn't the time for long goodbyes and stubbornness. Nialla points the horse toward home, nudging him to go. He whines, unwilling to leave her.

"Why doesn't he listen?" Nialla wonders.

"He considers you his ward," Gallandhal explains. "He *is* meant as a warrior's mount."

"He knows his duty," Nialla smiles. She grabs a hold of his harness and looks right into the animal's eyes. "I release you, horse lord. Duty now binds you to find your way home again. Tell my mother I am safe."

Ryallamere snorts and bumps the top of Nialla's head with his chin. There's a sad look in his eye, a longing to stay with her until the end. Yet, his duty demands he yield, and so he does. Nialla watches him leave with a heavy canter. She waits until he disappears into the distance before turning to the wildwoods ahead.

"He will find his way," Gallandhal reassures. "Horses are clever animals."

"Maybe he'll run into Sackery's unit on the way back," Nialla hopes.

"Only if they don't find us first," the bird suggests. "Are you ready? It won't be an easy trek on foot."

Nialla nods and steadies her breath. "I'll be fine."

Gallandhal takes flight and weaves through the trees. She lets off a bright song that pulls Nialla onto the old forest road. Her music is so loud. As they travel farther, Nialla realizes that the forest's sounds beyond the threshold boldly covet the air, and her footsteps drown under the hillocks and leaves. She would lose herself in the windfalls without the cadence, a beacon in a vast ocean of a hundred vibrant tunes.

As she journeys most of the day, Nialla can hear birds singing ever more colorfully. Alive?! Herds of deer prance across the path, large bucks leading them. Beavers in the creeks, building their dams as large black bears wade in the water, catching fish. A far cry from the bleak emptiness that embodied these woods during the Reign of Crows.

So, there is life, after all? Not all of it abandoned this place.

"Everything's changed," Nialla tells Gallandhal as they break camp after a night.

"Change defines the Wilds," Gallandhal replies. "Should it stop, it will die. A lifeless, barren landscape."

Nialla runs a hand through dark-brown dirt, which is healthy with worms, feeding the plants. "But it isn't lifeless? I thought you said even the spirits would avoid this place if they could. There is a story here! Hopefulness. This wilderness brims with it from root to leaf, from the rocks to the high canopy."

"What do you mean?" Gallandhal issues. "I am not blind. Life grows, but the critters know better."

"I don't understand. Do you not see it? So beautiful, all these songs."

Gallandhal turns to the girl with puffed feathers, confusion in her violet eyes. "Perhaps I am overly focused on our destination?"

Nialla grimaces as the shadows creep on her like tendrilled vines. "That voice? I hear it again."

"Maybe I am deaf as well? A voice? I hear no voice."

"How can you not?!" Nialla challenges, the trees flinching as her tone cracks.

Gallandhal lowers her head and softly asks: "What does it say?"

"I don't know. Maybe a warning? It talks about a . . . cave . . . an end in . . . violence? The words confuse me," Nialla states. "They blur together. It's hard to tell, but I promise you, I can hear them. Are they screaming?! From everywhere, all at once. Cries? Painful ones. I-I don't . . . I don't know?"

The white bird draws back. "There are no voices but ours," Gallandhal tells her, quiet and forlorn.

"Perhaps the spirits took up residence and choose now to stay hidden?"

Gallandhal shakes, fluttering her wings as if a chill suddenly crawls down the back of her feathery neck. "Do more than listen, then. Take your chance, little one. If the woodland spirits are indeed here, they owe you fealty. Don't be afraid. Tell them your name."

Nialla stares at the bird, then blinks. These wildwoods speak to her, but the words are very foreign. She was small the first time she heard them, a cold and distant light, but it is a language that life understands. She closes her eyes to feel a semblance of every song and chord surrounding her.

Emotional ... Powerful ... Soft ... Strings ... Drumming ...

"I am Nialla," she utters.

"Louder!"

"My name is Nialla Elendsah, Princess of Ilhivendal and Calidor, daughter of Galron and Cyridel! Will you hear me?" Then, she smells that musky stench filling the air as the shadowy mist draws away. Nialla snaps her head to attention just as the trees multiply and grow. "We are not alone."

The wilds fold unto themselves, creating a mirrored image, upside down and sideways. The land Nialla stands on becomes an island. She can see where the edge drops, a dark abyss with a shimmer of water at the bottom she *knows* isn't there but is enough to force her back a few steps.

Gallandhal jumps onto her shoulder. "Nialla?!"

The girl spins as a high laugh surrounds her, and the trees stretch and whine.

A white figure, small and fast, dodges the thickets and shades, bright yellow eyes clear against the black. "Must I hear? Or can I speak true? Did you forget another name they call you? Or was that on purpose?" Irimara iterates. "You follow me?! Do you know where I bring us?" The fox walks into the open and sits, arrogant and secure.

"No."

"Liar!"

"Why do you attack me?"

"Do I attack? Or do I hide in plain sight?" Irimara growls. "It seems we each have many questions to answer." The fox disappears into a dust cloud, her voice still ringing in the girl's ears. Here and there, always on the move.

"I only asked one," Nialla murmurs. "Is this another illusion?"

"Another lie? Yes, indeed. What do you think? Does the fisherman ask where the water is when he's on the boat?" the fox's voice falls from all directions. And all the while, the bright shadow darts between the trees. "You and I are on this road. Together or apart, it does not matter. Neither of us will like where it leads."

Irimara fades into view again, taking a firm stance on the black island's edge.

Gallandhal squawks. "Murderer!" The bird spreads her wings to appear larger, talons digging into Nialla's shoulder.

"Spoken insincerely," Irimara laughs. "Death follows me as it follows you! All of us? Murderers."

Nialla notices the fox speak, but it isn't with anger. There's a wisp to the creature's tone, soft and sorrowful like autumn leaves falling on sand. Nialla pushes forward. Then, she stops just as quickly. She bumps into something hard. *Is it a wall?* Nialla feels around. She can't see it, but it *is* there, solid as a rock.

She takes a few steps back, Gallandhal's talons clinging to her tighter. From a distance, another figure arrives. It walks toward her, slow but steady. "What are you doing—?" Nialla attempts to ask it, squaring her shoulders and narrowing her eyes.

The figure appears as a dim blue light until it halts an arm's length away. Nialla stands her ground as the face comes into focus. She is a young woman with a noble expression and dark, braided hair, like a younger version of her mother. At least, it is what Nialla imagines her mother to look like if she were young again.

It's not until the other mirrors Nialla that she realizes the truth.

Nialla raises an arm, and the woman does the same. Nialla tilts her head, and the other parrots the motion. Nialla reaches out a hand to touch her, stopping when she hits the unseen wall. Their hands press together as if looking at each other through silver glass. *But this isn't a mirror?* There's nothing between them, the girl or the woman.

"You're cold? Like the bark on a tree," Nialla details. "Another false impression?"

The woman takes a deep breath and sidesteps the barrier. Nialla watches as she disappears into the clouds bordering the island. Irimara merely sits there, waiting to see what either of them do.

"Only in part," Irimara answers. "Do you know this place?"

Nialla returns her attention to the fox. "I've stood in these woods in my battle with the Crows." She clenches her fist, nostrils flared. *Why does she play these games? What purpose does it serve?* "They betrayed you. Sold you out to Heluvian, who then hunted you like vermin."

"You can ignore vermin," Irimara seethes. "He hounded us

like the very course of history depended on it. Icurian failed to act. He left us to fend for ourselves. What would you do if everything you loved were to die? What if you found your mother butchered? Your friends beheaded, their skulls on spikes to serve as a warning to others?!"

Nialla frowns. "Is that why you killed Amerllie?"

Irimara closes her mouth, her yellow eyes beaming forward, unable to hide the soul behind them. "Her death was unavoidable," she admits. Irimara's voice fades under the wind, attempting to hide the uncertainty of her tone.

"Unavoidable? Was she *that* much of a threat to you? Is that why you attacked her?! Attack me?"

Gallandhal leans forward and whispers in her ear: "Be careful, little one."

"I needed to draw your protectors away," Irimara confesses. "Amerllie was a young cub that left the den. Predators must take opportunities. A strike at the right time makes the herd panic, leaving the rest vulnerable."

Nialla squeezes her fists tighter until her knuckles are white, causing the trees to wither and shake. Even the fox's illusion hears her fury and wanes for a heartbeat. It is enough for Nialla to see through to the Wilds on the other side of the pitch blackness shared between the fox and the girl.

"You speak of her like some abandoned puppy in the streets," Nialla seethes.

"And if I didn't kill her, another would have! Soldiers? Old age?" Irimara argues. "Time kills all things. Even us! And there are monsters in these woods that are far worse than me, little cub. Don't believe me? One perches on your shoulder this very instant! Shanashéron, Daughter of Aerrovoshal."

"The woodland beasts answer to me!" Nialla decries.

"Like they did Clesturia? Or are you only another tyrant building off others' failures?"

Nialla draws back, quiet for a moment. "I am *not* like them."

Irimara sits a little taller, unafraid of the girl. "Neither were the Crows before they were buried alive." She pauses, staring hard at Nialla with those yellow eyes. Then, she runs off into the fog, folding the trees behind her so Nialla can't follow. "Is that why the Mórhathan also hunts me?"

"I don't know what you mean," Nialla whimpers, less than confident. "He is my friend."

"Friend? Like a bird to a tree—which is friend, and which is slave?"

"He is not my slave," Nialla refuses.

"Is he not? As the Mórhathan approached you those years ago, did you *not* invade his mind?"

Nialla shakes her head. "He came to me. He protected me! He listened."

"He protects these wildwoods, little cub. Don't you understand? And your song calls louder than the trees," Irimara states. "That is what I am trying to teach you! But first, you must *want* to learn, to know the truth of what happened years ago. You are only a few steps away now."

Gallandhal loosens her hold on Nialla's shoulder as the white bird settles unevenly. "She describes the Dead Caves, so called because—"

"Because it is where my people had their last gasp," Irimara finishes. "Here I am. A survivor?" She appears again beside Nialla, like a phantom. She is so close that her musky stench nearly overwhelms the girl's senses. Nialla reaches out to touch the fox, only for the image to pass through her fingers like ink in water. "My kind were tricksters. Our illusions . . . half-truths, mirrored and mimicked."

"You aren't really here?" Nialla asks.

"No. I am. Out of sight," Irimara admits. "Safely at a distance."

"You are an idea that made it past the death throws," Nialla swallows.

Irimara laughs. "You could always find out how close those words are to the truth." The images fade away as the path through the forest gradually opens. "It is dangerous to walk in the dark when stepping off the road. Follow me. Let me be your light."

Gallandhal jumps off her shoulder and flies after the fox. "Filthy wretch!"

Nialla runs to keep pace through the trees, cutting herself on low-hanging branches and vines. It is a hard trek as she hits a field of tall grass before coming out the other side at a cavern etched into the cliffs.

The bird lands on a rock outside the entrance.

Nialla looks up at the mountains, out of breath. "Where did she go?"

Gallandhal dithers. "Inside? Irimara's tracks lead in and out, so this is likely the fox's den."

"Or a mass grave," Nialla worries. She looks at the size of the rocky entrance, tall and wide, with only darkness inside. "This is it, isn't it? Is this what Irimara wants to show me? It feels . . . Empty? I sense a heaviness in the air. Tell me you feel it, too?"

"I feel it," Gallandhal answers. "Death lingers here."

Nialla breathes, but she can't fill her lungs. It hurts. Her eyes flutter, and her throat dries like she suddenly needs water. "What's inside?"

"The name speaks for itself, does it not?" Gallandhal says, slumping forward. "I don't know, little one. Not anymore. I never took the chance to find out. You already know everything I do. And there is little use for me telling you again. She's inside, along with whatever truth she wants to tell you."

"She was afraid of you," Nialla scolds.

"Pride got the better of me."

"You called her filth."

"And is she not? After all this, can you doubt it?"

"Yes," Nialla frowns, stepping toward the entrance. "Should I follow her?"

"A wiser bird than I would argue against it. But—? After what she said, there is a reason for doing what she did. And it wasn't merely out of malice." Gallandhal shivers coldly as a soft wind flows out of the cavern. "Something tells me there's a threat looming over our heads. Inside the cave? Maybe. Be cautious, nevertheless."

"You'll stay here, won't you? Until I am done?"

Gallandhal flattens her feathers. "Your friends likely aren't far behind. If possible, I should warn them."

"My Sackery?" Nialla begs the question. "I could use his courage." She moves closer to the caves but feels the wind pick up and push against her. *It is a sensation I don't feel often—the cold. Dark waters scare me more than anything, but the cold? It is unnatural.* "Maybe I should wait?"

"That would only work to the fox's benefit," Gallandhal cautions. "And if this is a trap?"

"It'll be more dangerous if others are with me," Nialla considers.

"The choice *is* yours."

"But you *will* be here when I come back?"

"Do you want me to be?" Gallandhal returns.

"Yes? Maybe. It depends on what's on the other side," Nialla expresses.

"The only way you can find out is by plunging deeper into the abyss," Gallandhal urges. "Steel your heart, little one. Raise your chin when all sense abandons you. Stand as a single bright note in the choired sea, a land of silence, whispering until you become the crescendo."

"That isn't helping much," Nialla shudders.

Gallandhal tilts her head and drops her eyes. "My apologies."

"Can you tell Sackery to wait for me?" Nialla begs the favor. "Should he find his way here?"

"You have my word," the bird agrees, offering a respectful

curtsy. "Remember what I said about friendly faces? Don't trust them." Nialla watches as the Shanashéron takes flight and vanishes over the trees. "We'll be waiting for you when it is over!"

And with that, Nialla is alone, now more than ever. Does she feel a tremor in her hands? She squeezes her wrist and breathes to calm her nerves. She wraps all her provisions in her cloak and lays them flat on the rock by the cavern's entrance. It is better to keep them out here, where they won't weigh her down.

Nialla walks over to the cave's threshold, stairs hewn from the stone leading her inside. This place isn't natural. There are etchings across the surface and script along the foundation. She can still read them, but they don't make sense. Nialla recognizes the clearest words, chiseled in Iírdunic runes, the tongue of her forefathers. *Carry the torch and light the braziers of Alinmarthal*, it says. *Only sorrow ahead. Stand by the doorway to a space between worlds and hold it shut. Beware. Only doom survives.*

"Icurian?" Nialla whispers. "Did you inscribe these?"

Nobody answers. She shouldn't expect anyone but the fox and her tricks.

Nialla takes a breath and follows the only way forward, cold and dry through the dust.

— *Nialla delves into the Dead Caves* —

— 16 —

VISAGE

Sackery keeps an eye on the Mórhathan as the party follows the lumbering creature south along the mountains. Iben and the Jhalamar march in a wide pattern, searching the woods for the fox's tracks as they push deeper. *I commend their efforts, even if I suspect where this road already leads.*

"Strange how the Great Bear doesn't attend us," Iben points out.

"And what are *we* to him but a few motes springing his stride?" Sackery suggests.

Every few leagues, the massive creature stops and claws at a tree. Iben and Sackery found those markings on the trail before. Yet, the reason was a mystery then. Sackery knows many animals rub against vegetation to leave their scent and remove their winter coats. And bears? They would peel the bark as the Mórhathan does. It has taken a few days for Sackery to conclude why the mighty woodland spirit would play to such behavior.

"Master?" Ivette nudges him.

"Steel your wits, Jhalamar. Eyes high and be ready," Sackery tells them. "Even for our friend, these are unfamiliar lands." The Mórhathan glances at Sackery and his companions as it trudges forward on the path. He shakes his head as if guessing what's on the old warrior's mind.

A bright song floats down from the trees. Sackery looks and spies a white bird jumping from branch to tree branch, keeping a steady pace with the group. "Gallandhal?" Sackery last saw her at Hugh's Cabin, flying off toward Wilhimusk. He questions why the Shanashéron is with them now. *Does she know? Has she followed us these past few days? No. I would have noticed.*

Gallandhal watches their road but doesn't fly down to speak with him. It is as if she's only ensuring they march in the right direction.

Did you beat us to the end of this chase? Sackery riddles. *What should I expect?*

As the group plunges into a field of tall grass, Sackery loses sight of Iben and the Jhalamar. He retraces his steps, finding the Captain with only three others. "Master Greywolfe?" Iben asks. Sackery puts a hand on the man's shoulder.

"Let's tighten up," he quietly orders him.

"I'll make the rounds," Iben agrees. He steps off to spread the word, disappearing behind the dense grass wall. Moments later, Sackery hears the man shouting for everyone to regroup.

"Find yourselves! Close ranks in the center!" He repeats it. "Close ranks!" One by one, the party follows the voice and rejoins Sackery in following the Forest Guardian. "Count heads! Who's left? Soldiers?!" Camdyn and Kennen are the last to return, cuts on their skin left by the edges of the leafy barbs. "You'll be fine."

The Mórhathan grunts and tilts. He blazes a path through the grass, quickening his pace.

Sackery hears a voice ahead—a woman's tone, sad and beautiful. She sings high and low, the only sound for leagues. There are no wild birds or music in the trees in this stretch of wood. All that remains is what comes out of the ground. And now, there's life?! It's unlikely a coincidence.

Something isn't right. I shouldn't trust what I see. Trust only my gut and what I smell.

Icurian's warnings haunt him with every step.

"I know that melody!" Iben utters, pushing fast ahead.

Emerging through the grass in the Mórhathan's wake, the party finds themselves at large cliffs married to the mountains rising from the other side of the clearing. Hidden among the crags and dirt is a large cavern stretching a quarter way up the height.

Sackery raises a hand and halts Iben and the others. He sees a familiar face. Sitting on a rock by the cave's entrance is a woman dressed in green, silver, and blue. Shadows obscure her features at first. As Iben and the Jhalamar move toward her, the Mórhathan circles the meadow, only for the woman to look up and smile. Her eyes land on Sackery. *I catch a subtle musky scent.*

"Lady Miralifrim?" Iben asks, confused.

"My friends," the woman offers.

Sackery stands there, less surprised, glaring at the woman's glowing figure. "Where did you come from?" He looks to the clearing's edges, questioning how she could have beaten the party to this place. "Lady Cyridel?"

The Mórhathan stops circling the field, scratching at the dirt with his root-like claws and growling unhappily.

Cyridel looks at the Forest Lord, almost cheerful. It is like she's confident the massive creature won't harm her. *Or maybe he can't?* Sackery wonders if *that* could be true. Regardless, she looks awfully at ease and gladly finishes her song, undeterred by the creature's threats:

He is a warrior,
Braced against the wind, without his shield,
Desperate is his hour, his standard torn,
Trampled by the soldiers dying all around,
Together, his swords do reign, a dark steel reflection,
As a shadow falls over Ilhivendal,
Low the flags fly under the glare of a red-orange sky,
And as dust gathers on the mounds,
Bodies lay still, his friends bare on the stoney shore,
A fallen star from the black above,
Like a flare from a distant, raging fire,

And the warrior stands, a silver for his pride,
For where the masked-king walks,
Doom falls upon his dead, dying house.

Sackery thumbs his sword's pommel. He moves to the side to better view the woman's face, studying her cautiously. Cyridel's false image returns the stare and smiles. "You are far from home, old warrior. And farther still without your horses? Oh, Vedrethal."

"You speak with her voice," Sackery decides, "but not her words. You were to stay with Nialla at Wilhimusk. And yet? Here you are, deep into the Wilds—a yellow tint to your eyes, Daughter of Ilhivendal."

The false impression frowns. "You care about these people?" She rises from the rock and walks toward him, stopping uncomfortably close. Enough so that Sackery feels her breath on his cheeks. *Is it her breath?* His fingers wrap his sword's hilt. *Or is it the wind?*

"It is my duty. Always my duty," Sackery derides, holding his ground.

"But is it only a duty to you? Or is it something more?"

Sackery steps back. He hears a whine from beyond the cavern's threshold—a whistling noise, like a flute. "What is that?" he demands. "Who's in there? Surely not a minstrel-poet."

"Most likely Nialla," the false Cyridel tells him. "She went inside."

Iben and the Jhalamar turn to each other with surprise, hands on their weapons.

"My Nialla? Why would she—?" Sackery begins to ask but again notices the yellow tint in the woman's eyes. He focuses on them, the clear shine of their color. Those are not *her* eyes, *her* words, or *her* smile. "We left three, four days ago. How did you beat us here? Why *are* you? These caves are dangerous. And why did Nialla venture into this morbid place *alone* if *she* is, as you claim?"

Cyridel bares her teeth at him, foxlike and fierce. She holds her stare for the longest time, not a word from her tongue. The Mórhathan lets off a low-tone growl, kicking up more dirt, agitated. Sackery glances in the creature's direction, unsure and worried.

We can all feel it, this woman—? Not a woman. She isn't our Cyridel.

"She met an anomaly at the village," the false impression finally answers. "She decided to follow two days ago to its source, racing through the fields and brambles. She found *this* place, these Dead Caves, as you know them. That's when you arrived, Sackery of the Vedrethal. Along with these pale imitations of your warrior-kin."

"Are you the one who killed Amerllie?" Sackery questions, drawing his blade a little from his side. "Tell me."

"Should I tell you? Or have you already guessed *what* this is, Vedrethal?" the false impression confides. "Nialla *is* here, lord. She *needs* to make sense of it. Not the most delicate approach, I admit, but I am unwilling to beg the mercy of somebody whose sword was once at my neck."

"I don't know what you mean?"

"You do, Vedrethal. Do not play innocent. Inside is no more dangerous than the beasts that gather here, if you ask me."

Sackery narrows her eyes at the woman. "Is this charade meant to confuse me?" he demands. "Why not conjure Pict and Hader to stand guard? They wouldn't have left your side had both of you come to this sad place."

Her expression drops like she doesn't know those names. The false Cyridel quickly catches herself and squares her shoulders.

Gallandhal swoops down from the trees and lands between Sackery and the image. The white bird looks at him, then at the false impression of the woman they know. "She is an illusion," Gallandhal warns. "Her name is Irimara, and she—?"

"I know *what* she is," Sackery regards. "Neshulha. A fox spirit from Dal Rarhavonn."

"Master Greywolfe? Are we still—?" Iben begs the question.

Sackery raises his hand and gently quiets him. "It is all right," he tells the man.

"Is it? Are you not afraid of when the fox bites?" the false Cyridel derides. She walks amongst the Jhalamar as if surveying them. They draw their swords, their spears. Unsettled. Much as the Mórhathan. Cyridel—or whatever wears her face—stops within the crowd and frowns. "You need to leave this place before you get hurt. All of you! Everything I do is for a reason."

Sackery takes a defensive stance, hesitant to draw his sword further—Aru il Endril. "And *what* reason is that? Why would my girl come all this way? Was it so you could lure her into a trap? Will you let me see her? Or is it a lie? An illusion to march my company into a monster's den?" He slightly pulls his hand back. *Every time I draw my sword, blood spills,* Sackery recites. *Now isn't the time for rash action. I mustn't act first.*

"What'll happen inside this cave isn't for you," the image warns. "Nor your party far afield."

Sackery clenches his jaw. "Why? Because she's your prisoner?"

"Did I suggest she was? Nialla arrived by her own accord. With help from the bird, she followed me like a stalker in a graveyard. I did nothing but show her the way, isn't that right?" She looks at Gallandhal, who writhes uncomfortably. Cyridel's visage smiles again, tilting her head with an artful thankfulness. "It is as it should be. As it *must* be for all of us to survive past this hour."

"The fox whispers. Don't listen to her! Her words play on your emotions," Gallandhal hollers. "She's dangerous."

"Enough! All of us *are* dangerous, but you chased *me,*" the image cries. "I did not ask you to come."

Gallandhal jumps to a tree branch above the field. "Your people were hunted!"

"Like animals! Would you like to finish the job?" the false one demands.

"It was a mistake. And I didn't condone it," Gallandhal murmurs. "But now? A child's dead! What is *that* if not hostile?"

Irimara scoffs. "Instruction." The visage shifts her attention away from the bird and toward Sackery. "I wondered if you would have remembered me. During those years with Icurian? You visited our home—such bright days, forgotten by most. But I remember you, the boy with the sword who played soldier by the island. Oh, Vedrethal." She utters the final word with a twist on her tongue, full of hate. Almost as if she uses the name as an insult to *him* and *his* brethren, the Vedrethal of the Order.

Sackery looks beyond Cyridel's image to see a white fox sitting by the cavern entrance, clear as day. *Out in the open? She's not trying to hide.*

"It's not something I would forget," Sackery admits. He takes a breath, stepping past the false impression and toward the fox. "Let's drop the masks, shall we? I want to talk. You? Me. All of us, here at the end of this search you've led us on, friend."

"You would speak to a murderess?" Irimara asks.

"No. I would speak to the one who could answer for their crimes," Sackery bites angrily.

Irimara lets Cyridel's image dissipate, stepping forward in her true form. Sackery eyes the white fox, a subtle glow surrounding her, the way her fur catches the sunlight as it breaks into the field afore the cavern. "I had my reasons, Master Vedrethal. Always a reason."

"No reason you give me will ever be good enough!" he shouts with a crack. Iben and the others jump, surprised by his tone.

Sackery clenches his jaw, exhausted by the game. He never once raised his voice in their presence in such a way, even during the hardest days when he would push them to their limits from dusk to dawn and dusk again. "You came to us? Attacked the soul of our people?! Those I swore to defend."

"And I would do it again," Irimara says, laying her paw down.

"Why? Tell me!"

Irimara sits straight and raises her head. "Icurian made a promise. He said he would keep us out of his war so the Neshulha could live in calm solitude. *He promised.* All those years? For what? A rebellion nobody remembers?!"

"Icurian broke many promises," Sackery tells her. "I still have the scars. Many of us do."

The fox scowls at him, a heavy sense of loss in the yellow of her eyes. "Do you think I don't know?! Vedrethal?" Irimara speaks the title again with such contempt. "I am not blind to those responsible! Vedrethal? You and I understand what it means to walk alone."

"Then why add to the misery?"

"A word once given should never be forgotten," Irimara decides. "First, she must witness the consequence. This is my task, my burden . . . my purpose. The suffering of an entire race lives on inside these caves. Whispers? Darkness all around us."

"Nialla had nothing to do with the crimes against your kind," Sackery defends.

Irimara seethes like a rabid hound. "The scars don't heal! They only fade, and I must look at them. Maybe others can forget? Not me. The fur doesn't grow back. You should know *that* better than anybody. Carrying on makes the pain left behind that much stronger. It is hard to see past the hate."

"And you led the girl *here* of all places?"

"Isn't it odd? Do you even know *where* we are?"

Sackery grimaces. "The wilds at the edge of the known world?"

"At the border where many roads cross, a place where time and space intercede," Irimara describes. "One of many doors."

"Nialla can't return what you lost back to life," Sackery tells her.

Irimara shakes her head and softens her posture. "I don't do this for my memories. Those days are gone! A promise was made, and it *will* be kept. By me?! For *her* sake, not mine. Everything inside those caves is a prelude. Nialla *must* face it, as I must. That is our trial—our fate, born and raised."

Sackery takes a breath and raises his blade, aiming it at the fox. "She won't do it alone. Let me pass. You aren't the only one with a promise."

Icurian's voice echoes in his thoughts: "*Every time you draw your sword, blood will spill. A curse more than a gift,*" the man had said. His father's words are a cautionary tale. "*Do what you can to avoid it, but realize this, son. That weapon is a pledge. You do not draw it unless you intend to use it.*"

Irimara takes a guarded step back, only for the Mórhathan's growls to get louder as it lumbers toward her with menace. She clearly understands her odds, but the fox isn't powerless.

Sackery knows that she can make them see whatever she wants. *Was she trying to offer an olive branch?*

"Let her do what she came here for, Vedrethal," Irimara offers him a chance. "That's all I ask."

"And what is she meant to do?" Sackery demands.

Irimara raises her snout, amused by the question. "To bring down the mountain and stop the bad from becoming worse. Deny it as you might. You could say the war never ended for some, but now we stand at the cusp of another. You still fight the battles in your head—as you sleep, when you dream?! Always with a sword in your hand, never a petal of kindness."

"Words spoken like they come from a distant place?"

"Should they not?" Irimara asks. "We don't have to draw more blood."

"Blood is already drawn, Irimara. Do you not see it in the water?"

"Along with the rest of the filth," the fox speaks mournfully. "Fine. I *am* your enemy. And you *are* mine, Sackery Greywolfe." She jumps forward and bares her teeth, but that was a mistake. The Mórhathan suddenly roars and charges at the small white creature. Iben and two others roll out of the way. Irimara closes her mouth and vanishes into a fine mist. *Another illusion?* A failure to end it before it started.

"No! Hold your ground!" Sackery shouts to the Jhalamar. He rushes to the Mórhathan, raising a hand to calm him. "Easy now, friend. Take it easy." The bear growls and snaps, eventually snorting at him, angered by his interference.

"What just happened?" Iben asks.

"The fox played us! She wasn't here," Ivette answers. "She must be close?!"

The Mórhathan snarls and beats the ground with his great paws. Sackery backs away, too aware of the creature's strength and power. He turned the tide against the Crows at Mireaderal. He's in a near-feral state, acting out his instincts. Irimara had announced herself as an 'enemy,' and the Forest Guardian answered the threat.

Iben turns to him, his sword still ready: "What do we do now?"

"We fight off the fox's defenses and push into the cave," Sackery decrees. "That's what we'll do."

Gallandhal finds a perch on the Vedrethal's shoulder. "I am sorry for this."

"No time to apologize," Sackery tells her. "You did what you could. Irimara *is* dangerous, as you said. And not the sort of danger you'd confront willfully. Heluvian feared the Neshulha. He had his reasons."

"And the fox has hers," Gallandhal offers.

"Prepare yourselves!" Iben orders.

"Nialla and I chased the fox after she approached us at the village," Gallandhal dithers. "The girl wants you to wait outside. Don't go after her! Please? I don't know what's inside the caves, but it isn't our place to jump into the middle of it! You'll only do more harm."

"Are you saying I should do nothing?" Sackery weighs.

"Sometimes it is the best course," the Shanashéron suggests.

"No. I stayed my hand once before when faced with a threat. Never again! Eyes forward."

"This is a mistake, Vedrethal. Nialla said—?"

"I have a duty, Gallandhal. And I will see it done," Sackery decides.

The bird draws back and flattens her wings to her sides. "Do as you will, then. I will not help you."

"Then find a spot on high and stay out of our way," Sackery orders. "Be safe."

Gallandhal lowers her head and breathes deeply, only to fly off and perch above the cave's entrance. "Don't trust your eyes, Master Vedrethal. Trust your gut and what *feels* right. I don't want anyone else getting hurt."

Sackery frowns. He knows the Neshulha can fool the senses in the heat of strong emotions. "Everyone? Call out anything . . . unusual. Anything that shouldn't belong to our environs. She'll trick the eye as much as the mind."

Iben and the Jhalamar establish a circle around him, waiting to hear more of a plan.

"Should we rush for the entry?" Ivette begins to ask.

"No! We draw the fox out," Camdyn suggests.

"Stay together!"

"We are well trained."

"Fight to the last!"

"Fight as one!"

"Or die," Iben utters grimly.

The Mórhathan grunts as he stares at the cave's entrance.

Sackery tracks its gaze and points: "Look forward! Ready? Expect anything out of the hole."

He can feel vibrations underfoot—a bright figure stepping from the cavern, dressed in armor under a white cloak. Sackery's hands tremble. The old warrior narrows his eyes at the figure and the mask it wears, shrouding its eyes. *There's a swelling in my throat.* Sackery looks to the others. Even the Mórhathan amply retreats several wary steps backward.

Iben grips his sword and comes alongside Sackery. "Master Greywolfe? Who—? Or *what* is that?"

Sackery bumps Iben's shoulder. "Follow my lead, Captain," he says, signaling everybody to close ranks. "I told you stories about the man who raised me, did I not?" The others reorient themselves, catching his worried tone.

The figure draws a long, elegant spear, the metal humming like music from its haft to the fine tips on each end.

"Yes. But is that important now?" Iben asks.

"Might be, if *he* is real. Your very lives may depend on it," Sackery admits, not enthused by the company's response. He locks his sword and taps his foot, counting the seconds. He breathes deeply before letting it out again. "Because I know *that* mask. Survive *him* if you can. An illusion can only hurt if you let it." His body reacts as ice runs down his arms, his fingers stiff.

Sackery beats his chest to wake the fire in his blood.

— 17 —

AT WILHIMUSK

Cyridel steps quietly by the children asleep on the floor.

Elundjir built the Hall of His Name on the road into Wilhi-musk as a feasting house for his neighbors to partake in his joys—brewing ales, smoked meat, and keen conversations, all to relish the days. During the warmer seasons, the settlers kick back at the tables after toiling in the sun for long hours. In the autumn and winter, the hearths offer light and heat on colder evenings.

It is the sturdiest building in the village and their refuge when danger knocks at their doors.

Cyridel had stumbled on such places during the decades she spent as a wanderer. She always found them . . . troublesome, a place where folk drink too much and forget their manners. Raised in Ilhivendal, the Míran-Ellúndar had their share of tea houses and public gardens, but never anything so raucous.

Nineteen years since they laid the first cornerstones of Elundjir's Hall, Cyridel still doesn't see the appeal. *Perhaps I never will?* Most days, there's so much noise that she wouldn't hear somebody talking to her an arm's length away. Smoke fills the space at night, the fumes collecting in the deep recesses above them before flowing out through the roof's openings, making the air stuffy and unpleasant.

Tonight isn't one of those nights, Cyridel grimaces.

With the fox on the prowl and Nialla rushing off to confront the creature, Cyridel must comfort the settlers. She's ordered them to occupy Elundjir's Hall while the Jhalamar remain alert. All the better to keep them safe. A few dozen families with only a handful of guards? Even as she walks the rows between the sleepers, helping soothe their worries, the air feels dry and empty, but not from the smoke. Ever since Amerllie died, these people have lived as though every ounce of cheer turned into the ashes on the girl's pyre.

Cyridel notices several younger boys pretending to sleep while whispering stories under their blankets. She kneels and rests a hand on one of their backs: "Do try to get some rest, won't you? These nights will go faster if you dream." The lad looks up at her, astonished. He opens his mouth, but his tongue becomes twisted. Cyridel smiles at him kindly and turns to the others.

"Our apologies, Lady Miralifrim," offers the eldest of the boys. "We miss our beds." The rest all nod.

"I am sure you do, little man," Cyridel speaks softly.

"Can we go home?" another boy asks.

"Soon. After the danger's past us."

"And when will that be?"

Cyridel offers a solemn frown. "When the others get back."

"And how much longer is that?"

"A few days? A week? I don't know. I wish I did, but I don't," Cyridel admits. "That's why all of you need to get some sleep. Take advantage of these quiet days when you're not busy helping in the fields. Soon enough, your parents will take you home. Listen for the bells, and they'll tell you it's safe."

"But the bells only ring when there's trouble," a third boy points out.

"Like when somebody dies," a fourth adds.

"Like Amerllie."

Cyridel holds her breath. "And what do you know about Amerllie?"

"That some wild animal killed her," the eldest boy answers.

"Yes. Out in the fields, where your families work," Cyridel explains. "That's why the others went to find it with Master Greywolfe. Until they return, it isn't safe to leave the village. And the feasting hall allows us to keep an eye on everyone."

"And will they kill it? The animal that killed Amerllie?"

Cyridel chews her tongue, weighing her words carefully. "Are you worried?"

"My father went with the Lord Vedrethal," the eldest confesses. "I am worried about what will happen if they don't kill it. Could it kill them, instead? Will they bring my father back like they did my uncle? He died at Mireaderal, my mother said."

"That was before you were born," Cyridel frets, noticing the bite in the lad's tone. She breathes, unsure how to feel about a youth who can so easily speak of death. He's not Nialla. They may look the same age, but these boys only lived a fraction of her life. "Sackery is the greatest warrior I have met in all my years. He can do what nobody else can do, friends. A simple wild animal is nothing to him. Once it's dealt with, everything will be fine." She lies.

It won't be the last threat these people face. The next may not come until these boys are well into adulthood, but it *will* still come. *Perhaps they will be the next generation to take up arms as the Jhalamar of Wilhimusk?* Cyridel wonders. *Aspirants of the Vedrethal? A seed for every flower in the garden. Soldiers. That's who they'll be.*

"I'll make sure they go to sleep," the eldest boy agrees. "We promise."

She nods, satisfied. "I will hold you to that, Orswarvin, Son of Iben. And I will give my praise to your father."

Cyridel reads the pride in the eldest's eyes. She rises and walks to the windows, leaving the boys to their schemes. She paces back and forth along the wall, counting the heads of everyone in the feasting hall—Ankara and her husband among them, with Yeavengeritt by the doors, speaking to a small group.

Over the years, local artisans added wooden reliefs to the

walls—designs of horses, birds, and the dwellers by the river. An elderly seamstress made tapestries to compliment the works, illustrations of how these people came to settle the land in many colors and threads. Cyridel's favorite depicts her family's crossing of Arún Ouandin and the audience with Lord Rasterforn in Trebunor's ruins. Another is the battle with the Crows at Mireaderal, the Lady of the Mountains holding her own beside the Riders of Calidor against the witches and their army of thralls.

"Lady of the Mountains," Cyridel whispers, a name given to her daughter in these images.

A cold breath pushes against her, knocking her off-balance. "Ansolas," it utters.

Cyridel looks out the window. She notices the light eking over the eastern ranges. It's the middle of summer, and dusk falls late, meaning it's nearly dawn. Six days ago, Sackery and the Jhalamar departed. Nialla left with Gallandhal two days later. That's seven days since Amerllie died.

All I can do is bide my time until they return. Cyridel rubs her throat, feeling the tension. *Should I have told those boys otherwise?*

She ordered Hader to stand guard at the road leading into Wilhimusk. Pict makes rounds between the Solitary Hill and Elundjir's Hall. Olynn and Rod remain here in the ale house, watching over the families who've come to shelter in these walls.

"How long does she expect us to keep these folks here?"

Olynn asks Yeavengeritt.

"As long as it takes," the old man tells the warrior.

"All is quiet outside," Pict reports.

Cyridel turns her eyes to the man and blinks. "Thank you, Pict."

The sentinel lowers his head to her before heading back for another patrol.

"See? Nothing to worry about," a husband whispers to his wife. "Should anything come near the village, it won't get past the Jhalamar."

"But it already has!" another woman shouts. "Why do you think we're in this hall?"

"Amerllie died when they had their full number. Now? It's only four."

"The rest had gone with Master Greywolfe and Captain Iben."

"When do you think they'll return?"

"They've been gone for days."

"Almost a week!"

"What do we do if they don't come back?"

"They're hunting some wild animal. Not a monster."

"How do we know it wasn't a monster that killed the girl?"

"Because *our* Vedrethal told us it wasn't. Do you doubt him? He's never led us wrong before."

Another voice sounds louder than the rest, waking a few children. Cyridel turns her ear: "I was there when he ventured off to take on some 'gafling' on his own. Lord Rasterforn had to

go after him with all his men, and only half of them returned."
The whole room quiets as they listen to the doomsayer.

"I remember, too. Our riders carried the Vedrethal home.
He was in a bad way."

"How do we know this isn't any different?"

"Because the young lady Nialla went after him."

"Did she? To what ends? She went alone!"

"She is our patron! She hums to the fields, and the wheat
grows."

"These are fertile lands. Maybe the dirt makes it so? Or the
easy winters?"

"Have we been lucky for twenty years? No. I don't think so."

Hundreds of villagers squeezed into the feasting hall. Cyridel
feels the heat coming off them, and it isn't just the smoke
making it hard to breathe. Never once had she heard them
voice these doubts. Seven days is a long time to ask them to
keep faith without answers to their questions.

Yeavengeritt meanders through the aisles, calming tempers.
There's a pessimistic glare in his eyes. He stops to pray with
some of the others as he makes his rounds, the old man with
a silver tongue, who'd seen too much while living under the
mercy of Clesturia, Alanssia, and Raenia. Finishing the prayers,
Yeavengeritt pulls away, retreating into his more reclusive shell.
Like a shimmer, it's still there. Most people won't see it, but the
old Maithandír can't hide it from Cyridel. She was there when
the darkness that shrouded his eyes had cleared, and he could
see the sun again.

"Lady Miralifrim? All seems well enough," Yeavengeritt offers.

Cyridel folds her hands and turns to him. "Is it? The others don't seem to agree."

"Only because they don't know what to expect," he counsels. "Too few of them remember that night the Crows attacked them at Trebunor. I warned you all to flee, and you didn't. Instead? You let Master Greywolfe march off alone, thinking they were only monsters."

"He survived," Cyridel smiles. "As did you."

"Did I? Many nights, I still dream about searching for wood to keep the fire in the tower alive," Yeavengeritt sulks. "All to ward people away. And what did you do? You followed it to a ruined city that lost its battle two hundred years prior."

"We won the fight that followed," Cyridel reminds him.

"You killed the Crows. Yes. You freed me. Allowed me to go anywhere I wanted."

"And yet? You stayed with us! I always wondered, why *did* you?"

The old man's eyes flicker as if he wasn't expecting the question. His jaw quivers as his mouth opens: "And where else could I go? Trebunor was no longer my home, especially with humanity taking root there."

"You could have gone to Invala Dailn," Cyridel tenders. "King Herranol?"

Yeavengeritt's face sinks when she voices the name. "Have you ever met Herranol? I did once. A true monarch. And a lordly figure who drove those like your Grandfather into the Long March across the Arún Ouandin. You made the reverse passage years ago. Cyridel? You understand the dangers of that road. No idle feat."

"Such were the stories my father told me. And more followed in his footsteps. Herranol's very son? Prince Aéandal took up the name 'Freeheart' and mentored with Rauhnníal Badinhorn," Cyridel tells him. "He traveled with my brother, Erathil, when I was only a girl in Ilhivendal."

The old man smiles. "Another reason to avoid returning if the man's only son abandoned him," Yeavengeritt admits. "But this place? It's a simple life. Quiet. Apart from recent events, I found peace here with these people. They look to me and offer thanks."

"You were a soldier. Your role was to guard the walls of Trebunor," Cyridel reminds him. "And now? What *are* you?" She squeezes the man's hand to comfort him. He flinches with her touch and pulls away, tears in his eyes—the cost of bad memories.

"Just a man? My life fell apart as I stood on that wall. We took a side, then we lost," Yeavengeritt whispers. "All this? These people? Our biggest challenge is gathering the harvest before the flood season. I found more dignity in *that* than simple, martial glory."

Cyridel looks softly into the pale shine of his eyes. He is no longer the starved madman of when they rescued him. "But the harvest doesn't keep us safe," she says, matching his tone, stretching every word with a note of pain. Cyridel didn't intend it to come out that way, but it does.

Yeavengeritt notices. "Are you okay?"

"No? I don't know," Cyridel tells him. "We always knew somebody would find us." She shifts her attention to the people in Elundjir's Hall, these *folk* who took after them and made a home alongside hers. "Another bump in the road."

Yeavengeritt lets out his breath. "Nialla is a forceful girl. And our Vedrethal is out there, too. Don't let these troubles weigh you down, my lady." He speaks to her with a low, worn tone, yet a peaceful one. "You should rest while there's still some night left. Pict and Hader will manage fine."

"What about Olynn and Rod?"

"Them, too."

"Because they are Jhalamar?"

"No. Theirs is a dignity of another kind. A sworn task. Duty."

"A duty to keep us safe?" Cyridel frowns. "Soldiers to die. Doesn't that seem . . . cruel?"

"A soldier's life is always cruel."

"Will any survive?"

Yeavengeritt hesitates, clenching his jaw. "Perhaps?"

"That isn't an answer," Cyridel refuses.

The man looks at her, unsure how to respond. Yeavengeritt won't say it out loud, at least. Cyridel reads it in the lines of his face. *He is worried.* Twenty years on the fringes, the harvest being their great challenge, a race against the weather. *Are we ready for our lives to change again?*

Cyridel wasn't ready when she left Ilhivendal with Nialla in her arms. Word came about the dragon Morenarch's defeat at the Battle of Aardan and Galron's death at Aamelian's Ford. Sackery appeared a stranger to her months later, a letter in his hands with her love's last wishes.

She has tried to live up to his memory for their daughter's sake.

Cyridel notices others staring at her from across the feasting hall—distant admirers, those who respect the 'Lady Miralifrim,' as they call her. She looks out the window, the darkness quietly dropping behind the hills. Yeavengeritt stays close. She listens to their muffled voices off the walls:

"Why does she always look so lonely?" a woman asks.

"Lady Miralifrim? She's not alone."

"She has us! All of us."

"Is that true? She hardly speaks to anyone other than the children."

"She always has sad eyes," a little girl reads.

"The fair lady has a lot on her mind, little one," the mother says. "She isn't sad."

"Then why is she crying? Don't you see?"

Cyridel takes a breath and drifts to an unlit corner, feeling her cheek. *Am I crying?* Yeavengeritt follows her, too polite to interrupt. He notices it, too. He stares as the tears roll down her face, her skin red and soft. "I *am* crying. Aren't I? As anyone *should* on days like these when the light of the dawn reaches over the horizon. All else is left quiet while the birds bask in the warmth and let off their morning songs. Does it remind me—?" She stops.

Yeavengeritt frowns. "Cyridel?" he queries, overly familiar.

"Lady Cyridel?" another voice asks.

She turns to find Ankara wrapped in a blanket, her face pale as ice. Nialla's oldest friend, but still with the air of a small girl about her. Cyridel smiles. Amerllie looked so much like her. Their eyes are the same, mother and daughter—stark blue, near white, like stars in the night sky.

"What's wrong?" Cyridel begs the question.

"Everyone's looking at you," Ankara whispers.

Cyridel looks past the woman and realizes it's true. Everyone still awake has their eyes on her, standing in the shadows. As the moments pass, others stir from their dreams, and the more attention she garners. The interest unnerves her. Cyridel doesn't *want* their concern. She doesn't *need* it. Yet, they give it to her, regardless.

Jhalamar Pict enters Elundjir's Hall, back from his rounds. He stops at a table near a firepit, scanning the room and the many long faces now looking at him. The man finds Cyridel and hurries across the main floor. He breathes through his mouth like he was out on a run. His jaw twitches, clicking his teeth, planning his words. All traces of a man with a message. And the way he grips his sword's hilt so tight as he walks? She reads his anxiousness.

Pict cups a hand over Cyridel's ear and whispers: "Horses on the eastern road."

"Our horses?" Cyridel inquires. "Or a wild herd?"

"Yes? *Our* horses. At least, Hader thinks so," Pict answers.

"And their riders?" Yeavengeritt overhears. "Sackery?"

"Not with them, lord," Pict tells him.

Cyridel tucks her hands into her gown. "Were they sent home alone, or—?"

"I don't think there's an 'or' there, Lady Miralifrim," Pict discerns.

"No? And why is that?" she begs for clarification.

"No saddlebags. They took the gear they carried. Which means—?"

"Our people are on foot," Cyridel realizes, crossing her arms. "Sackery? They must've trekked into the wildwoods."

"Most probable," Yeavengeritt agrees.

"Did you get a count of how many made it back?"

Pict straightens his neck and squares his shoulders. "I did not."

"Jhalamar Hader?"

"He went to lead them into the village."

Cyridel politely nods and veers off toward the door. "Collect the Stable Master. We'll go and help corral the herd and settle them. Olynn? Rod! Come with me. Yeavengeritt? Gather who you can. We can finally do something other than wait now."

"Of course, my lady," the old man stipulates.

Pict's expression gladdens when she says it. "Right away, Lady Miralifrim." He pivots on his heel and calls for volunteers.

Cyridel presses her palm against an ache in her side. *Sack-*

ery? Did you plan to delve into the Seclumor? The tension in her throat makes it hard to swallow. *And should you find Nialla, what will the two of you do against this fox? Are you prepared? Truly? Irimara, the Last of the Neshulha.*

As she stops at the entry to the feasting hall, Cyridel hears a set of questions on many tongues:

"Where would Iben and the Jhalamar go without their horses?"

"How will they return?"

"It's quite the hike on foot."

"What if they're lost? Do they need help?"

"Is that why Nialla left? To find them? Help them?"

"I hope they're not hurt."

She puts aside these worries and heads out into the quaint twilight. The sun won't fully peek over the eastern ranges for another hour. Still, Cyridel can already see the light brimming a brilliant yellow haze where the horizon meets the valley.

It doesn't take long before she hears the horses whimper and snort as Hader wrestles to bring them together. Cyridel raises an eyebrow, watching the warrior chase after the animals as they avoid the man. She only counts five or six of the beasts. Not the twenty that set out with Sackery and the others. Even the mare Ora seems unwilling to heed commands. She knocks the man into the dirt as he attempts to grab her reins.

Cyridel rushes to Hader's side and picks him up. "Damnable beast," he curses.

"You need to be gentle with them," Cyridel tells him. "And

they will respond in kind. Horses are prideful animals. Intelligent. They feel as much as we do. And right now? They're scared."

"Scared?" Hader chuckles. "You sound like your daughter."

Cyridel frowns. "Nialla can speak to them in ways even I can't imagine."

She reaches out a hand and approaches the old mare. Ora burrs and swings away from her with genuine annoyance, stubbornly refusing to calm down. Cyridel laughs as the animal canters around her, mocking the attempt.

"Arí behn naír ecü maíe vaern, ane nidias?" Cyridel whispers. "Aren't you a wonderful sight?!" The mare slows down and pokes her arm with her snout. Cyridel steals the opportunity to scratch behind the animal's ears. "There. Don't you see? A delicate touch and a soft voice. That's all it takes."

"She normally doesn't need it," Hader scoffs.

Cyridel smiles and raises her chin to the warrior. "No, she doesn't." The woman locks eyes with the proud creature. "You feel it, don't you? That cold wind on your neck?" Ora snorts and lowers her head. Cyridel moves with her, graceful as a dance. "Where is he? Our Vedrethal? Can you tell me?"

Ora side-eyes her as if barely catching her words. *You understand me. I know you do, friend.* Cyridel presses her forehead against the mare's muzzle, matching the creature's breath. At that moment, the stress in Ora's muscles loosens. *You understand. You are safe with me.*

The settlers from Elundjir's Hall help corral the other beasts.

As the morning rises, a thin fog descends. Through it, more of the herd arrives from the hunting party in threes and fours, a steady stream, until all twenty reach the outskirts. Only Nialla's mount, the stallion Ryallamere, hasn't returned.

Cyridel walks with Ora to the stables, removing the saddle from her back. *Pict was correct. Somebody took the saddlebags and the gear, leaving only the riding harnesses.* The mare whimpers and grunts, poking her again, troubled. Cyridel feels the creature wince under her touch, her core sunken, shivering like she's trapped outside in the dead of winter.

"It's okay. I am worried, too. Nialla left a few days ago. You didn't happen to see her on your way back, did you?" Cyridel asks the question, but it stretches hope too far to expect an answer from the mare. "No. I didn't think so. You're all right. I am sure they will be fine."

Ora surrenders a low-pitch whine.

She doesn't believe me.

Cyridel takes a brush and strokes the animal's mane. Her coat is filthy. No injuries? But it's hard to see under all the mud.

"Rest for now. Better give our people a few more days before we send out another search." Cyridel's knee buckles when she repeats the sentiment in her head. "A few days?" It's a grim thought, mired in doubt.

Wilhimusk's best trackers went with Sackery into the Wilds. Pict and Hader would be next if the party had trouble they couldn't handle. *Could they tackle a foe the others could not?* Although dutiful, the others were right. The Jhalamar haven't been able to keep Irimara from approaching Nialla thus far. That is why the girl decided to follow Gallandhal in pursuit of the fox—to face the challenge head-on, with all the fear and doubt set aside.

"Alone?" Cyridel shudders. "Always alone."

She stops grooming Ora and puts away the brush. Cyridel kisses the mare before offering her a barley patty. She walks outside after. By then, the others finished corralling the rest of the herd, leading them to their pens.

Pict and Hader meet her halfway to the Solitary Hill.

"That should be it. All twenty-one," Hader tells her, "including the old mare."

Pict itches his nose. "Clever animals. Wonder how long it took them to find their way home?"

"Long enough. Ora is tired," Cyridel offers. "And stressed? She *did* lose her rider the last time she went into the Seclumor."

"It would explain why they seem riled," Hader suggests. "Master Greywolfe must've set them loose days ago."

"How far are the Wilds? Three nights?" Pict asks.

"Depends on how far and fast you ride," Hader answers.

Cyridel tucks her hands into her sleeves. "The hunt took them into the wildwoods and the monsters lurking there. They wouldn't risk the horses. Jhalamar Pict? Hader? How long would it take our people to return?"

"On foot?" Pict begs the question.

"At least another week, if not a fortnight," Hader offers.

"Either way, it'll take several days longer to travel the

distance," Pict finishes.

"Wouldn't they have sent a messenger back with the herd?" Cyridel finally questions.

Yeavengeritt joins them with Olynn and Rod. "Maybe they felt the entire company had to push ahead? Sackery *is* of the Vedrethal. He fought against the onslaught at Mireaderal for days before Rasterforn's forces reached him. Alone? So, imagine what twenty of him could do."

"A valiant last stand," Cyridel says under her breath.

Hader surrenders a frown, standing next to her. "Or maybe they didn't feel the need to?"

"Which only adds to the speculation," Yeavengeritt claims.

"Isn't speculation all we have? Only the horses returned," Cyridel reasons.

"All but one," Yeavengeritt corrects.

"Ryallamere," Pict whispers.

"Nialla went southeast," Hader recounts. "Should we go after her?"

"No. Gallandhal said that Nialla had to face this alone," Cyridel refuses. "That it was safer that way. And against a foe that can turn your greatest allies into your worst enemy? All we can do is wait to see who else makes it back." She lets her words linger for a minute.

The villagers walking the outer ranges start yelling her name. "Lady Miralifrim!" They point at the fog over the southern hills. "Lady Miralifrim! Look there!" Cyridel snaps her eyes in that direction. She notices the silhouette of another horse fast approaching Wilhimusk.

"Isn't that—?" Hader questions.

"Ryallamere!" Pict blurts out. "Nialla's mount!"

"Twenty-two," Yeavengeritt utters.

Cyridel steps forward as she watches the stallion quickly cover the distance. Ryallamere jumps a fence, knocking several handlers aside. Cyridel marvels at the creature's tenacity. A half-dozen villagers attempt to corner the animal, but the warrior of a beast runs through them, outsmarting them. He throws off the ropes that intend to tie him down.

He is indeed a fighter, Cyridel muses.

"Tire him out! Keep him on the move!" Hader shouts.

"What happened to him?" Cyridel asks. She eyes the scratches on the beast's side.

Yeavengeritt joins her in watching the villagers scramble after the horse. Olynn and Rod jump into the fray as others attempt to cut off his path. Ryallamere spins on his hind legs and . . . freezes when he lays eyes on Cyridel. A force takes hold of the beast, calming him into a subdued adherence.

Everyone hesitates. The handlers look at Cyridel as if there's dirt on her face. Or maybe they're waiting for her to tell them what to do? She doesn't know. Instead, she walks to the animal, feeling the wounds on his side. "Poor boy," she whispers.

"Miralifrim?" Yeavengeritt mutters, coming alongside her.

"He's angry," Cyridel explains.

"What happened? These scratches?" Hader asks, out of breath.

"It's like he grazed a thorn bush and galloped away," Pict suggests.

Cyridel pivots toward them and hums. "Perhaps? Have the Stable Master look the animals over," she orders, gently dabbing the stallion's thighs with a dry cloth from her belt. The beast flinches. *The cuts have already started to heal. A couple of days old? At the very least.* "They need care before we take them out again. Marshal fighters in the meantime. Anyone who can hold a weapon. We should prepare for what could happen next."

Yeavengeritt takes a step back. "My lady?"

Cyridel doesn't answer him. She doesn't quite know herself at the moment. Olynn and Rod don't wait for her to explain. They run over to the Quartermaster and begin calling out names. Meanwhile, Pict and Hader work to bring Ryallamere into the stables.

"People need to keep their minds off things," she whispers.

"Cyridel?! Isn't that a little drastic? A call to arms? What do you intend to do? Go after them?" Yeavengeritt demands, grabbing her wrist and forcing her attention. "Are we to equip farmers and field hands? They aren't soldiers. Not like the Jhalamar. Shouldn't we—?" He jumps in fright as the horses in the barn suddenly become riled when Ryallamere enters through its doors.

"They're afraid. Because *he* is afraid," Cyridel tells him.

"Ryallamere?" the man begs the question.

"He'll lead the herd when Ora retires. They already know it, so they sense the fear. Nialla rode him across the Southern Plains and into the wildwoods. That's how he got those scratches. It must be." Cyridel whistles Nialla's Lullaby and soothes the air over the grass, creating a somber tickle in her ears.

"They left days apart," Yeavengeritt voices. "Strange how they almost returned together?"

Cyridel finishes her tune and takes a breath. "Isn't it? Strange, indeed. It is almost like a verse: 'The horses all come running one faithful day, against the light, led astray.' I wonder how far it was before they turned back. Were they let loose at the edge of the forest? Or did they travel deeper inside? Did they stop to graze? Or did they run full sprint across the leagues?"

"I don't have the answers to those questions," Yeavengeritt confesses.

"No? But the horses do," Cyridel tells him.

"Do you think your daughter's in trouble? Master Grey-wolfe?"

"They'll always be in trouble. But—? I don't know," Cyridel discloses. "It is a lot to read from only a few scratches. Yes? And that worries me. Returning home without their riders? A call to arms will make our people feel safer, even if it's only an illusion."

"You want to lie to them?"

"I want us ready for the worst."

"What about Nialla? Sackery? Can they fight this alone?"

"And what would you have me do? Join them?"

"I don't—? No. I don't know."

"Neither do I," Cyridel frowns. "And I hate it. This wait?! I feel blind. Like I am stuck here, unable to help. Everyone keeps asking me if it'll be fine. And I have no idea! All I can do is drown out the noise that separates me from my girl."

Yeavengeritt lowers his head, sharing her grief. "Can you feel where she is? How far she's gone?"

Cyridel can hardly keep her eyes open, flooded with tears. "I don't know. It doesn't work like that. Our 'sense' comes from our ability to notice things. It's not a 'power' as most would think. So, I don't *feel* where she is, but I feel the air getting colder. She must be close."

"Close to what?" the other asks, stepping within arm's reach.

"A past never meant as hers," Cyridel recites.

Yeavengeritt's eyes widen as if confused by her words. She shrugs. They hold their stare for a short while before she encourages him to go. He hesitates, but she insists. Eventually, her friend departs with the grace of a stubborn moose. She watches as he steps toward Elundjir's Hall. Then, she feels a shift. A cozy wind sets on them from the south. A ripple of warmer air? It ignites a fire in her blood.

She hurries after the man. "Yeavengeritt?" Cyridel prods, a hand on his shoulder.

The Maithandír swallows as he turns. "Yes?"

"Before? You never said why you stayed with us," she points out. "Not really?"

Yeavengeritt looks away. "Did I not?" He smiles, then frowns. "You need me here, don't you?"

"We have the people looking out for us," Cyridel tells him. "Why not go home? Even to see how it's changed?"

The other's frown becomes a pained, sunken expression. "Are you asking me to leave?"

"No. I—? I want to know why you chose to stay?" Cyridel asks more directly. "You aren't bound to us. We don't hold a debt over you. Nothing's keeping you here. Why not return to that life you had before the Crows destroyed Trebunor?"

"And what keeps anybody in a place other than feeling they belong there?" Yeavengeritt begs the question, squeezing a tremor in his arm. "Yes. I spoke of Herranol, but . . . he isn't the reason. And the Crows of Mireaderal? They didn't destroy Trebunor. No. They infected the place! One bad day. That's all it took. And before your daughter restrung my strings, I had lost my battle with the dark."

"But—? I thought Nialla cleared your mind?"

"Perhaps the girl merely played the right notes?" Yeavengeritt shudders. "People forget. Scars can hurt long after a wound mends. You can't escape it. So, I need her to . . . What do you call it? Feel intact? Sane? Yes! That's the word. 'Numb the pain,' others call it. And the farther away she is, the more it grips me. On my best days, I still feel like broken pieces of glass held together by glue."

Cyridel offers Yeavengeritt a warm smile. "You're afraid that if you leave, that pain will return." She notices the old man taking an unwilling breath. He opens his mouth, but she touches his cheek and stops him. "It's okay. You don't have to speak a word."

Yeavengeritt resigns with a nod. He steps away, leaving her alone in the field outside Wilhimusk.

"Don't let this place be where your story ends," Cyridel utters. "Promise me." He can't hear her. At least, she hopes he doesn't.

She looks over at the stables, at the horses corralled. Satisfied the animals are well cared for by the villagers, Cyridel drifts back toward Elundjir's Hall after the old Maithandír. Along the way, she hears a voice in the breeze—deep and familiar. *Are they singing to me?* She turns to the hills overlooking the village.

A figure's there, dressed in blue, watching them from afar. *Another illusion?*

Cyridel walks toward the hill where the figure resides. Then, she blinks, and he disappears like he was never there. She's left breathless.

"No?! You died," Cyridel whispers sorrowfully. But the sound of *his* voice haunts her. Her heart quickens. *There are no ghosts. Only memories.* Except, the figure on the hill was *no* memory. She's noticed him in the past, but always at the edge of her sight.

"Rise up again, fly high and free," the voice sings, soft and pleasant.

"Catch the wind," Cyridel answers.

"Feel the beat," it finishes.

Silence follows. And it leaves Cyridel with an emptiness in her stomach. *That melody? Here? My mother's lyrics! It could only come from Ilhivendal. Gallandhal knew the words before.*

She learned it from somewhere. Is it possible—? No. It's not from him. It can't be!

Somebody's out there, playing tricks, reflecting *his* presence. "My Galron?"

Out of habit, Cyridel clenches the jewel hanging from her neck. But it feels . . . cold? She looks at the rock and frowns. The rough edges could always stretch light into brilliant shades of white. Now? Those colors fade, failing to catch the glancing warmth of the sun.

Cyridel touches the blue scrap of cloth she tied around her wrist. "Is it true? Can you be alive?"

— Village of Wilhimusk —

— 18 —

THE DEAD CAVES

As she lowers her foot, there's a sudden crunch under her boots. She looks down. "Bones?" Even in the dark, Nialla can tell they litter the ground. Old bones. Small bones? Overly brittle. Nialla winces as she takes another step, snapping an oddly shaped skull to bits. "Fox skulls?"

Nialla sweeps the remains aside as she moves forward through the black.

The rocks in the cavern are sharp and jagged, chiseled out of the mountain, then melted into slag. Nialla cuts her hands and forearms as she works her way through. Without light, she's left to feel her way across the walls.

A flash of white ahead, a ghostly figure darting around the corners. She catches a musky stench.

Irimara watches Nialla from the small crevices. She knows it's the fox. Those bright yellow eyes lead her farther into this dark place.

They come to an intersection with three branches off the main corridor. Nialla stops and listens. Down the left, she hears her name in a whisper: "Nialla ... Nialla ... Nialla ... " It doesn't end. She can't see *what* speaks it, but the noise is bleak and monotone. *Not the fox's voice, that's for certain.*

From the center pathway, there's more darkness. And a shadow in the darkness, blacker than black. A face? It stares at her with pale eyes, hissing resoundingly. Nialla's skin crawls. She steps toward the figure, and it answers by stepping toward her.

The figure speaks low and muted: "Hver kemur?" it asks, vibrating the very stone. "Komdu fram." It sounds ... Excited? Like welcoming a childhood friend.

Down the far right and final tunnel, she notices a luminous, wispy ball—a cold light floating in the air like a warning to stay away. It speaks no words and doesn't react like the others. The light purely stays there, like a candle left on a windowsill on a frosty winter night.

Nialla's muscles tense. "What is this? Where should I go?"

The fox comes alongside her. "Isn't it obvious? A simple choice. One of many," Irimara utters. There's a serene presence about her, less violent than before. *Is it true? Does she want to teach me?* The fox looks at the girl and nods, soft in her features. "Can you guess what it is?"

"I—? I don't know," Nialla admits. "Three paths?"

"Each darker than the last," the fox iterates. "All lead to the same place."

"Another illusion? A *false* choice, then?"

"No. You could argue taking the first step is the *true* choice. Perhaps the only choice? *That* is hardly an illusion," Irimara says. She merely sits and waits, staring peacefully at Nialla. "And what's on the other side, you may ask? To a humble few, a crossroads in more ways than one, little cub. For others, a chance to find themselves elsewhere."

"Gallandhal didn't know what I'd find," Nialla retorts. "She warned of a different threat."

"Did she? And what *is* the threat? Death? Or the false promise of a doomed man," Irimara weighs, "doomed to fail?"

"Is this why you killed Amerllie? To ask me these questions?"

Irimara takes a breath. "Yes? Or—? No. Maybe not. She wanted to warn Sackery about me," the fox dims, her ears flat against her head. "These bones? You see them. My people? Killed by the Vedrethal. *His* brethren. Would you trust your life with somebody who hurt your family? Those who loved you the most?"

Nialla frowns. "I am here, aren't I? With you? Alone."

"And without a butcher," Irimara adds pointedly.

"Sackery wouldn't have hurt you," she argues.

"Are you certain? Look around you, little cub. You see them. Their faces? At the very least, you hear them as you walk," the fox says, miserable and lonesome. "Memories? Voices locked within the rock. We close on a sensitive moment. A dangerous one."

"What are you telling me?" Nialla demands.

"That you mustn't forget what you see in this place," Irimara instructs. "You can't break some promises. No matter how much you try, events conspire to make them happen. Some call it destiny. Others? A fate never ours. We live cruel lives, abused by whatever powers serenade us from the black above."

"Anánturial? My mother calls it the House of Ansolas."

"That is what the Ellúndar call her," Irimara scoffs. "Ansolas? A sister born of light to brother darkness."

"She created the Singers of the Immortal Songs," Nialla recites. "Music of Creation?"

"Your father's warm light. Full of hope? Unexpected. A power in *your* blood, little Vedreron."

Nialla drops back. A breeze pushes against her. She touches the cavern's walls and closes her eyes, feeling small vibrations throughout the mountain. She can sense thousands of little imperfections—the holes in the stone, the minuscule fissures. The rocks crack at her fingertips, and dust falls in plumes atop her head. *Does it hurt? Does the earth cry for me to stop?* Nialla submerges herself in the noise and tries to understand.

Then, there are voices behind her, back the way she came.

Irimara rises to her feet, narrowing her eyes. "Others approach."

Nialla blinks and takes a breath. "Sackery?" She draws away from the wall and starts back toward the entrance, away from the crossroads and whatever lies beyond. "They found their way! I wonder if they can—?"

The fox moves to block the way out. "No! The task is ahead, not behind you."

"But they came all this way?!"

"Yes. For *me*. For my crimes," Irimara declares, puffing out her chest and widening her stance. "I killed the child. Your friend? So, I must confront the Vedrethal—a slave to his duty, as I am a slave to mine. Otherwise, he won't give up the hunt. These caves are the consequence of what his siblings did. Like me, he should face it, too."

"Then? What should I do?"

"Take the first step, little cub. You'll decide what that means."

"And once I get to the other side? What will I find?"

"A question for us both to answer."

"Or—? Or I could stop this now. I can make the mountain swallow you whole."

Irimara looks at her and tilts her head. "You could, indeed. And what does that accomplish?"

"Justice for Amerllie?" Nialla suggests. "For my friends." She closes her fist.

The fox raises her chin ever slightly. "Don't you mean revenge? Take it from me, little cub. You'll starve before you can sate that hunger, wanting more as the red stains your hands. By the end, you'd betray all your loved ones to feed it." Irimara backs away from her, unsure of Nialla's attitude. "But the choice is yours. Always yours. I declared you my enemy the day I learned where to find you. And revenge? I could settle for revenge, but that's not the only thing I want anymore."

Nialla reads the sadness in the fox's yellow eyes. After a moment, the girl nods to the creature. Irimara steps back with bemusement. She breathes slowly and drifts down the tunnel toward the entrance, white fur melting into the darkness, wordless. *Cold? No. Afraid. Too afraid to speak.*

Nialla returns to the corridor. She follows down the center pathway, hugging the walls. No sign of the dark figure. An illusion? Or the cave playing tricks on her. Nialla can't tell. She doesn't even know if her eyes are open or closed. It's too dark. There's a draft, a soft hum down the tunnel. A chill in the air the deeper she goes, a bad sign whenever she feels it. Cold is the world's natural state, and *she* isn't a part of the natural order of things.

The air becomes heavy as she steps into a space where the echoes deepen.

Nialla rubs her eyes as the cavern expands into enormous depths. Illuminate flowers bloom a wonderful golden light at her ankles, pushing back the darkness creeping in from every corner, but she doesn't attend such marvels. Rather, her focus rests on the tree before her, massive in size. Its branches stretch far and wide like a magnificent crown, digging into the mountain above, which molds itself around the ancient weodemair.

A waterfall dances on the other side of twisting footpaths and flat rocks, filling the deep recesses of the chamber like some innate reservoir. Such pools feed the strange plants throughout the hollow, veiled behind a thin mist. The sight sends a wave of awe into Nialla's throat and chest.

Nialla can't move. She leans forward, tapping her fingertips to the rhythm of her mother's lullaby. "You'll dream of a world you've never seen," Nialla whispers. The familiarity fills her with courage. "A life of love and dancing in the light." She clenches the Ancestrum Stone that hangs over her chest, warm in her palm.

She notices the bones piled against the tree's great roots. Not human bones, but . . . canine? No! Foxes. Hundreds? Thousands. Every one of the Neshulha that had fled the onslaught and found themselves trapped. They would not escape.

Nialla loses her sense of time as she traces the cavern into her mind's eye. Looking at the ancient oak, she struggles to pull away from it. The weodemair seems to enchant her, but it isn't trying to draw her in like some predator luring its prey. No? Instead, it reaches out, like wrapping her in a blanket by the hearth on a rainy day. "A home you've never known," Nialla finishes the verse and breathes. It is almost like the tree's attempting to speak to her through soft rumbles and shifts in the rocks. And underneath? A deluge of decay in the rich, black soil in which it rests.

"A sad place, isn't it?" Irimara begs the question. "Do you see now the cost of blind servitude?"

Nialla turns. The fox limps into the chamber from the left tunnel, her coat reflecting the golden hue of the flowers.

"How did this happen?" Nialla murmurs. "Is this place an illusion? Or is it—?"

"I am too tired to conjure something else so intricate,"

Irimara denies.

"Sackery? And the others?"

"Will be kept busy with a shadow from the past."

Nialla swallows, unsure what that means. Irimara looks at her and reads her discontent, dropping her ears and sitting at the edge of the path. Out of breath, the fox stares at the tree for a long while. *Is she here? Or is this another false impression?* Nialla can't guess. All she knows is that the draft causes the fox's fur to move, and the musky scent hits as much now as before.

"Is this what you wanted to show me? All this?! And this tree?"

Irimara nods. "Icurian called him the Grandfather Tree. His name? Gallindrusk," she explains. "In the youngest days, this is where life took its first roots. The eldest of the weodemair trees and the near oldest thing in this world apart from the dirt and the stars in the skies."

"It's beautiful. And this is where your people died?" Nialla wonders.

"Slaughtered," Irimara mourns. "This is where I survived."

Nialla frowns, a tear rolling down her cheek. She can hear whispers through the rocks, the memories the Neshulha left behind in the very earthworks of the cavern. She looks at the tree. He calls to her through vibrations in his many limbs. *"Kom frem, min venn! Kom frem,"* Gallindrusk beckons. She holds her breath. The words are different than before, but Nialla recognizes it as the voice calling her name at the cross-roads . . . *Come forward, my friend! Come forward.*

Irimara stares at her intently. Then, she circles her and stops at the tunnel where Nialla emerged into the chamber. "And you took the center path? That is good. It means you'd rather live in the present. My sisters took the road on the right. Such was their *want* for a brighter future."

"But you came from the left?" Nialla points out.

"Do you think it strange? I carry my people's history," Irimara states. "I *am* the last."

"Meaning you can't escape the past," the girl understands.

"No matter how far I run to get away," the fox agrees.

"And when you said each path gets darker than the last? You meant—?"

"Sometimes what comes merely exists as petty chance," Irimara stipulates. "Often, that brings hope, an opportunity to do better. Yet? For so many others? Uncertainty leads them down roads best left untraveled. Many choices lie ahead of you, little cub. All of them difficult."

The fox eases down to the ledge just below the walkway.

Nialla watches, then goes after her. She stops before the drop. It strikes her how difficult it is for Irimara to descend the rocks. *Is she injured? She favors her left side and badly tries to hide it.* The fox catches her stare and plants herself midway down amidst the Grandfather Tree's outstretched roots and the bones that covet them. She looks back at the girl with a worn yellow shade in her eyes.

"It's all right. It's mostly safe," Irimara urges, a weakness in her tone.

"Are you sure?" Nialla asks.

"Can you be *sure* this isn't a trap?" the fox asks.

"I don't think you would do that."

"And why not? After what I did? All I had made you see?"

"You *want* me to think this is only about revenge," Nialla fades, shaking her head. "And seeing these remains of your people, how can it be anything else? But there's more to you, isn't there? Yeavengeritt calls it a deep shade reflection. All that emotion? It radiates off you like water in a rainstorm." She climbs down after the fox, the cavern's flowers getting brighter as she passes them.

"And how far would you go to save the ones you love?" Irimara demands.

"You can't undo the past! And if we could, I would know Ilhivendal," Nialla settles, "from more than my mother's stories! We wouldn't have had to wander for sixty years! Or search for a place to call home? Or lay our heads in the dirt for how many nights?! And my father? He would still be alive."

"Is he not?" the fox begs the question.

Nialla catches the other's words and nearly stumbles over the ledge. She takes a breath and steadies her balance. Portions of the rock face crumble when she lends too much weight to it. Sweat drips down Nialla's collar as she backs away, throwing an intense glare at the white fox. Then, she finds footing on stable ground near the pools. More bones line the shore, with skulls that do not belong to any fox.

Human skulls. Soldiers? No. Vedrethal.

"Don't lie to me. No more illusions," Nialla seethes, tightening her fist. "Why did you bring me here?!" Around them, the weodemair tree's roots shift and murmur, reacting to her fit of anger. "Tell me, or I will leave this place."

Irimara opens her mouth as her ears suddenly flutter. "Because I want to bury the past to save the future," she tells her. "*That* is why I led you here. To have you rip down the mountain and close a door between *our* world, and all other worlds. And I can't do it without you, little cub. Or somebody *like* you."

Nialla kneels to one of the soldier's bodies. The rusted armor is like that worn by Sackery in his Vedrethal attire. She notices a sword in the dark and picks it up, wiping off the dust with her sleeve and allowing the light blooms to reflect off the tainted metal. "I don't understand," Nialla admits.

"Neither does the fox," another voice speaks, soft and thoughtful. Irimara's yellow eyes widen, clearly surprised by it. She looks to the cavern and at Gallindrusk, who merely burrs, shrugging off the idea it was him. "She's brought you to a graveyard, knowing its true nature. Unaware of the *real* danger."

Irimara growls. "Is this a ghost in my head?"

"Another voice among the hundreds," the faceless offers.

The air leaves Nialla's lungs for an instant. There's a tall woman with broad shoulders there by the waterfall. At first, she believes it is her mother with her raven hair and long braids. The woman steps to the side and into better light, showing her silver eyes and a scar on her cheek.

"I thought I said no more illusions," Nialla tells Irimara.

"This isn't me," the fox warns.

Nialla looks at the woman again. She notices cuts on her hands and bruises on her arms. And her clothes? Torn at the sleeves as if she waded through a battle to arrive here at this very moment. There's a metal spear in her hands, and it sings a tune of its own, fine points on either end.

Nialla forgets to breathe. "Are you—? What *are* you? A shepherd of the dead?"

"A blue woman? No. Although, I do look the part," the older speaks. "Please? We haven't much time."

Gallindrusk, the Grandfather Tree

— 19 —

FATHER AND SON

His armor feels heavy now, pressing on his shoulders. As he lifts his arm, the weight fights him.

Sackery shrugs it off and finds his balance, sword in hand, joined by men and women to his left and right. He's trained them for twenty years in the warring arts. Sackery trusts their abilities. But? All of them are looking at the man in front of them like newborn calves do a staarag. Now, he doesn't know if those years were enough.

"Icurian? You can't be real," Sackery mourns, a tightness in his throat. Everything about the figure is exactly how Sackery remembers him—from his narrow stance and harrowing mask, even that steady warmth in the silver of his eyes that betrays his noble nature. "It doesn't matter. No. You aren't him. Just another memory that's haunted me for most of my life."

The figure merely stands there, eyes fixed on him. Sackery's knees feel weak, his fingers numb.

"Am I just a memory? More of an image, less than a ghost?" Icurian demands.

The Mórhathan lumbers along the outer field, measuring the shade's worth as it waits at the cavern's entrance. Sackery doesn't know what the wild spirit understands. Still, the fact that the bear hasn't lunged at this false Doomed King means the Forest Guardian is wise enough to know the ramifications if it is indeed the 'real' Icurian.

"There are no such things as ghosts," Sackery recites. "I don't know *what* you are, only that you're *not* him."

"Such doubt doesn't grow well on you, little warrior. Although? I see you're traveling with others again. That *is* good. I am glad for you," the other says faintly. *And with Icurian's voice?!* Iben and the Jhalamar flinch, a chill on the back of their necks. Sackery tries to remain steadfast.

"I have for a while now," Sackery admits, raising his blade and pointing it at the false image.

Icurian steps forward, the ground cracking at his boots, thunder falling as each foot lands. The trees in the clearing's edges shift away, opening the space into an arena. Sackery doesn't want to fight here. The ground is soft and uneven, a perfect field for their opponent. But he'll fight if there's no other choice.

The false image stops an arm's reach away from the Jhalamar's front ranks. Iben steadies his men. Sackery inches ahead of them, not knowing what to expect. He presses his sword's tip against the Doomed King's breastplate, and . . . it's solid? Icurian wraps his fingers around the metal and steers it aside. Sackery clenches his jaw. *He's real. But he can't be real, can he? One of the fox's tricks*, Sackery decides. *Another illusion? Made corporeal by some means.*

"Everybody seems nervous," Icurian says. "And yet? I am alone."

Iben clears his throat. "We are the Jhalamar of Wilhimusk! And we are duty-bound to the Lady of the Mountains. Disarm so we may pass and ensure her safety. There's no need for violence."

Icurian chuckles. "No need for violence? I wish that were true."

Sackery can see Icurian's eyes through the mask, like water in a fountain under a full moon. Those eyes don't break away from him, devoting his attention entirely to the Vedrethal. For the Doomed King's false visage, it is as if Iben and the others aren't here, standing alongside father and son.

"What else is in the cave?" Sackery demands.

Icurian tilts his head, taking a few steps back. "Something I won't allow you to intrude on, little warrior."

"Do you think you can stop me? We fought each other before."

"Oh, I remember," Icurian returns. "Last time, I was so tired. Of war? You won because I surrendered. And the world now suffers as a consequence. Our conflict had ended, but it opened the door to another. Nobody stopped fighting! I've made many promises, Sackery of the Vedrethal. I broke every single one. No more."

"Just let us inside," Sackery urges. "Please? I don't know if you're my Icurian—or the fox wearing his face. You sound like him, mourn like him. Maybe you *are* an aspect of him she's using to toy with me? I don't know. One way or another, I am getting into that cave."

"To kill the fox?" Icurian begs the question.

"Only if she doesn't leave me any other choice," Sackery decides.

"No! That's a lie people tell themselves to justify their cruelty. Irimara had a choice to murder a child," Icurian describes. "Do you know why?" He stretches the last words to let Sackery mull over the question. "It was to draw you away from your ward—to avoid you. All so she could speak to the young one's mind, my thrice-born grandchild. To make her understand the responsibility that was once mine."

"Stop talking like him! You are *not* the man who raised me."

"No? I *am* a shadow of a remnant. We urged the fox on this path! Now? You must let events unfold."

"And accept what comes after? No. I should've killed you when I had the chance."

"Endúcar forgave me," Icurian dithers. "Someday, maybe you will, too. And yet—?" A sudden roar cuts him off mid-thought.

Sackery reels back and tightens the grip on his sword's hilt. Like a storm, the Mórhathan charges Icurian from behind before anybody else can react.

Icurian pivots and veers, locking his spear's haft into the bear's maw to keep its teeth from wrapping around his neck. In a show of strength, Icurian pushes the creature backward. The Mórhathan growls as it fights against this shift, beating the dirt with its massive paws. In an eager move, the bear attempts to hook Icurian with its claws, but the false image ducks under the creature's body and shoves his spear's fine point into its wooden gullet.

The Mórhathan rears in pain, lashing violently at the ground in an attempt to crush Icurian under its enormous weight. The false image guards himself against this, taking hold of the creature's jaws and twisting its neck. SNAP!

Iben and the Jhalamar gawk as Icurian shoves the Mórhathan off him. After all, this was the 'beast' that snuffed out the fallen songs of the Crows at its rampage at Mireaderal. Such is the proof needed to show the true power of the Doomed King versus those of his former kin.

Sackery looks on. He can see the tension in Icurian's jaw where his mask doesn't cover his face.

"Master Greywolfe?" Iben questions. "Sackery?"

"Stay back!" Sackery warns. "Stay together! Don't engage him."

Icurian rises from the Mórhathan and retakes his spear from the carcass. "Such a beautiful creature, the Great Bear of the Seclumor Wilds. Master of the Forest Lords? A Guardian. Mightiest of spirits brought low by the trill of a darker melody." The false image of the man breaks away from the bear and nods respectfully to Sackery and the Jhalamar.

"Does he taunt us?!" Iben calls.

"No. That's genuine," Sackery tells him.

"How do we fight that?" Ivette frets.

"Some of you were at the battle with the Crows," Sackery iterates. "You saw what they did and everything they could do. Their songs were quiet things next to the tune this one plays. The very earth will work against us. It'd be sensible to take off our armor."

Iben and the others turn to him with shock. "He just killed the beast! Without our armor, we'll be—?!"

"Dead? Like our friend here?" Icurian questions, laying his palm against the Mórhathan's snout, gentle with his touch. "Can you kill a wild spirit? Or is this another game we play? Vedrethal." He says the name with such *hate*, a tinge of yellow in the silver of his eyes. Neshulha illusions can only hurt those who believe them. Icurian taught him *that* sullen truth. They'll trick, maim, counter, and lead astray, but they can't outright kill somebody. Not by themselves.

Sackery swallows. "Armor won't protect you if he's real. And if he's not—? Push forward! That's all we can do."

"You'd waste their lives to fight a shadow?" Icurian asks.

"No. To fight you," Sackery snarls.

"That's very brave of you," the image feigns. "Would you like a moment?"

"A moment?" Iben asks. "Why a moment? What does he mean?"

"To ready ourselves," Sackery answers.

"Because it won't make a difference," Icurian clarifies. "Now or later? My only goal is to spend time."

Iben and the Jhalamar all surrender glances to each other. Icurian stands there, waiting again. Sackery's heart quickens, his breath suddenly shallow. He turns to the others and nods. "I hope you're right," Iben agrees, removing his bracers, breastplate, and pauldrons, leaving only his cloak and sword. Sackery does the same. And the weight he felt suddenly lifts off his shoulders and frees him of the burden.

Others don't lose their armor—Ivette, Camdyn, and Kennen. They hesitate, not agreeing with the reasons.

Sackery can see the tears in Ivette's eyes. She looks at him, heavy with her breath. And it makes him afraid. It's the same look the woman gives him when they spar in their practice drills and battle games. Everything the Vedrethal's taught her since she took up the sword to call herself Jhalamar? It embodies her—*his* reflection.

"No," Sackery utters.

Ivette shakes her head and charges with Camdyn and Kennen to catch the shadow on the back foot.

Icurian drops into a defensive stance and laughs. The man dances with the trio, dodging their throws and parrying their thrusts. The false image kicks out Ivette's knee, sending her face-first into the dirt. Camdyn and Kennen rebound to defend her, but he slaughters them with a single fluid motion of his spear's fine point. Icurian is like a blur—elegant and efficient.

He moves as Icurian should, drawing blood quickly and almost without effort. The man was never one to relish the kill. That doesn't mean he'd shy away from brutality. He drives his spear into Ivette's chest with enough force to shatter the plate, the metal collapsing her ribcage.

Gallandhal flies down from above to intervene, but the doomed lord swipes the white bird aside.

"Is this it?!" Icurian demands. "Are these your students? Vedrethal?! These—? Pale imitations?" He runs his hand along the spear's haft, wiping off the blood. "Arrow-fodder to feed the tide. You might as well have suffocated them in their cribs as infants."

"What do we do?" Iben cries. "Ivette? She's—?"

"Hold your ground," Sackery redirects. "Let him come to us!"

"But will it be enough?" Icurian seethes.

There'll be time to mourn later, Sackery reasons. *And I know Icurian. This fight would already be over if that's what he wants.*

"My lord?" Iben compels his attention.

"He's stalling us!" Sackery explains, focused, here and now.

Iben presses against Sackery's shoulder as they group side-by-side with the remaining company—seventeen against one. Sackery's fought worse odds and won. Icurian taught him to persevere, no matter what—to hold out in a fight and win, even when losing a battle is the only way to get there. To survive! And whether this is the real Icurian or not, it's a near-perfect impersonation.

Icurian stands there, welcoming them one final time before

the storm.

Sackery peers at the cave behind the false image. *Why not let me see what's happening inside?* He's left to wonder.

Icurian's gaze snaps to the nearest Jhalamar in the front ranks, lunging like a spider to its next meal. He plunges his spear through the man's throat, ripping it out. The others panic and swing too wide, missing their marks. Icurian weaves and dodges to escape each throw while closing the distance with the defenders. He takes chances with his free hand to break arms and twist wrists to disarm the fighters as he cuts them down where they stand.

Sackery pushes to the center with his sword, Aru il Endril, to meet Icurian's spear, Rhongomyniad.

The two men test each other's defenses, steel on steel. Sackery's muscles scream as he rolls his binds, staying patient. All the sound around him becomes muffled as his blade scrapes against the spear's metal haft, making him recoil. He fights through it, working his angles, looking for an opening to use and better the odds.

It holds Icurian's attention enough for Iben and the others to flank the man, ready to strike.

Icurian catches them and steps out of the way at the last second. Sackery falls forward, swinging his arms to stay upright. Iben and the Jhalamar stop their attack to allow him a chance to find his footing. Icurian rushes to skewer another of their number, answering their reluctance with contempt.

Most of the others have now lost their discipline. Icurian

walks between them, twisting and controlling the battle with his spear in his right hand, attacking with a sword he's taken from one of the fallen in his left. Iben does his best, but he can't get close enough to scratch the man, let alone draw blood. Nearly all his soldiers are down. Icurian conquers them, two and three at a time, until there's only a handful left.

Sackery must engage with Icurian as a wolf does to a dragon. "Move back!" he orders, wanting the survivors out of his way. Iben collects everyone still on their feet and retreats from Icurian in the field. Sackery raises his sword and aims it at the man's heart.

Icurian meets him, blow for blow—he fades, deflects, advances—with little room to maneuver. Calm. Deliberate.

"I won't make the first mistake," Sackery declares.

"You would die if you did," Icurian returns boastfully.

Sackery presses the moment and tackles Icurian into a tree— the two swinging around the trunk like birds dancing on a fountain's edge. Sackery thrusts the point of his blade at a flaw in the other's guard, but the Vedrethal quickly realizes the feint as he attacks an opening that isn't there. Icurian catches Sackery's wrists and snaps his arms upward, squeezing until his grip weakens, and he drops his sword.

In a desperate bid, Sackery raises his foot and twists free, separating Icurian from his spear.

Icurian laughs as the duel turns into a brawl. Sackery trades punches with the man, going for his core. However, no matter how much power he throws behind his fists, his jabs bounce off the Doomed King like balls of yarn on solid rock. Icurian steps fast, letting loose a single powerful blow to Sackery's chest, then as quickly, grabs the Vedrethal by the throat and slams him against the tree, the trunk bending from the impact. Sackery's bones crack as his neck and arms go numb, blood in his mouth.

"You do *feel* real," Sackery utters through his teeth.

"Why fight me? Vedrethal," Icurian asks, such disdain in his tone for *that* word. "A memory? That's all I am. It doesn't matter what happens between us. All that matters is that Nialla and Irimara finish their task. You can't win this one, son. And if you do? All the people you protect will die."

Sackery struggles to find his breath. "Because of you?"

Icurian's hold on his neck loosens, and he looks away. Sackery notices a shimmer in his eyes, the tears behind the mask. "The fox can hardly control the cadence of those like me. We called ourselves the Vedreron. A new name for a new life? I was known as the Chronicler of Anánturial, the Wordsmith—a keeper of stories."

"Until you became a doomed man," Sackery derides, "doomed to fail."

"That is the role I played as a sour note darkened our songs," Icurian admits.

"Then let me inside," Sackery pleads. "Let me help her!"

"You would only help a more dangerous foe."

Sackery's eyes widen. "Then join us!"

Iben and the others rush to get the Doomed King off him.

Icurian turns and stares them down, stopping the attempt dead in its tracks. Iben locks eyes with the man, unsure about risking more of their lives, only for that old soldier's glare of his to land on Sackery. Icurian notices and tilts his head, amused. He lets go of the Vedrethal and saunters into the woods like the battle is more of an annoyance than a threat. Sackery gasps for breath as the Captain takes a knee to aid him.

"Here I thought I saw the worst of it at Mireaderal," Iben attests, shouldering him to the open field.

"He's stronger than the Crows," Sackery tells him. "And faster? Every move planned out."

"Can we win this?" the other asks.

"I don't know," he admits.

"Do we stand a chance?" another begs the question.

"He walked right through us!" a third says, breathless.

"Where did he go?"

"Did he retreat?"

"No."

"Did we wound him?"

"How? He shrugged it off! All of it."

"Vedrethal?" Iben demands. "What do we do?!"

Sackery eyes the man for an instant before standing on his own. His soldiers litter the ground—either dead or wounded. *Mauled? Like the act of a monster in a rage. Some? Stabbed or skewered. Most seem to have deep cuts or broken limbs, injured but alive.* Around him, only five remain of the twenty he set out with from Wilhimusk—only five who can still fight, Iben and Sackery among them.

"Our way to the cavern is a clear sprint," Sackery notices.

"Do we make for it?" Iben asks.

"It's likely another feint," the Vedrethal weighs.

"Then, what do we—?

"Form a circle."

"And defend from all sides?"

"Icurian won't let this end," Sackery explains.

"We can't fight him," a survivor cries.

"We should run!" another argues.

"Abandon Nialla? No. You heard the fox! She's here."

"Yes! So, we'll fight," Sackery tells them. "Survive! That's what we'll do."

"Protect each other?" Iben wonders.

"I don't see any other way," Sackery admits. "My sword? Where—?"

"Still where you dropped it," the Captain grimaces.

One of the Jhalamar quickly runs to retrieve the blade, offering the hilt to the Vedrethal. Sackery accepts it with a weakness in his arm, almost like the sword is heavier in his hands. His fingers twitch as he notices the blood smears on the steel. *Did I nick him? No. There's too much.* It is as if he'd cut a swath through a battlefield.

He looks to Iben, who merely frowns, his blade clean, but the edge is out of alignment. Ruined? As if he tried chopping wood with it.

Sackery falls into a defensive stance within their circle. The wind blows hard into the field from the wildwoods. The trees moan as something takes over them, pressing them together toward the center, a slow and laborious process. The soil folds over itself, creating ridges and steeps that work to entrap the survivors.

"I don't like this," Iben admits.

"No running now," Sackery whispers.

"So? We'll hold our ground," Iben states.

"Whoever's the last, find Nialla. Get her out."

"What about the fox?"

"She'll play with us until we can't lift our arms," Sackery tells him. "This isn't the real fight."

Behind the trees, Sackery notices shadows—figures moving from place to place, filling the wood's edge.

"He's over here!" somebody calls.

"No? This way!" Iben corrects.

"I got three on this side!"

Sackery looks in all directions. Then, Icurian appears from the woods, spear in hand, followed by a second, more gnarled version of the man, shaped into being by a cluster of leaves, sticks, rocks, and dirt. Another emerges . . . then another, and another. Dozens. *More illusions? Wild shades of a doomed man, doomed to fail.*

The false Icurian takes a step before the masses. "Isn't this familiar? An onslaught in the woods, the odds stacked against you. Whereas with the Crows, it was a thousand against one. Now? It will be a hundred against five. Vedrethal?" He speaks the title again with a deep-set growl. "One final lesson."

— 20 —

OASIS OF ANSOLAS

She reads the fatigue on Irimara's face.

Nialla breathes as she turns to the other woman. A mirror's reflection? Only the face looking back isn't wholly hers. She's much older, a lifetime gone by, showing through the creases around her eyes and a faded scar on her cheek.

"Do you know this place?" the older asks.

Nialla swallows. "This is where the Neshulha hid themselves."

"Our ancestors had them clawing at the walls," the woman utters. "Fear? That's what drove them to such an act. Can you still taste it in the air? It's stale. Death wounds the very earth. Such wounds open doors that must be closed before worse finds their way through."

"A door? I don't understand," Nialla dithers. "How are you here? Who—?"

"Between worlds is an endless black sea," the older says, kneeling to match the younger girl's height. Nialla can feel the woman's breath on her face. There's a warmth to it that she can't quite describe, but it makes her feel safe. "And to sail those misty waters is a perilous journey."

"A journey?" Irimara asks. "You speak of the stars above?"

"No. Something else," the older describes. "Anamares nya eloran."

"Waters of Passage," Nialla recognizes.

"A Space Between Worlds," the older clarifies.

"And you knew to come here?" Irimara wonders.

"Is that a surprise? I had lived this day before," the older softly laughs. "But finding my way back? That *was* a challenge."

Irimara's ears fold as she lowers her head. "We didn't want to fight their wars." She shifts the cavern into a lush garden with a view of the stars over their heads, water at their feet, and a strong, vibrant weodemair where the elder Gallindrusk stands. "Icurian promised to keep us away from Heluvian and his Vedrethal." Images of white foxes fill the chamber, running from a savage blaze, the smoke encircling the Great Tree. Neshulha, by the hundreds, shelter under the weodemair's limbs, crying out to their loved ones. Many would collapse, the adults fighting alongside their cubs for breath as the air smothers them. "It was a false hope. And all we had? Gone."

The woman reaches a hand and allows the Neshulha to catch her scent. "Icurian's words don't fade with time," the older consoles. "And survivors? They usually want to leave that pain behind. It is hard to go on living when your entire world forgets you exist." She looks at the fox as she speaks, gentle in her tone.

"I won't ever forget," Irimara resolves.

"And that is why she confronts you," the older says to the younger.

"To teach me?" Nialla asks.

"Small chances to make things right," the older confides.

Nialla stares at the woman. She touches the other's face, warm like her breath, a softness under the dirt and scars. "A life I had never known," Nialla whispers. The older smiles as she leans forward to kiss the younger on the head. "Are you real? An illusion?" she asks as the other pulls away.

The woman shakes her head. "Not an illusion. They call *us* the Lady of the Mountains."

Nialla frowns. "A fate never meant as ours," she utters. For the first time, the moniker has a purpose to it. As the younger breathes, so does the older. And, as they breathe together, the air ripples throughout the cavern, causing the light blooms to sway. "Do you know the song from our dreams?"

"Our mother's lullaby," the older recites. She takes the younger's hands and presses her forehead against hers lovingly. "You dream of a world you've never seen, a life of love and dancing in the light, beyond the ranges stands—?"

"A home you've never known," Nialla ends the verse.

"Strength flows between us," the older says. "Our songs comfort us."

Nialla closes her eyes and listens. She can see a city on fire and a ship drowning under a great wave. Stars disappear from the skies, one by one, until none are left to sparkle in the night. Once she opens her eyes again, she notices the seriousness on the older one's face.

"Your memories?" Nialla asks.

"Ours," the older nods.

Irimara watches them, a dullness in the yellow of her eyes. "What happens now?"

"A harbinger comes," the older warns. "Ethernal. One followed me."

"What do you mean? I don't—?" Irimara begs the question.

"An enemy of ours. He'll catch up soon."

"Soon?" the fox asks. As she does, Nialla's breath turns foggy.

"Irimara? My friend," the older stands. "Can you show me home again? I'd like to see it."

"Your home," the fox asks, "or mine?"

"Aren't they the same? Show me the house on the cliffs by the pond," the older describes, "and the mountains that stand our walls." She brings out her weapon, a fine metal spear, and shows it to Nialla, the tapered ends melding into the haft. It is an elegant tool for a powerful warrior.

Iírdunic letters etched into the side spell out a name: 'Rhongomyniad,' it reads.

Irimara regards the spear as if she recognizes it. The fox's stare weakens as she turns to the younger Nialla, letting out a weary sigh. Swift and seamless, the cavern shifts again, this time to the gardens at the Houdicar. The stars and tree disappear, as do the light blooms throughout the expanse. Colorful birds dart across a vast blue sky under the sun afore the valley.

Nialla raises her head and smiles. She knows it isn't real, but she's glad to see it, nevertheless.

"Your home? It *is* a lovely place," Irimara offers, panting heavily, strained by the effort.

"But the smell isn't right," the younger notices.

"Neshulha trick the eyes and mind," the older explains.

"Enough to fool the heart in a moment of passion," Irimara says.

"To defend themselves," Nialla realizes.

"If only it had worked," the older whispers.

Irimara looks at the woman, tears soaking into the fur around her eyes. She opens her mouth to speak, but the fox doesn't voice her thoughts.

From the waterfalls, another figure appears, colossal and dark. Nialla counts four sinewy arms, striking an almost regal silhouette, and bladed spears in each of its four hands. The titan of a being wears thick bone-white armor over a black robe, a golden light spilling through the cracks at its joints and mask, legs built for jumping vast distances. *Is it a monster? Or something else?* Nialla doesn't know. The image of the house on the Greencliffs vanishes, and they ready themselves.

"What is that?" Irimara asks.

"A voyager from very far away," the older states.

"What does he want?" Nialla wonders.

"Us? All of us," the woman answers. "Nells? Finish your task.

And be quick."

"My task?" Nialla asks.

"The fox brought you for a reason. Go to the tree. Speak to him," the older commands. "Gallindrusk's roots grew into the very bedrock of the mountain. He can bring it down and close shut the open door."

"He will resist," Irimara warns.

"As much anything that wants to live would resist," the older agrees.

At the waterfalls, the Ethernal Harbinger doesn't wait. He charges forward. The older pushes the younger out of the way, and she meets the foe head-on, fast and fierce. The pools ripple with every blow they make, metal on metal, fist to rock, and bone to dust.

Sackery had taught Nialla some measure to wield a sword, but the skill the older displays is well beyond those lessons. Songs fill the chamber as she watches the woman match this dark warrior, the voyager from 'far away,' as the woman called him.

Nialla looks at Irimara, the fox that played with her dreams and murdered her friend.

"Go now, little cub. I will help where I can," Irimara tells her.

The girl clenches her jaw. "You still have Amerllie's death to answer for."

"First? Survive. Then, I will accept your judgment."

"You better! I'll find you if you don't."

"I would expect nothing less, little cub," Irimara utters,

letting off a low whimper, her ears flat against her head. For some reason, Nialla believes her. Irimara offers her a nod before running off to join the battle. "Fast to the tree! Go! Reach the crown!"

Nialla blinks. Her heart races inside her chest. She looks at the path leading to the tree's heights. *How do I do this?* The weodemair's massive trunk has grown slanted like a stairway extending out of the rocks, the pools filling the chamber at its roots. Nialla swallows. It'll be an awkward climb, hand over foot.

As she lends her weight to the lowest limbs, a sudden sour note rushes at her from all directions. Nialla covers her ears, reeling from the noise and the pain. Gallindrusk had overheard their intent. "I don't want to hurt you," she pleads. "Please?! Listen to me!" But the ancient weodemair burrs ever louder, and his roots squirm.

Gallindrusk lashes out, wildly swinging his branches as she clambers from one limb to the next.

Another crack erupts among the rocks below. Metal rings as the battle with the Harbinger descends into the shallows, the older putting the fiend on the defensive with powerful thrusts of her spear, fine points splitting the air. She pierces the warrior's bone-like armor, its golden blood spilling from the wounds.

Mindful of her footing, the younger scales the old weodemair. A branch sweeps up and smacks Nialla in the face, sending her over the ledge and into the cold waters of the cavern's rocky foundation. She falls under the surface, gasping for breath. No way out.

A darkness enwraps her and drags her deeper into the abyss. Like a rock, Nialla sinks. She can no longer distinguish between the surface and the depths. *Sackery isn't here to carry me anymore*, Nialla fears, losing heart. *I don't want to die.* Her vision blurs as the last bubbles escape her mouth. Then, she hits the bottom.

She is a seed held in gentle hands. "Ansolas," whispers a voice from nowhere.

Nialla opens her eyes, breathless . . . *Am I dead?* She languishes in the solitude, a weight on her, unable to move. The tree's great roots stretch toward her, swathing her in a tight shell. A flood of new thoughts enters her mind—brighter days under the sun, a thousand lifetimes passing by her too quickly for her to read.

And in the shadows, there's a whisper of another name. "Aeterhet?" The word sends ice into her throat, causing her to choke. In a panic, she digs into the tree's presence from inside the cocoon, his songs as vibrant as a sunlit meadow:

"Is this how the world must end?" Gallindrusk utters. "Or is it a new beginning? A second chance?"

"Please? Help me," Nialla forces out the words.

The weodemair groans and waits for a long while, deep in thought. "We helped many throughout the years," the tree burrs. "None demanded we die for their cause. You have the trill of a familiar song about you, little seed. It brings imbalance where you walk, forcing creatures to act against their will."

"I do not demand," Nialla defends. "I ask, and they answer me."

"And now you ask us to kill ourselves?" the weodemair questions.

"No? I don't know," she admits. "I don't understand it. All I know is that I am afraid, and I don't want to die." Nialla wraps her hands around her throat, unsure how long she can hold her breath, pushing out her thoughts in a language they both can speak. "Not here. Not like this."

The tree pauses, weighing his options. "A second chance," Gallindrusk decides. "Rise then, little seed. We shall speak candidly." Nialla can feel the tree's roots vibrate and loosen, opening the cocoon and letting the darkness consume her again.

Something *white* approaches her in the water and bites ahold of her collar. Nialla feels a soft tug on her, lifting her to the surface. She coughs as they breach, with Irimara dragging her toward the rocks. And when they reach solid ground, the whole cavern hollers like a wind beating drums!

The light flowers bloom brighter, and the Grandfather Tree emits a song that earns the Harbinger's attention. Its severe gaze lands on Nialla. The older lunges forward, but the Ethernal warrior takes the blow, grabs the woman by the neck, and throws her violently against the stone.

Irimara nudges Nialla with her snout. "Get to your feet! Don't die here, cub."

Nialla's still gasping for air, muscles unwilling to move. "I can't—?" At the shore, there's red in the water. She touches her face and pulls her hand away, blood on her fingers from a cut on her cheek. Gallindrusk left his mark when he struck her and sent her over the edge.

The fiend halts and laughs at Irimara and Nialla, blocking their way out, their only chance to run.

"And what is this? Or yet, who are you? The fox, I know, but you—? I do not," the Harbinger chides, his voice like gravel. He leans forward, a golden hue showing through the cracks of his bone-white armor. Nialla scrambles to her feet and looks hard at the creature. She notices his eyes—not human eyes, rather, six burnt-orange irises encased behind the rough iron of his mask. He blinks at her, tilting his head before pulling away with a growl. "Can it be? Your face?! So clear to me. Are you the younger of our enemy?"

Irimara steps forward, laying her paw firmly on the ground. "Stay away from her!"

Nialla uses her sleeve to wipe the blood off her face. *After everything Irimara did, does she protect me now?*

"Step aside, little fox. Your fight is lost," the Harbinger derides. "Your tricks are old, don't you see? A chase across the misty waters? She's brought me to this place, to the very start, a moment when she was still but a fawn." His many-eyed stare veers away from the fox and burns through to Nialla.

The fox looks back at her, a glimmer in the yellow of her eyes. "I am sorry."

"Irimara?" Nialla wants to speak.

The Harbinger raises his arms and stomps toward the two of them, ready to cut the fox down. Gallindrusk roars, lifting its roots from the rocks, forcing the dark warrior to hesitate. He tucks in his arms and braces against the storm.

"Go!" Irimara shouts.

Nialla rushes through a torrent of wood and water, pulling herself back onto the weodemair's limbs.

The dark warrior evades and sidesteps, deflecting and redirecting the roots and branches meant to slow him down. Irimara dances with the carnage, creating false images to lead the Harbinger into attacking mist and shadows. Never in her life did Nialla think a being could take on so much, with such malevolent wrath, and remain almost gleeful as he takes each break and fracture. She doesn't know how long it will hold him back.

Nialla climbs until her fingers bleed, her knees bruise, and the cut on her cheek throbs. She reaches the weodemair's crown, where the branches sprout from the heartwood. She lays her forehead against the bark, slowing her breath, feeling its roots and limbs stretch for hundreds of leagues through the mountains. There is so much life, big and small, from the birds to the frogs, the bears, and the deer. Nialla can hear all their songs unabated—raw and untampered, crude and undressed.

Gallindrusk stirs, resisting her thoughts. "Stop this, little one. For all our sakes, do not force me."

"We have to do this," Nialla whispers. "Please? Don't you see?

If we can't stop it—?"

"I don't want to die. All that I am?" Gallindrusk pleads. "It would be gone."

"Your voice doesn't have to fade! Let me take your memories, bring them anew."

"Another chance? That is a burden no single mortal should carry."

"But what if I merely hold it for a while? A seed?! Planted in the daylight for all the world to see."

"Out of the darkness? A new growth, much like me?"

"A second chance," Nialla tells Gallindrusk. "That, I promise you, Great Tree."

She draws back, lids fluttering as they readjust to the dark. Nialla cries, only for Gallindrusk to lower a branch and wipe the tears away. "There is darkness hiding in the bleak corners of the world, little one—sacrifice and pain," the tree burrs. "But I hear you. I see it. A star's light to touch all our songs. Make us bright."

The branch unfolds to reveal an acorn no larger than her thumb. Nialla hesitates, feeling a heat come off it. A fire burns inside the shell, the memories of whole generations. Nialla accepts her charge and stuffs it under her garb, hoping she can keep it safe.

The Harbinger climbs onto Gallindrusk, cutting through wood, stone, and failed promises—three arms swinging in perfect unison. The last one has Irimara in its grasp, held by the neck, strangling her with its three-fingered fist. "Enough!

No more tricks," the fiend shouts. "No more illusions!"

Nialla rises to her feet and stares him down coldly. "No."

Fissures erupt throughout the cavern as Gallindrusk rips his limbs from the mountain.

The dark warrior snarls. "Is this it? Desperate is your hour, indeed. Mere rocks won't kill me." He tightens his grip on Irimara's throat, causing the fox to whine. Nialla looks at her, lips dry, unsure *what* to do. "I survived the death of my world when our sun died. Do you know what true cold is, child? I do. I know a frost that bites harder than any beast! A winter that causes fire to freeze like water in a pond."

"I don't care," she rejects. "Let her go!"

"Do you know what she will do? Because of this wretched skunk, my brethren scatter among the stars, aimless as sailors without a shore," the warrior bemoans. "A trickster? *She* can lead armies astray and turn allies into foes. I see the hate in your eyes for her, little fawn. You hate the fox, do you not? She took something from you! She always does. Neshulha? Their story can end before *this* last one can hurt anybody else. I can finish it with your blessings."

"She *did* take someone from me," Nialla utters. "My friend? Amerllie."

"Just say the word, and the fox will breathe her last," the Harbinger squeezes. "For all our sakes."

Nialla's jaw clenches, looking again at the yellow hue of Irimara's eyes. Is it fear? Sadness? The fox had led her into the wilderness these past few days, playing with Nialla's mind like a child plays with a doll. She made her see things—dark things, preying on her silent terrors.

"No," she decides. "I said, let her go."

The warrior raises his chin and chuckles. "No? Then, you forfeit your revenge," he says, closing his fist. "Her life is mine!"

"No!" the older shouts.

A metallic shine pierces the warrior's chest, ringing out until the source impales the tree beside Nialla—the fine spear her elder wields. Nialla falls back, startled by the ferocity. Golden blood flows from the Harbinger's wound, contrasting the black cloak he wears under the bone-white armor. From behind, the woman rushes the warrior.

Irimara breaks free of the monster and joins the younger at the tree's heartwood crown.

Nialla watches with the fox as the older hammers the Harbinger to his knees—hand and fist, her strength cracking his false steel with great force. "You aren't the first your master sent after me!" the woman taunts. "Champion of a dead world? He takes one from every planet he conquers." The fiend tries to grab her, but the older takes his arm and snaps it. His bone-like shell crumbles as every impact turns it into dust. "Each of you that dies, you take the last memories of your people with you!"

The dark warrior seethes. "Fouled in death?! He leads us to a promised land."

"No. He corrupts you. Enemy of Life? A doom upon the stars," Nialla's older scoffs. The woman presses her hand against the defeated Harbinger's helmet, those six eyes fixed on her. "I will see you again in Iánturial." She closes her fist, and the iron mask shaped to his face shatters, revealing the charr-skinned being underneath.

"Fight as you might, Light Maiden. It won't be enough."

"No doubt. That's why I won't come alone."

In a final motion, the woman twists her wrist, collapsing the Ethernal Harbinger's skull. Whatever he used to be, all that's left is a corpse that falls over the side and plummets into the pools under the tree's roots. His blood mixes with the water, like ink spilling from a well as he sinks, turning it a golden hue.

Nialla breathes. "Is it done?"

The woman looks at her briefly as she trudges to the heart-wood crown, exhausted, retaking the spear skewered into the bark. Irimara moves aside, fearful of what comes next. "Almost, little one. You must quickly leave this place," the older warns. "Gallindrusk won't give you much time." The tree wrenches more limbs out of the rock, and new fissures form throughout the cavern.

"And what about you?" Irimara begs the question.

"I will return to where I am needed," the older woman concludes. "Back to the door before it closes. Others await me there."

"Others?" Nialla wonders.

"Our friends. Most with familiar faces," she says, looking at Irimara. "Some? It's difficult to know." She presses her thumb into her palm, uncertainty hanging in the air as the cavern splits open, letting sunlight break through the rocks overhead.

"Do you have the seed? Good. Plant it in your garden at the Greencliffs. Let it grow. New life will spring from its branches. Protect it." She steps to the side, kneeling to Irimara.

"How can you be real?" the fox asks. "They didn't—? Well, they didn't tell me much, it seems."

"Didn't they? Odd that you should ask me such questions," the older admits. "Thank you."

"That creature said it knew of me," Irimara notions.

"This isn't where the story ends," the other says warmly.

"But I—?" the fox hesitates. "I thought things would be different?"

"And why can't they be?" the older asks, looking again at the younger. "Lives will be lost because of what we'll do. Sometimes? I miss the quiet of a simple life." The woman clenches a pair of jewels at her chest, a glow showing through her bruised and bloody knuckles. Nialla's eyes can't break away from them. She touches the Ancestrum Stone hanging from *her* neck and realizes they are the same pieces of a whole. One of them, at least. But the other? Nialla knows the rough edges, the soft glint, and the chain from which it dangles. It is her mother's birthstone, the Fallenstar of June. "You'll need each other. Trust me. Now? Let's get to solid ground."

She walks past the fox and the girl and descends the branches to the bottom of the cavern. Nialla follows her alongside the fox. The woman's stride is graceful and rigid. Even with a clear pain in her side, she holds her shoulders high while barely swinging her arms as she moves. It is as if she walks knowing others are watching her, unwilling to let her lassitude show.

Nialla catches the other's wrist. "And what happens now?!"

The older stops and turns to the pair with a weak smirk. "A simple choice. One of many," the woman recites. "From here, all you can decide is which path to chase. Will you take the straightest road? Or will you veer off course, becoming lost in a sea without stars?"

"I don't understand," Nialla frowns, tears down her cheeks.

The woman takes the younger by the hands. "Can I tell you a secret? Neither do I, little one. And that's the trick, isn't it?" she tells Nialla. "You're fighting a war that started before our time. Today was a battle, and we won it. Barely. Tomorrow? There'll be another. There'll be no end until I find a way through the fog and back again."

"Are you looking for something?"

"My courage? The man who raised me."

Nialla's eyes widen. "Sackery? Is—? Is he lost?"

"Yes. But I will find him," the older says, determined.

"Where did he go?"

The cavern rumbles again, and boulders drop from above, crashing onto the weodemair's fat trunk. Nialla swallows, only for the older to answer her with a gallant smile. "Farewell, Nialla—Princess of Calidor and Ilhivendal, Daughter of Galron and Cyridel," the woman lists, "Lady of the Mountains."

Nialla gasps for breath as dust fills the chamber. "Goodbye."

Irimara tugs on her sleeve with her teeth, signaling their need to go. Without another word, the fox and the girl retrace their steps to the entrance as the caves buckle. Nialla looks back only to see the older image of herself disappear into the dark as the light blooms fade under the debris and rocks.

Gallindrusk lets out one final roar as the cavern collapses on top of him.

Nialla lost in the Dark

— 21 —

THE LAST STAND

Sackery moves, careful not to leave the safety of their circle. He can taste the blood in his mouth, so he spits it out. Gripping his sword, angling the blade straight, the Vedrethal nods. His muscles clench as he prepares for the onslaught.

Icurian sends his shades forward. Iben and Sackery come together to protect their flanks while the Jhalamar survivors swing up and under, covering each other as they move in unison to maintain a perfect dance. The shades dissipate when their blades run through each mass of wood and leaves. Icurian creates more and throws them into the fray, not caring how many succumb to the cold, hard resolve of Vedrethal tradition.

Even for their prowess to hold the line, Icurian continues. These shades aren't meant to win the battle for *him*, only exhaust *them*. And as arrow-fodder, they do their jobs, thinning the circle's number until only Iben stands with Sackery.

It's when the dirt softens under them, and their feet sink into it, stopping their dance, that Sackery fears the end comes.

Iben and Sackery press their backs together, fending off the last few shades. Icurian marches on them, releasing whatever power holds the two in place as the shadow nears. Iben recovers first and rushes the man. Icurian cuts him down like a rock splitting a river.

Sackery adjusts his stance and breathes. "Enough! Nobody else dies!"

"Do you even have anyone else left?" Icurian asks. "How does it feel?! Wasting lives? Only to fail."

"Not while I stand with my sword in hand!"

"I am not trying to kill you."

"Liar!"

"I have never lied to you, little warrior."

Sackery lunges forward. Icurian sidesteps and kicks out his legs from under him, throwing him into the dirt. Sackery wildly swings as he falls, nicking the Doomed King on the shoulder. *Pure luck, not skill.* Icurian yelps and thrusts his spear's point at the Vedrethal, frenzied.

Gallandhal sweeps down from above, throwing the Doomed King off-balance. "Stop fighting!" she shouts.

Sackery ignores the bird, taking his chances to avoid getting skewered. Icurian's quick and relentless, however. He makes jab after jab, attempting to impale Sackery while still on the ground. The lord crushes the latter's cloak with the heel of his boot to pin the Vedrethal down. As the spear comes again,

Sackery veers, and it misses, striking the dirt instead. Sackery rolls onto the haft, using the momentum to plunge his sword past the gaps in the lord's armor and into his side.

For an instant, the Vedrethal cheers. "Ha!" But it's a dreary, mock rejoice of mixed emotions.

Icurian reels back, gasping with surprise. "Faster than I thought?"

Sackery rises to his feet and sinks the blade deeper, refusing to stop, even as Icurian looks at him with a fearful glint in his silver eyes. "Afraid? How does it feel?" But he notices a shift in the other's face, only for the reality to dawn on him. Sackery can *see* his face, no longer behind a mask. "Icurian?"

His features melt into Iben's grizzled mug. "Greywolfe? Master, I—?" Blood trickles into the corners of the old soldier's mouth. The man feels around the wound where Sackery had driven Aru il Endril into his flesh. "I-I was f-fighting him? Icurian?! But it was y-you? Was I fighting you?"

"Captain? No. What—?" Sackery stammers. He gently lowers Iben to the ground, only for the illusion to dissipate completely, and the field returns to a woeful peace. A wave of cries hits his ears as the realization sinks into his stomach. "I don't understand. How?! She couldn't have—?" Sackery looks to the others and the man in his arms. Even the Mórhathan stirs where it had fallen, left in a daze. "Irimara? No?! She didn't—?"

Somebody shouts for his attention. "Greywolfe?!" But the sound doesn't wake him from his shock.

Another voice calls. "Lord Vedrethal?! He's over here! We

found him!"

Sackery drops his shoulders as Ivette and others rush to his side. "What is this?" he utters. Many of the Jhalamar are hurt or scattered across the field. And the blood on his sword? It was *not* an illusion. "The fox made us fight each other?" It is the very power Heluvian feared that had *his* Vedrethal hunt the Neshulha to near extinction.

Ivette shakes him. "Master Greywolfe?! Can you hear me?"

"My Jhalamar?" Sackery begs the question.

"Master?! Are you okay? He's all right!" Ivette shouts.

None of it happened. But it did? Sackery knows it did because it still feels so real. He *felt* when he hit the tree. *Was it all my people trying to stop me?* He *felt* every time his sword met with Icurian's spear, Rhongomyniad. *Was it against those I trained?* He *felt* his blade cutting as he sank it into—?

"Iben?!" He looks down, the Captain still awake. "Iben? My friend."

"Sackery? So, it *was* you I fought," Iben mourns, his tone almost peaceful. "That was a good fight."

"Don't move," Sackery urges. "We'll get you help! Ivette?"

The woman shakes her head. "I don't know if we can," she tells him.

"Don't worry about me," Iben confides. "I don't—? You?! Nialla? She needs you more than I do, Vedrethal." He reaches for Sackery's hand and squeezes it. "Ours is a duty. And I am glad for it, no matter the name of the halls I am sure to walk."

"You're not dead yet," Sackery refuses.

Iben smiles at him kindly. "You'll find another to lead your band of wayward soldiers. And if I survive? My fighting days are behind me. Maybe my son can rise to the task?" he weeps. "After all, what good are forebears if they don't want their children to outshine them? Isn't that all a father should want?"

"After this," Sackery recoils, "you'd let me train Orswarvin?"

"Nothing would make me prouder," Iben coughs, straining his voice.

Gallandhal lands next to him, a sad look in her violet eyes. She breathes deep as she stares at the man in Sackery's arms, the blood on his hands, the water down his cheeks. The Shanashéron lingers for a long while, unsure what to say that could uplift their downtrodden spirits.

"I tried to warn you," the bird whispers. "I saw it all. Icurian? It felt like him. Moved like him."

"But it wasn't him," Sackery accepts. "How many did we lose?"

Among the Jhalamar, most are on their knees, exhausted, faces in their hands. Sackery counts them. Ivette and Kennan are somehow on their feet—bruised and battered, with new dents in their armor, taken with pride. Camdyn works the rounds, handing out water to the survivors. Most appear alive! Confused but alive. He looks at the Mórhathan as it rumbles, shaking off a nest of shattered rocks and broken trees.

But they died? Sackery frowns with a shallow breath. *Was it all an illusion?* He doesn't know what the others saw or who they fought. All he *does* know is there's a girl who still needs him. Even beaten into the ground as he is, Sackery will do his duty as Nialla's custodian.

"Ivette?" he pleads.

"This isn't your fault," she offers solace.

"But I charged us head first into it," he murmurs.

A softer voice rings out. "Sackery of the Vedrethal," it whispers.

He looks up at the fox standing over him, a frown in her eyes. She raises her chin, almost amused by the anger on his face.

Sackery's jaw tightens. "Irimara?" Ivette and Kennen raise their swords to the creature, but she does not flinch. "Are you here? Or elsewhere?"

"Never where you'd think I am," Irimara admits. She looks at the others and unfolds her ears. "Your people? They've a strength to them, do you know that? You fought a valiant stand, as my kindred had fought." He notices the wounds on her body and neck, red staining her white fur.

"Nialla?! Is she—?"

"No. But it's almost over now," Irimara tells him. "Do you know? Most people didn't appreciate Icurian. And of late? I'd argue you fail to understand the girl. Nialla views the world in ways you and I can hardly imagine. All those songs? Music played on chords stretched across the sky." She looks at Gallandhal, confident and peaceful.

Above them, the mountain collapses, and a fervent roar breaks the wind.

Sackery falls forward, losing his breath. "Nialla?!"

From the dust and the ruin, a shape takes form from the entry to the caves. Those among the Jhalamar that can stand, they stand with haste. A dust plume washes over them, turning the very air grey. Sackery hears a cough, and the shape staggers onto the rocks on the other side of the field.

"Greywolfe?" Iben asks through his teeth.

"Jhalamar?" Sackery begs of Ivette. "Do you have him?"

"Don't worry," the woman confirms. "Go!" She takes the Captain in her arms.

He nods to her, rises to his feet, and hurries to the small figure by the cavern's entrance. Nialla's there on the ground, soaked and covered in mud. Sackery lifts the girl and carries her into cover by the trees, where the air isn't as thick. "Can you hear me? Nells?!" He traces the cut on her cheek and cleans it with water from his skin-flask.

"Sackery?" the girl stammers.

"It's me! You're all right."

Nialla's eyes flutter open, worn and drained. "What happened to you?" She touches his face.

"A fight I wasn't ready for," Sackery admits. He holds her tighter, wiping the crud off her face with his sleeve. "We set out to hunt a wild animal. Instead, we found someone . . . far more dangerous. A few of us are hurt. We'll have to find a way to get them home."

"Irimara?" Nialla mutters.

"You know her name?" he questions.

"She led us here," the girl weakly chuckles. "Gallandhal? She's a better tracker than you."

Sackery lets out a laugh. He looks up, but he finds the fox has fled. He wonders if she was *ever* here or if it was merely another false image. "What did she want? Why so much effort? I had seen many things in my life, but that—? She played with our minds and made us fight each other. All her anger?"

"She *was* angry," Nialla weighs, pulling herself upright. "At least, that's how it started, I think."

"Did she give you this cut on your cheek?"

"No. But, I don't—? I'm tired."

Sackery nods. "So am I, little one."

The Mórhathan approaches, lumbered footsteps beating the soil. He lowers his snout to the girl on the wayside, catching her scent before letting out a great yawn. Nialla smiles and presses her face against the creature, taking an acorn from her tunic to show the wild spirit. Sackery watches, not understanding the reason behind it. By the end, the Mórhathan moves away, widening his stance, and musters a roar that startles the Vedre-thal, shaking the dust from the trees.

Most of the others warily stare at the noble brute as it plods through the trees afterward, disappearing into the wildwoods.

Sackery breathes. "Care to explain?" he asks Nialla.

"Not really. Though, he *did* tell us to leave," the girl answers. "Is that all he said?"

"No. And that's okay. It's between the two of us."

Nialla pushes off the ground and wobbles to her feet. She leans on Sackery's shoulder and finds her balance. As she breathes, a wind sweeps through the field, clearing more dust from the air as the mountain crumbles, shattering the horizon.

"Master Greywolfe?!" another begs the question.

Sackery looks to Camdyn. "Yes?"

"This ground isn't stable. We can't stay here!"

Sackery hooks his thumb onto the strap that attaches his cloak to his back and nods. "Then let's get the wounded to safety," the Vedrethal instructs. "Everyone who can walk, assist those who can't. This fight took a lot out of us, but we'll be stronger for it next time." He looks to Iben with Ivette, still trying to stop the bleeding from the man's side. He may survive the wound, but the concern is infection. They'll make camp and tend to their casualties.

Gallandhal hops alongside them. "We should hurry before the landslide buries us."

Sackery looks at Nialla. "She's right. Let's move! Nobody gets left behind."

"Aren't you curious about what happened?" Nialla clumsily alludes.

"Tell me later," Sackery tenders. "Promise me?"

"I promise."

He swings an arm across Nialla's shoulders and shakes the dirt from her raven hair. "Good," he accepts. The girl doesn't look at him, but Sackery can see a void in the silver of her eyes. She had witnessed something inside the Dead Caves beyond her years. *What did the fox do to her in there?* He doesn't know. Only that she's gripping the jewel hanging around her neck so tight that her knuckles are stark white.

It is what we always feared by settling down, Sackery muses. *Our enemies would find us, and they did.*

But he must abide by her word that she will talk to him when they are out of danger. For now, they move on with diligence. Sackery leads Nialla and the Jhalamar west through a forest of haze and echoes. Even as they travel farther from the mountains, it only gets worse. Gallandhal flies ahead of them, looking for a clear area to rest.

It's a long march back to Wilhimusk without their horses. Six days ago, they set out on a task to hunt the animal that killed little Amerllie. It'll now take longer while carrying their wounded, failed in their pledge. Irimara escaped, and the Jhalamar are no longer in any condition to track her down again.

"He felt so real," Sackery whispers. "How did the fox do it?" He replays the battle with the false Icurian in his head. "The way he moved, his voice, his very presence . . . Every detail? Nearly perfect." And that loathes him to ask Nialla candidly about the subject. She holds the Ancestrum Stone as if the very course of her life depends on keeping it close, but it isn't his place to question such things.

All he can do now is carry the injured, one by one, until they are home.

— 22 —

THE STRANGER

Irimara climbs to the top of a distant hill overlooking the road into Wilhimusk. She's far enough away that people won't notice her. After recent events, it's better this way. *For me. For everybody.* She did what she came to do, just not how she thought it would go down.

The girl and her followers have made it home. Irimara escorted them secretly, staying hidden on the roadside day and night, keeping the predators away.

A quaint breeze ascends the overlook, making the grass dance in the girl's direction. Irimara watches as Nialla stops mid-step and turns toward the hill. Their exchange lasts moments—long enough for the air to fall starkly cold and the wind to blow harder. They are two dots to one another, but Nialla's eyes pierce the distance like a drestel sand-borrower stalking its prey from tunnels under the Akkadvar sands.

Irimara hears the stranger's footsteps as he walks up the hill to join her. The fox glances at the blue-cloaked man for an instant before lending her attention wholly to the village again. He patiently stands there, waiting for her to talk first. Irimara merely puffs her chest and doesn't give him the satisfaction.

"You'll have to speak to me at some point," the man implores.

"Must I now?" Irimara questions. "Verhan? That is a silly name."

He betrays a frown from under his hood. "One of several I have, but also what the Aenümorians call me," the man admits. "It means 'father' in their tongue. And this far south and east? It's a safe bet to use without many being wise to it. The only name they'd know here is 'Endúcar,' and there's more than a few called *that* in Calidor."

"How about 'Galron,' as others may recognize?" Irimara chides.

Verhan falsely smiles. "Why this fascination with my names all of a sudden?"

"Because of what you put *me* through," Irimara decides. "Did you know what would happen?"

"In the caves? I could assume," he shrugs.

"But you weren't certain?"

"No. I am never without some doubt." He sits beside her in the grass, running a hand over the emerald blades, letting the wind tickle his palm. "But that crossroads was one dear to your heart. Icurian agreed it wasn't ours to close. You also couldn't do it alone, so I sent you to somebody who could."

"Your daughter? She thinks you're dead."

"Everyone thinks I am dead," Verhan states. "It's safer."

Irimara folds her ears back against her head. "Safe?! No. It's cruel."

"Killing that child was cruel," the man derides.

"And what was I to do? She would've told the Vedrethal," Irimara tells him. "Sackery Greywolfe is many things—a soldier above all else, what his *kind* did to mine. But I did my best. I showed her the truth. I made her find the strength to push on and follow me through a nightmare. It took a lot to get her there."

"You'll find no rebuke from me," the man says, taking a deep breath.

"Then why do I sense it wasn't enough?" Irimara begs the question. She watches as this Verhan raises his hand to catch the empty air. Faintly, the cold disappears behind a warm, southerly breeze. He flips his palm to the sky, letting out a soft whistle, and the wind altogether stops. "Is that necessary? You'll risk notice."

"Nothing we do is enough. And it all has a consequence," Verhan speaks mournfully. "Every verse is tied together in the cadence of our lives. Each tone plays off another—a single beat followed by a matching note. All of it works in harmony. And yet? It's easy to upset when one piece falls out of rhythm."

"I don't understand," Irimara admits.

"Nobody does," Verhan chuckles. "Not really."

"And what we saw in those caves? That dark warrior?"

"A harbinger for things to come," the man coughs. "You drove him off, can I guess?"

"Your daughter killed it with her bare hands," Irimara tells him.

Verhan looks at her with surprise. "That isn't—?" He stops and runs the possibilities through his head. "A place where time and space confuse themselves. *Mionaid le cothrom, meòrachadh nas sine.* You saw another glimpse of her, didn't you?" *A chance moment*, his words mean, *an older reflection.*

"More than a glimpse," Irimara states, lifting her head to show the wounds on her neck.

"Maybe you should've let Sackery join you in the caves," Verhan weighs.

"I'd be lying to say the notion didn't tempt me," Irimara confesses.

"And by the look of it, the choice took all your strength."

"Fighting two battles at once? It would've been easier to let him die."

"You didn't intend for him to find you. Like a good soldier, he did. He always does."

"Regretfully. And the bear? What am I to a beast like that?"

"It's difficult, these lives we lead. Nialla still needs him, much as she'll need you."

"I promised I'd answer for my crimes."

"Then answer for them," the man encourages.

"And face how many centuries of judgment? All for some girl nobody will remember in a decade."

"Nialla will remember. She has a garden where she plants flowers for those who move on to the other side," Verhan says with a glad smile. He nudges Irimara, a kindness to his silver eyes, much like his daughter. Old? And yet, not old enough. "People say we all die twice. The first is when our spirit leaves the body and passes to Iánturial. And the second—?"

"When the last one to remember us no longer does," Irimara whimpers.

"We've yet to die our second death," Verhan comforts. "And that little girl you killed? She'll live on."

Irimara turns away, burying her nose into the dirt. "Her name was Amerllie."

GARDEN OF MEMORIES

Cyridel accepts the acorn from Yeavengeritt, handing it off to Nialla as they set it into the ground.

Her daughter picked a nice grassy patch by the pond with plenty of dirt and not too many rocks to disrupt the tree's growth. Cyridel looks over the valley to the vast yellow fields and distant blue peaks of the Lurhan Mountains and the Arún Ouandin. *When last did anyone plant a weodemair?* She doesn't know. *Centuries? If mortal hands ever did touch them.*

Sackery stands with his Jhalamar in a circle around the Houdicar, hands on their sword hilts.

Nialla covers the acorn with rich, black soil. "She'll need a name."

"She? You already know that?" Sackery wonders.

"Don't you? I can hear her voice—soft and shallow, like a child. She asks for daylight."

"Sacred are the names we give to trees," Yeavengeritt tells her. "Are you certain?"

"Gwyndrasil," Nialla proposes.

"Tree of the Damsel?" Cyridel begs the question.

"And why not?" Nialla asks. "To remember Amerllie."

"A weodemair should choose a name for themselves," Yeavengeritt explains. "But it's been so long since—?"

"It is a good name," a brighter voice interrupts. Cyridel's eyes widen. Sackery and the others draw their weapons as the white fox reveals herself in the grass, her yellow eyes beaming at them. "Perhaps I should have announced myself first? I am sorry. That was rude of me."

Cyridel scrunches her nose as she catches the musky stench the fox extrudes.

Nialla stares hard at Irimara, rising to her feet. "You actually came?"

"I had nowhere else to go," the fox says.

"Irimara? You could've run," Sackery glowers, "and we'd never find you."

"Is that a life to lead? I did a terrible thing to you. Your people? They deserve a chance to face me."

"And what do you expect will happen?" the Vedrethal asks, turning his blade so the metal reflects the sunlight.

"That you'll kill me? Justice," the fox weighs. "As the old ways dictate."

"And snuff out the last of your kind?" Nialla mourns.

"Mine is already a dead race," Irimara accepts. "There is no return for the Neshulha. Not anymore. That is a hard truth. And someday? The last child born to the Known World will fall asleep, never to open its eyes again. Our great journey in a cycle of rebirth, a watchful rest until the hour comes when darkness surrenders to new life."

"Is that what your people believed?" the girl asks.

"That is the promise each of us share," the fox whimpers. "Every living creature."

"We are all a part of this song we call life," Cyridel offers a quiet solace.

Irimara lowers her ears as she meanders out of the grass, staying low to the ground, uncertain. "I am sorry, little cub."

Nialla looks at the fox and frowns. She reaches a hand toward her, and Irimara sniffs it before drawing back. Sackery and the Jhalamar close their circle, blades still drawn. "No! Please?! Leave us," Nialla shouts.

Sackery turns to her, confused. "Nialla? But I—?"

"I said leave, Sackery. Yeavengeritt? Can you take them?"

"Of course, my lady," the old man agrees. "Master Vedre-thal?"

Sackery narrows his eyes at the fox, a heat coming off him like a rock baked under the sun.

Nialla drifts to the man and squeezes his arm, getting him to lower his sword and point it at the dirt. "Please?"

"After what she did," Sackery asks doubtfully, "are you sure?

"No? But this is my choice, and I will make it."

Sackery lets out his breath and nods, defeated. Cyridel

touches her friend's shoulder as he walks by to ease his worry. He returns with a cold stare for only a moment before following Yeavengeritt and the others down the path toward the village. He leaves her with an empty sense in the pit of her stomach.

Cyridel finds a quiet spot in the shade by the Houdicar to lie down. She's close enough to listen as the girl and the fox make amends, but she wants to stay out of the way so they can have that chance. It's the least she can do. She will act as their witness.

"Nialla? I am—" Irimara begins.

"All that you showed me?" the girl interrupts.

"Your nightmares. A chance to face your fears," the fox admits.

"You can read my thoughts?"

"Feel them. My kind can sense the songs in strange ways," Irimara tells her. "Icurian once told me he felt strongest when he could feel the wind, the rain, the clouds above, and the dirt under his feet. You can feel them through a sense of warmth. Subtle vibrations? Mine is more like paint on a canvas, with thick brush strokes and vibrant colors."

"Is that why I often don't feel the cold?"

"Unless there's another close by with an off-key to their tone."

"Who *am* I to you?" Nialla demands.

"You saw *who* you are, the same as I did," Irimara confronts. "Who you'll become?"

"That older version of me?" the girl murmurs.

"I don't understand how such things work," the fox admits.

"All I *wanted* was to destroy that place. And you? I thought the only way you'd agree to help was if I made you angry enough to tear the roots from the mountain and perhaps bury me along with it."

"And how did you know where to find me?" Nialla wonders.

Irimara lets out a weak, amiable laugh. "You have a presence where you walk, little cub. And unlike me, you are not alone."

"Alone? You don't have to be," Nialla quietly offers.

Cyridel raises her head as Irimara's ears unfold, almost surprised.

"What do you mean?" the fox asks.

"I won't forgive you for what you did to Amerllie. But—?" Nialla looks briefly at her mother, water in her eyes. Cyridel smiles, offering her a confident nod, a nudge toward the idea that whatever she decides, it'll be all right. "Maybe you can stay here with us? Protect these folks as your atonement."

"You would let me live?" Irimara breathes. "Me?"

"I have seen what revenge does to a person," Nialla whispers. "All that needless hate? I shouldn't want that for anyone." As she stands there, the breeze causes every flower in the garden to turn in the girl's direction. Like soldiers mustering in a field for a parade, they cheer her name, reflecting her gaze. "And I don't want that for me."

"You may not have a choice," the fox warns. "History is our fate."

"Maybe? But not today," Nialla decides.

Irimara sits, her fur glowing in the sunlight. "I don't—? What can I do?" The fox glances at where they planted the weode-mair's seed, her yellow eyes pale against the green. "Where should I start? How does one make amends for killing a child?"

"You can make me a promise," Nialla suggests.

"A promise? To what end, may I ask?"

"That you'll be there when I need somebody to remind me of the person I must become."

"And *who* are you?" Irimara brightly charges. "Tell me."

"I am Nialla Elendsah, the Daughter of Galron and Cyridel," the girl speaks loudly and self-assured. "I am . . . Princess of Calidor and Ilhivendal, a child of the Endúcar and the Lady of the Mountains." Cyridel notices as her daughter stops and gathers her thoughts, only to whisper: "The Girl on the Hill who likes to sing when it rains."

"No. That is *not* who you are," Irimara denies. "You are simply Nialla—a flower in a wider meadow beset by a storm." She raises her head and speaks proudly. "Others gave you those names, but they don't make you who you are, do they? Take it from a lonely fox. Our lives? You saw who you might become, but the journey to get there? You'll find no lack of pain or loss."

"I am afraid," Nialla admits.

"As am I, little cub."

"This isn't the end," Cyridel speaks out.

"No. It isn't," Irimara concurs.

"Then let us start anew," Nialla offers, "to forge a path ahead."

Irimara sits up and puffs her chest, bowing to the girl. "I am yours," she vows.

Nialla indulges with a smile and scratches behind the fox's ears, taking her leave down the Greencliffs to Wilhimusk, a lighter weight to her footsteps. She has said her peace. Cyridel stays and lounges in the shade, watching as Irimara wallows in front of the house, unsure what to do next. She isn't what Cyridel had expected of the villain that caused them so much trouble these past few weeks. The white fox catches her gaze and flicks her tail nervously.

"So, you intend to stick with us?" Cyridel asks the creature.

"Yes? Should your daughter's offer prove genuine," Irimara answers.

"Do you think she would lie to you?"

"You'd know better than me."

"Would I now? A most clever thing to query."

"Is it? Or am I merely looking to protect myself?"

"Every living creature needs shelter from a thunderstorm."

"And yet? Even the strongest tree can topple if the wind blows hard enough."

"That is why we need as many roots as we can grow," Cyridel suggests. "Don't you agree?"

The fox shudders. "This won't be easy."

"No, it won't. Though, isn't that how the river flows? Getting the others to trust you after everything you did? It'll be hard, no doubt," Cyridel mourns, folding her hands into her lap. Before, when Nialla had warned her about the Neshulha, Cyridel had thought it was a dream acting out. She later imagined a fiend on the prowl, stalking them day and night. "But you'll find a way to make things right. You aren't a monster out for blood. Simply a lost soul."

"You once wandered the world for decades," Irimara murmurs. "I walked it for centuries."

"Were you alone that whole time? Any family? Friends?"

"Any family I had died in those caves. It left me enraged. Resentful enough to kill a child that did me no wrong."

"And yet? You felt it was your only course." She looks at the pond and the sunlight blooming off the water's surface. "Amerllie enjoyed swimming in the Little River," Cyridel describes. "It's difficult to say how truly close she was to Nialla. A decade is merely a breath to an Ellúndar babe, growing one year for every ten that passes to human eyes. My daughter will someday bury everyone she'll ever meet. And that, too, is a hard truth."

Irimara perks her ears and slowly comes alongside Cyridel, finding a sunny patch by her feet to settle. The fox tilts her head with an odd curiosity as her eyes land on the blue cloth tied to her wrist. "My lady? About the figure you saw by the hill?"

"You showed me the face of somebody I loved," Cyridel tells her. "That was cruel."

"It was, and I am sorry. But—?" Irimara pauses, eyes still on the blue ribbon. "You should know the songs of the Vedreron stem from a single chord in which to pluck. As I create images in their form, they are not wholly mine. An illusion can become them if they are alive, as *he* did when *he* spoke to you."

"My Galron? No?! He died?"

"No memory could turn a false impression against me."

"What are you saying?"

"Only what you're willing enough to accept," Irimara admits. "Loss is a natural part of life, even when others rip that life from you and make you walk an endless road. All we are? We are from the choices we make. But no matter how dark things get, hope comes—"

"From the unexpected," Cyridel utters. "Galron used to say that—a solitary verse, *his* verse."

Irimara lowers her head, her breath shallow. "Do not tell Nialla. I made a promise, and I share it only with you."

Cyridel feels a sharp ache where her heart sits under her breast. She twists and curls, closing her eyes as she fights back against the pain. She lays back and breathes through her nose, slow and measured, and the sharpness dulls into a quiet throb.

She notices the dried blood on the fox's white coat when she opens her eyes again. "Are you hurt?"

"From the battle in the caves," Irimara describes. "That warrior with the four arms?"

"Let's go inside. I'll clean the wound," Cyridel offers. "Would you like that?"

The fox closes her mouth. "I—? Yes, I would. Thank you."

— 24 —

THE TWO KINGS

He dunks under a branch and steps into the campfire's soft glow.

"Another chance meeting with the family who believes you dead?" the other begs the question.

Verhan grimaces before finding a seat next to Icurian, the glint of the flames in his silver eyes. "I went to ensure Irimara wouldn't go too far," he tells the man. "Do you know what she did? She killed a child."

Icurian shakes his head. "The white fox suffered greatly in the past. She yearns to share that pain, no matter who's at fault. We understand *that* better than most, do we not?" He takes a deep breath and lets it out, and their fire glows a little brighter.

"You have this curious habit," Verhan scolds. "You ask a question, but it comes off your tongue like a statement." He raises his fingers over the flames as he speaks, though he can hardly feel the heat.

"Do I? Curious, indeed," Icurian chuckles. "How did the battle play out?"

"The mountain collapsed," Verhan explains, "and the door with it." He stokes the fire, hoping to drive off the cold. It won't happen with Icurian this close, but after years of traveling with the man, he's made peace with the idea.

"Half the world will have surely felt it," Icurian says, rising to his feet. "And Sackery? Did you see him?" He walks to the edge of the tree line.

Verhan waves his hand, and the fire fades just a bit. He watches as the man stands there, a somber note to his tone. "You know as well as I do. As I understand, you fought him to a degree."

"An aspect of me did," Icurian admits. "Irimara tends to pull strings she shouldn't touch."

"As I said," Verhan iterates, "assurance the fox wouldn't get out of hand."

"Had you only intervened sooner to save the child?" Icurian suggests, closing his fist, and the woods shrink around them. "She's made victims out of all of us. Worrisome? Of course. Though, I can't say I am surprised."

"Wasn't this your idea?"

"She needed to reconcile her past, Galron. Much as I—"

"Don't call me that."

"Why not?"

"It is a personal name."

"Between you and the woman? Your tale is old, Endúcar."

"And I am tired of this argument."

Icurian smiles, returning to the fireside. "How long have you watched them from afar?" he demands. "How often does your daughter dream of the 'man-in-blue' that haunts her footsteps? Do you think you can run away from them forever? Every breath we take is a song all its own. You can hide it from the others, but the girl? She'll hear it soon enough."

Verhan presses his palms into the dirt, feeling the roots and the worms underneath them. "Like she did during her battle with the Crows?"

"Memories. Powerful tools for us. You may think me a villain, but I only did what I thought was right," Icurian explains. "And playing the part of a dead man? It's not 'safer' for them. You only deprive your loved ones of the time you could *be* with them. Listen to me, not as friends—?"

"Because we're not," Verhan scoffs.

"—But as somebody who understands what it's like to lose everything! Everyone I ever cared about came to hate me. Even after I led us against the Dragons of Islinin to free the people enslaved by them?" The man hesitates for a moment and looks away. "They once called me a hero! Aonarfudain?! 'One Who Stands,' they named me. A title? Yes. Much like yours, Endúcar."

"But? You didn't save everyone," Verhan laments.

Icurian returns his gaze to him, reaching to let his hand hover over the fire, his fingertips dancing with the floating embers. The wind lifts the ashes into the air, carrying them aloft into the night. As he breathes, the trees shift and shiver like grass in an empty field. "No," Icurian admits. "I did not."

"What happened?"

"Do you care to hear the story?"

"Whether or not I care has never stopped you before."

"I would never droll on without a moral," Icurian shrugs.

"Then?" Verhan urges.

"You already know a recent telling of it," the man says. "But the rest? A history so old they call it a legend. Mankind chose to stay behind after our pact for peace, fearing the dragons' wrath. We sailed from Géurdinhal, our foothold on the western continent, and said farewell to those we abandoned. Even then, I left somebody most dear to me."

"Rauhnníal told me," Verhan offers. "You found your love in Islinin? A human woman."

"One of my greatest regrets," Icurian mourns.

"That you found her? Or because you had to leave her?"

"Yes? Our terms for the war's end were difficult. Nobody won. Everybody lost."

"And? That's when you met Sackery," Verhan recalls.

"As a boy on the ship during the return voyage to Arún," Icurian says. "He hadn't even a name, then—some wayward child wandering the decks. The others of his kind were weary of him. His mother died to a Morkül-nazzok when he was an infant, while his father died in a hunt for her killer."

"Family is important to the Aens," Verhan stipulates.

"But without either parent, the boy had no family or clan," Icurian frowns. "So? I took Sackery as my ward and raised him to be a blade at my side. First of the Vedrethal, and the Master of the Order. A warrior-scholar, a true adept of the word and sword."

"Except? It didn't turn out how you wanted," Verhan remarks.

"No? It was better! I went back to Islinin alone. I stood on the shores of the land I left behind and held a child in my arms," Icurian describes. "He—? He was so new to the world that we didn't have a name for those like him. And I knew then I would not be the one to lead the lost tribes of men home."

"My Grandfather? Aamelian, King of Calidor."

"Child of my blood," Icurian recounts. "I decided to stay with him as long as possible. Decades? His mother passed early in his life, so I helped him until my duty forced me to carry on with my task. But before I left again, I taught him to listen! Open his mind? Find his strength."

"And you gave him another name."

Icurian looks at Verhan with pride. "Yours. Endúcar? My word for him."

"What does it mean? All my life, I've always wondered."

"Hope," Icurian describes. "My valiant hope for all mankind."

"Was this before or after you became the Doomed King?" Verhan derides.

"Before? I had set out to find the remainder of the Vinvidurfólk. After what the dragons did to them? I had to see if any had survived. They had the original claim to this world, did you know? Before *we* fell and made it ours. Ultheraal and his ilk were to protect them. *That* was their role."

He watches Icurian as the man stares into their campfire, a hardness to his eyes, almost dry from the blaze. "Born in the fires of the sun, a warmth that could breathe life into the land," Verhan recites from an old poem.

Icurian lets off a low whistle. Shadowy figures flicker from the ashes of the fire's smoke, fluttering at his fingertips. "Until a sour note corrupted their mighty songs. His name was Orthillian, an erratic trill in the cadence." He reshapes the images in the flames, now a garden filled to the brim by hundreds of others. "They called us the Eedian nya Ansolas—those few who were brave enough to confront him. A task that gave us a new purpose in Anánturial."

"You never told me this before," Verhan yields, sitting forward, attentive.

"It's not a story I like to relive. But? Events conspire to outpace us in this dreadful race," Icurian murmurs. "Orthillian seemed confused when we spoke to him. Angry? He said he didn't know of the trouble he had caused. That didn't stop us from sending our brother into the black abyss, hoping *that* would be enough to halt the spread and silence his tempo."

Icurian flicks his wrist, causing the shadow puppets to fight, each with a different masked crown. The shapes are familiar to Verhan, even as his eyes have trouble following the chaotic scene.

"You aren't talking of history anymore. This—?" Verhan

pauses, weighing his thoughts.

"We called it the First Betrayal," Icurian frowns. "And so, our tale begins."

A sudden gust of wind sweeps their campsite, bringing a newfound, aberrant chill. Verhan can feel it in his bones, drawing back to melt into his cloak. Icurian remains motionless, almost like welcoming an old friend into his abode. "And? What happened after this confrontation?"

"Brother Darkness. Anoan? He disagreed with our deeds, always the emotional, loyal servant to Sister Light," Icurian chuckles, reshaping the shadow puppets to show two new figures, bright and beautiful, with dark rings around their heads. "Ansolas told him she didn't want her children left cold and alone. Never alone! She couldn't understand how Orthillian's verse upset our other works."

"She loved him," Verhan suggests.

"She loves all of us," Icurian corrects.

"And yet? She was blind to his failings?"

"Can you blame her for it? We were blind to our own," Icurian admits soberly. "And what we did to him? It was terrible. Much like Irimara killing that child, we saw no other course. Our actions were desperate. Cruel? So, Brother Darkness made a promise to Sister Light. He would reach in and raise Orthillian out of that void."

"Didn't you fight against it?" Verhan frowns. "Argue it?"

"Our 'Bright Lady' decided, so it was no longer our place," Icurian answers. "Such are the consequences. Shattered was our trust in the bonds that balanced our ensemble. No matter what we did, we could not undo the damage. However, feeling that Anoan had lied to him, Orthillian murdered Brother Darkness at the edge of the abyss and cast his remains adrift. His body became Iánturial. His blood? It formed the Anamares."

Verhan witnesses the shadows reform into fantastic shapes and lines—Anoan's murder and Orthillian's rise, his crown flown backward like a wild elk's antlers. "He created the Space Between Worlds and the Shadowlands with his death."

"Life and rebirth, Ansolas and Anoan. A tale beyond return so ancient, I still have a hard time with it."

"Even now? Orthillian's still out there! Somewhere on foreign shores."

"Yes? A difficult truth to accept," Icurian murmurs. "And not all of us did! That makes me afraid."

Verhan watches as Icurian lowers his shoulders, wringing his palms. He can tell it is hard for him to speak of it. And yet? "Orthillian's conflict wasn't the only betrayal," he remembers. "Don't stop what you begun. Speak loud, Lord of Stories. Confess."

"We aren't to blame for what happened next. But? Another indeed came to us," Icurian weeps. "Our friend? Athulian said he wanted to help us correct our mistake. That he found inspiration with a new verse." The shadow puppets shift into the image of a crownless figure with bright robes. He approaches the others in the garden, three standing tallest among the masses—Heluvian, Icurian, and Enderian.

"You trusted him?" Verhan asks.

"Much as Orthillian had trusted us," Icurian returns.

"None of you suspected it was a ruse?"

"Athulian was Immaculate, the most noble of all our siblings," the other admits. "Lord of Justice? Some described him. He detested lies. But he saw what we did and took it upon himself to right the wrongs done to Orthillian. He declared his new lord as 'Aeterhet' before reciting his verse, exiling us from our home like we did our brother." A tear swims down Icurian's cheek. He feels it and wipes it away, fighting back the emotions bubbling to the surface.

"Justice and revenge are two sides of the same coin," Verhan offers a half-hearted solace.

Icurian smiles, then frowns. The man takes a deep breath. He raises his head and holds it there for a long time, only to release the air with a trill to his throat. "Because of our failures? Darkness sails across the endless black sea in iron ships, conquering worlds and taking a single champion from each to serve as soldiers of his Warriors Ethernal."

"Aeterhet," Verhan repeats, a foul taste on his tongue as he speaks the name.

"Enemy of Life, the Star-Eater, and the Golden Flame," Icurian concedes. "Alone? That's what our mother always feared for us. Now my brother searches for someone to make him whole again, a child crying out for his parents." With a subtle wave of his hand, the shadow puppets whisk away.

"You always tell such 'warm' stories to feed my bleeding

heart," Verhan shudders.

"They called me the 'Chronicler' for a reason. History? Another powerful tool." Icurian's eyes dull as the fire cools, the shadows darker on his face. "Look to the night sky. What do you see? Tell me."

Verhan looks and counts each tiny light in the black above. "Stars? A vast emptiness?"

Icurian nods. "You stare long enough, and you'll notice some lights disappear. So, I wish they were only stories. And the crossroads between worlds is the way through to ours. Each one we don't close—?"

"Leaves a way open for Aeterhet to walk through and hunt us down."

"Then our star will disappear, too. And this time? Numbers won't be on our side," Icurian warns. He closes his fist, snuffing out the last breath of the fire and leaving them in near-complete darkness. A silence befalls the pair for a while. Verhan raises an ear and listens to the crickets around them, unseen in the woods. "I am a darn fool."

"You won't hear any pity from me," Verhan contorts.

"And I expect none," Icurian accepts. "We once stood together. But? Most of us are now aimless, dead, or far worse. All because of me and my short-sighted crusade, wanting to save the world—a doomed man, doomed to fail."

"Icurian, I don't—?"

"No. It's true. All I had done? That's me. Icurian, the Exiled."

"All the more reason for me to stay and turn the odds,"

Verhan concludes.

"Our fight will be your daughter's soon enough. A hundred years? A thousand?"

"Each of us will lose a part of ourselves before the end."

"That's maybe the only way we'll survive. But for us to win? I don't know. I can no longer see the frontlines of this war of ours. Where do we stand? How do we fight? These questions wreck my mind day and night. And the answers elude me."

Verhan settles where he sits, lifting a hand over the smoldering ashes, feeling the heat at last. He hums a soft tune—the lullaby he used to sing to Nialla when she was a baby, unknown to the girl's mother. He followed his family throughout their wandering years, always close, always hidden. The fire's embers glow brighter as he hums, gaining strength until they spark a tiny flame anew.

"Hope from the unexpected," he utters. "And where should we go next?

"A question worth a hundred lives," Icurian quietly admits.